D1497525

Slooh
SPACE BOOKS

The Saturn Above It

An Anthology of Short Fiction About Space

Edited by Karen Stevens

For my mother, Patricia Stevens

My Star
ROBERT BROWNING

All I know
Of a certain star,
Is, it can throw
(Like the angled spar)
Now a dart of red,
Now a dart of blue,
Till my friends have said
They would fain see, too,
My star that dartles the red and the blue!

Then it stops like a bird; like a flower, hangs furled:
    They must solace themselves with the Saturn above it.
What matter to me if their star is a world?
    Mine has opened its soul to me; therefore I love it.

A list of acknowledgements to copyright owners appears
at the back of this anthology.

US website: www.slooh.com

ISBN: 978-0-9976211-0-5(US)

First printing 2016
Managing editor: Eliza Booth

Cover Photo: **Cristina de Middel/INSTITUTE**

CONTENTS

INTRODUCTION   *I*

SELMA LAGERLOF
The Eclipse   5

DON DELILLO
Human Moments in World War III   15

H.G. WELLS
The Star   39

STEVEN MILLHAUSER
The Invasion From Outer Space   59

C.S. LEWIS
Forms of Things Unknown   67

JOHN UPDIKE
Conjunction   81

HANS CHRISTIAN ANDERSON
The Comet   93

STEPHEN BAXTER
Last Contact   101

REGINALD MCKNIGHT
Uncle Moustapha's Eclipse   121

RAY BRADBURY
Kaleidoscope   135

MARGARET ATWOOD
Homelanding   151

J.G. BALLARD
The Message From Mars   159

STANISLAW LEM
The Seventh Voyage   177

VIRGINIA WOOLF
The Searchlight   205

JAMES FENNIMORE COOPER
The Eclipse   215

KURT VONNEGUT
Thanasphere   235

H.P. LOVECRAFT
Polaris   259

PRIMO LEVI
The Tranquil Star   267

PHILLIP K. DICK
Mr. Spaceship   277

RAY BRADBURY
The End of the Beginning   325

LEO TOLSTOY
The Coffee-House of Surat   335

Slooh   347

ACKNOWLEDGEMENTS   348

INTRODUCTION

Short stories emerge, wrote Emile Zola, "at that exquisite point where poetry ends and reality begins." When the short stories are about space both the poetry and the reality are amplified. The vastness of space seems to liberate the imagination and fears, expectations, curiosity are all intensified. A potent distillation of human hopes and anxieties emerges, rendering fiction about space particularly rich. The distinguished writers included in this anthology have boldly explored the uniquely human ways we react to the strangeness and enormity of the universe.

A walk through any library should convince you that the concept of space has long inspired, unsettled, humbled, befriended, and guided mankind. If one reason we read is to better understand ourselves, do we read about space to more fully comprehend not only ourselves, but perhaps, death and the other humanity-scaled issues that the enormity of space seems to stimulate? Just try standing outside under a full moon and not ponder the "big" questions.

However large the musings space may demand, we must still relate to all that infinity beyond the stratosphere through our human lens. The largeness of the unknown is otherwise difficult to hold and contemplate.

I

This anthology embodies the spirit of Slooh's mission of open access to the stars for all: a multitude of visions about what lies beyond our world are presented in these pages. A community of views, if you will. Although this anthology focuses on Western literature, subsequent collections will address other cultural perspectives. *The Saturn Above It* explores our contradictory views of the heavens; we have viewed them as the seat of the divine and an eternal resting place of souls, but also feared them as a menacing void from which aliens emerge. Do you think the mysteries of the universe can be solved? Or do you see space travel as a trespass? "Space," as represented in this collection's short stories, contains it all: it is a canvas for the writer as well as his times. Not only that, it is the starting or ending point of so much — it guides journeys, inspires both dreams and nightmares, sets us wandering and wondering...

I will leave you with a charming passage from Willa Cather's *The Enchanted Bluff* (1909). It encapsulates the pure wonder and promise the night sky can inspire:

After we finished our supper we beat the willow thicket for driftwood. By the time we had collected enough, night had fallen, and the pungent, weedy smell from the shore increased with the coolness. We threw ourselves down about the fire and made another futile effort to show Percy Pound the Little Dipper. We had tried it often before, but he could never be got past the big one.

"You see those three big stars just below the handle, with the bright one in the middle?" said Otto Hassler; "That's Orion's belt,

and the bright one is the clasp." I crawled behind Otto's shoulder and sighted up his arm to the star that seemed perched upon the tip of his steady forefinger. The Hassler boys did seine-fishing at night, and they knew a good many stars.

Percy gave up the Little Dipper and lay back on the sand, his hands clasped under his head. "I can see the North Star," he announced, contentedly, pointing toward it with his big toe. "Anyone might get lost and need to know that. "

We all looked up at it.

"How do you suppose Columbus felt when his compass didn't point north anymore?" Tip asked.

Otto shook his head. "My father says that there was another North Star once, and that maybe this one won't last always. I wonder what would happen to us down here if anything went wrong with it?"

...We lay back and looked, meditating, at the dark cover of the world....

"Queer how the stars are all in sort of diagrams," remarked Otto. "You could do most any proposition in geometry with 'em. They always look as if they meant something. Some folks say everybody's fortune is all written out in the stars, don't they?"

'They believe so in the old country," Fritz affirmed.

But Arthur only laughed at him. "You're thinking of Napoleon, Fritzey. He had a star that went out when he began to lose battles. I guess the stars don't keep any close tally on Sandtown folks."

We were speculating on how many times we could count a hundred before the evening star went down behind the corn fields *when someone cried, "There comes the moon, and it's as big as a cart wheel!"*

We all jumped up to greet it as it swam over the bluff behind us. It came up like a galleon in full sail; an enormous, barbaric thing, red as an angry heathen god.

"When the moon came up red like that, the Aztecs used to sacrifice their prisoners on the temple top," Percy announced.

"Go on, Perce. You got that out of Golden Days. Do you believe that, Arthur?" I appealed.

Arthur answered, quite seriously: "Like as not. The moon was one of their gods. When my father was in Mexico City he saw the stone where they used to sacrifice their prisoners."

...

"Must have been a big cat jumping," said Fritz. "They do sometimes. They must see bugs in the dark. Look what a track the moon makes!"

Perhaps, as has often been noted, it's during meditation on the alien that we are most human. This anthology offers a portrait of the human psyche and who we are — or could be — when we contemplate all that lies beyond Earth's atmosphere. Take what you will from these stories — they have been gathered with care and with a devotion to the power of words. Read long and prosper!

Karen Stevens
March 2016

SELMA LAGERLOF

Translated from the Swedish by VELMA SWANSTON HOWARD

The Eclipse

1922

There were Stina of Ridgecôte and Lina of Birdsong and Kajsa of Littlemarsh and Maja of Skypeak and Beda of Finndarkness and Elin, the new wife on the old soldier's place, and two or three other peasant women besides — all of them lived at the far end of the parish, below Storhöjden, in a region so wild and rocky none of the big farm owners had bothered to lay hands on it.

One had her cabin set up on a shelf of rock, another had hers put up at the edge of a bog, while a third had one that stood at the crest of a hill so steep it was a toilsome climb getting to it. If by chance any of the others had a cottage built on more favorable ground, you may be sure it lay so close to the mountain as to shut out the sun from autumn fair time clear up to Annunciation Day.

They each cultivated a little potato patch close by the cabin, though under serious difficulties. To be sure, there were many kinds of soil there at the foot of the mountain, but it was hard work to make the patches of land yield anything. In some places they had to clear away so much stone from their fields, it would have built a cow-house on a manorial estate; in some they had dug ditches as deep as graves, and in others they had brought their earth in sacks and spread it on the bare rocks. Where the soil was not so poor, they were forever fighting the tough thistle and pigweed which sprang up in such profusion you would have thought the whole potato land had been prepared for their benefit.

All the livelong day the women were alone in their cabins; for even where one had a husband and children, the man went off to his work every morning and the children went to school. A few among the older women had grown sons and daughters, but they had gone to America. And some there were with little children, who were always around, of course; but these could hardly be regarded as company.

Being so much alone, it was really necessary that they should meet sometimes over the coffee cups. Not that they got on so very well together, nor had any great love for each other; but some liked to keep posted on what the others were doing, and some grew despondent living like that, in the shadow of the mountain, unless they met people now and then. And there were those, too, who needed to unburden their hearts, and talk about the last letter from America, and those who were naturally talkative and jocular, and who longed for opportunity to make use of these happy God-given talents.

Nor was it any trouble at all to prepare for a little party. Coffee-pot and coffee cups they all had of course, and cream could be got at the manor, if one had no cow of one's own to milk; fancy biscuits and small cakes one could, at a pinch, get the dairyman's driver to fetch from the municipal bakery, and country merchants who sold coffee and sugar were to be found everywhere. So, to get up a coffee party was the easiest thing imaginable. The difficulty lay in finding an occasion.

For Stina of Ridgecôte, Lina of Birdsong, Kajsa of Littlemarsh, Maja of Skypeak, Beda of Finn-darkness, and Elin, the new wife at the old soldier's, were all agreed that it would never do for them to celebrate in the midst of the common everyday life. Were they to be that wasteful of the precious hours which never return, they might get a bad name. And to hold coffee parties on Sundays or great Holy Days was out of the question; for then the married women had husband and children at home, which was quite company enough. As for the rest — some liked to attend church, some wished to visit relatives, while a few preferred to spend the day at home, in perfect peace and stillness, that they might really feel it was a Holy Day.

Therefore they were all the more eager to take advantage of every possible opportunity. Most of them gave parties on their name-days, though some celebrated the great event when the wee little one cut its first tooth, or when it took its first steps. For those who received money-letters from America that was always a convenient excuse, and it was also in order to invite all the women of the neighborhood to come and help tack a quilt or stretch a web just off the loom.

All the same, there were not nearly as many occasions to meet as were needed. One year one of the women was at her wit's end. It was her turn to give a party, and she had no objection to carrying out what was expected of her; but she could not seem to hit upon anything to celebrate. Her own name-day she could not celebrate, being named Beda, as Beda has been stricken out of the almanac. Nor could she celebrate that of any member of her family, for all her dear ones were resting in the churchyard. She was very old, and the quilt she slept under would probably outlast her. She had a cat of which she was very fond. Truth to tell, it drank coffee just as well as she did; but she could hardly bring herself to hold a party for a cat!

Pondering, she searched her almanac again and again, for there she felt she must surely find the solution of her problem.

She began at the beginning, with "The Royal House" and "Signs and Forecasts," and read on, right through to "Markets and Postal Transmittances for 1912," without finding anything.

As she was reading the book for the seventh time, her glance rested on "Eclipses." She noted that that year, which was the year of our Lord nineteen-hundred twelve, on April seventeenth there would be a solar eclipse. It would begin at twenty minutes past high noon and end at 2.40 o'clock, and would cover nine-tenths of the sun's disk.

This she had read before, many times, without attaching any significance to it; but now, all at once, it became dazzlingly clear to her.

"Now I have it!" she exclaimed.

But it was only for a second or two that she felt confident; and then she put the thought away, fearing that the other women would just laugh at her.

The next few days, however, the idea that had come to her when reading her almanac kept recurring to her mind, until at last she began to wonder whether she hadn't better venture. For when she thought about it, what friend had she in all the world she loved better than the Sun? Where her hut lay not a ray of sunlight penetrated her room the whole winter long. She counted the days until the Sun would come back to her in the spring. The Sun was the only one she longed for, the only one who was always friendly and gracious to her and of whom she could never see enough.

She looked her years, and felt them, too. Her hands shook as if she were in a perpetual chill and when she saw herself in the looking-glass, she appeared so pale and washed out, as if she had been lying out to bleach. It was only when she stood in a strong, warm, down-pouring sunshine that she felt like a live human being and not a walking corpse.

The more she thought about it, the more she felt there was no day in the whole year she would rather celebrate than the one when her friend the Sun battled against darkness, and after a glorious conquest, came forth with new splendor and majesty.

The seventeenth of April was not far away, but there was ample time to make ready for a party. So, on the day of the eclipse Stina, Lina, Kajsa, Maja, and the other women all sat drinking coffee with Beda at Finn-darkness. They drank their second and their third cups, and chatted about everything imaginable. For one thing, they said they couldn't for the life of them understand why Beda should be giving a party.

Meanwhile, the eclipse was under way. But they took little notice of it. Only for a moment, when the sky turned blackish gray, when all nature seemed under a leaden pall, and there came driving a howling wind with sounds as of the Trumpet of Doom and the lamentations of Judgment Day — only then did they pause and feel a bit awed. But here they each had a fresh cup of coffee, and the feeling soon passed.

When all was over, and the Sun stood out in the heavens so beamingly happy — it seemed to them it had not shone with such brilliancy and power the whole year — they saw old Beda go over to the window, and stand with folded hands. Looking out toward the sunlit slope, she sang in her quavering voice:

> *Thy shining sun goes up again,*
> *I thank Thee, O my Lord!*
> *With new-found courage, strength and hope,*
> *I raise a song of joy.*

Thin and transparent, old Beda stood there in the light of the window, and as she sang the sunbeams danced about her, as if wanting to give her, also, of their life and strength and color.

When she had finished the old hymn-verse she turned and looked at her guests, as if in apology.

"You see," she said, "I haven't any better friend than the Sun, and I wanted to give her a party on the day of her eclipse. I felt that we should come together to greet her, when she came out of her darkness."

Now they understood what old Beda meant, and their hearts were touched. They began to speak well of the Sun. "She was kind to rich and poor alike, and when she came peeping into the hut on a winter's day, she was as comforting as a glowing fire on the hearth. Just the sight of her smiling face made life worth living, whatever the troubles one had to bear."

The women went back to their homes after the party, happy and content. They somehow felt richer and more secure in the thought that they had a good, faithful friend in the Sun.

DON DELILLO

Human Moments in World War III
1983

A note about Vollmer. He no longer describes the earth as a library globe or a map that has come alive, as a cosmic eye staring into deep space. This last was his most ambitious fling at imagery. The war has changed the way he sees the earth. The earth is land and water, the dwelling place of mortal men, in elevated dictionary terms. He doesn't see it any more (storm-spiraled, sea-bright, breathing heat and haze and color) as an occasion for picturesque language, for easeful play or speculation.

At two hundred and twenty kilometers we see ship wakes and the larger airports. Icebergs, lightning bolts, sand dunes. I point out lava flows and cold-core eddies. That silver ribbon off the Irish coast, I tell him, is an oil slick.

This is my third orbital mission, Vollmer's first. He is an engineering genius, a communications and weapons genius, and maybe other kinds of genius as well. As mission specialist I'm content to be in charge. (The word *specialist*, in the standard usage of Colorado Command, refers here to someone who does not specialize.) Our spacecraft is designed primarily to gather intelligence. The refinement of the quantum-burn technique enables us to make frequent adjustments of orbit without firing rockets every time. We swing out into high, wide trajectories, the whole earth as our psychic light, to inspect unmanned and possibly hostile satellites. We orbit tightly, snugly, take intimate looks at surface activities in untraveled places.

The banning of nuclear weapons has made the world safe for war.

I try not to think big thoughts or submit to rambling abstractions. But the urge sometimes comes over me. Earth orbit puts men into philosophical temper. How can we help it? We see the planet complete, we have a privileged vista. In our attempts to be equal to the experience, we tend to meditate importantly on subjects like the human condition. It makes a man feel *universal*, floating over the continents, seeing the rim of the world, a line as clear as a compass arc, knowing it is just a turning of the bend to Atlantic twilight, to sediment plumes and kelp beds, an island chain glowing in the dusky sea.

I tell myself it is only scenery. I want to think of our life here as ordinary, as a housekeeping arrangement, an unlikely but workable setup caused by a housing shortage or spring floods in the valley.

Vollmer does the systems checklist and goes to his hammock to rest. He is twenty-three years old, a boy with a longish head and close-cropped hair. He talks about northern Minnesota as he removes the objects in his personal-preference kit, placing them on an adjacent Velcro surface for tender inspection. I have a 1901 silver dollar in my personal-preference kit. Little else of note. Vollmer has graduation pictures, bottle caps, small stones from his backyard. I don't know whether he chose these items himself or whether they were pressed on him by parents who feared that his life in space would be lacking in human moments.

Our hammocks are human moments, I suppose, although I don't know whether Colorado Command planned it that way. We eat hot dogs and almond crunch bars and apply lip balm as part of the pre-sleep checklist. We wear slippers at the firing panel. Vollmer's football jersey is a human moment. Outsize, purple and white, of polyester mesh, bearing the number 79, a big man's number, a prime of no particular distinction, it makes him look stoop-shouldered, abnormally long-framed.

"I still get depressed on Sundays," he says.

"Do we have Sundays here?"

"No, but they have them there and I still feel them. I always know when it's Sunday."

"Why do you get depressed?"

"The slowness of Sundays. Something about the glare, the smell of warm grass, the church service, the relatives visiting in nice clothes. The whole day kind of lasts forever."

"I didn't like Sundays either."

"They were slow but not lazy-slow. They were long and hot, or long and cold. In summer my grandmother made lemonade. There was a routine. The whole day was kind of set up beforehand and the routine almost never changed. Orbital routine is different. It's satisfying. It gives our time a shape and substance. Those Sundays were shapeless despite the fact you knew what was coming, who was coming, what we'd all say. You knew the first words out of the mouth of each person before anyone spoke. I was the only kid in the group. People were happy to see me. I used to want to hide."

"What's wrong with lemonade?" I ask.

A battle-management satellite, unmanned, reports high-energy laser activity in orbital sector Dolores. We take out our laser kits and study them for half an hour. The beaming procedure is complex, and because the panel operates on joint control only, we must rehearse the sets of established measures with the utmost care.

A note about the earth. The earth is the preserve of day and night. It contains a sane and balanced variation, a natural waking and sleeping, or so it seems to someone deprived of this tidal effect.

This is why Vollmer's remark about Sundays in Minnesota struck me as interesting. He still feels, or claims he feels, or thinks he feels, that inherently earthbound rhythm.

To men at this remove, it is as though things exist in their particular physical form in order to reveal the hidden simplicity of some powerful mathematical truth. The earth reveals to us the simple awesome beauty of day and night. It is there to contain and incorporate these conceptual events.

Vollmer in his shorts and suction clogs resembles a high school swimmer, all but hairless, an unfinished man not aware he is open to cruel scrutiny, not aware he is without devices, standing with arms folded in a place of echoing voices and chlorine fumes. There is something stupid in the sound of his voice. It is too direct, a deep voice from high in the mouth, slightly insistent, a little loud. Vollmer has never said a stupid thing in my presence. It is just his voice that is stupid, a grave and naked bass, a voice without inflection or breath.

We are not cramped here. The flight deck and crew quarters are thoughtfully designed. Food is fair to good. There are books, video cassettes, news and music. We do the manual checklists, the oral checklists, the simulated firings with no sign of boredom or carelessness. If anything, we are getting better at our tasks all the time. The only danger is conversation.

I try to keep our conversations on an everyday plane. I make it a point to talk about small things, routine things. This makes sense to me. It seems a sound tactic, under the circumstances, to restrict our talk to familiar topics, minor matters. I want to build a structure of the commonplace. But Vollmer has a tendency to bring up enormous subjects. He wants to talk about war and the weapons of war. He wants to discuss global strategies, global aggressions. I tell him now that he has stopped describing the earth as a cosmic eye he wants to see it as a game board or computer model. He looks at me plain-faced and tries to get me in a theoretical argument: selective space-based attacks versus long, drawn-out, well-modulated land-sea-air engagements. He quotes experts, mentions sources. What am I supposed to say? He will suggest that people are disappointed in the war. The war is dragging into its third week. There is a sense in which it is worn out, played out. He gathers this from the news broadcasts we periodically receive. Something in the announcer's voice hints at a let-down, a fatigue, a faint bitterness about — *something*. Vollmer is probably right about this. I've heard myself in the tone of the broadcaster's voice, in the voice of Colorado Command, despite the fact that our news is censored, that they are not telling us things they feel we shouldn't know, in our special situation, our exposed and sensitive position. In his direct and stupid-sounding and uncannily perceptive way, young Vollmer says that people are not enjoying this war to the same extent that people have always enjoyed and nourished themselves on war, as a heightening, a periodic intensity. What I object to in Vollmer is that he often shares my deep-reaching and most reluctantly held convictions. Coming from that mild face, in that earnest resonant run-on voice, these ideas unnerve and worry me as they never do when they remain unspoken. I want words to be secretive, to cling to a darkness in the deepest interior. Vollmer's candor exposes something painful.

It is not too early in the war to discern nostalgic references to earlier wars. All wars refer back. Ships, planes, entire operations are named after ancient battles, simpler weapons, what we perceive as conflicts of nobler intent. This recon-interceptor is called *Tomahawk II*. When I sit at the firing panel I look at a photograph of Vollmer's granddad when he was a young man in sagging khakis and a shallow helmet, standing in a bare field, a rifle strapped to his shoulder. This is a human moment, and it reminds me that war, among other things, is a form of longing.

We dock with the command station, take on food, exchange cassettes. The war is going well, they tell us, although it isn't likely they know much more than we do.

Then we separate.

The maneuvre is flawless and I am feeling happy and satisfied, having resumed human contact with the nearest form of the outside world, having traded quips and manly insults, traded voices, traded news and rumors – buzzes, rumbles, scuttle-butt. We stow our supplies of broccoli and apple cider and fruit cocktail and butterscotch pudding. I feel a homey emotion, putting away the colorfully packaged goods, a sensation of prosperous well-being, the consumer's solid comfort.

Vollmer's T-shirt bears the word INSCRIPTION.

"People had hoped to be caught up in something bigger than themselves," he says. "They thought it would be a shared crisis. They would feel a sense of shared purpose, shared destiny. Like a snowstorm that blankets a large city – but lasting months, lasting years, carrying everyone along, creating fellow feeling where there was only suspicion and fear. Strangers talking to each other, meals by candlelight when the power fails. The war would ennoble everything we say and do. What was impersonal would become personal. What was solitary would be shared. But what happens when the sense of shared crisis begins to dwindle much sooner than anyone expected? We begin to think the feeling lasts longer in snowstorms."

A note about selective noise. Forty-eight hours ago I was monitoring data on the mission console when a voice broke in on my report to Colorado Command. The voice was unenhanced, heavy with static. I checked my headset, checked the switches and lights. Seconds later the command signal resumed and I heard our flight-dynamics officer ask me to switch to the redundant sense frequencer. I did this but it only caused the weak voice to return, a voice that carried with it a strange and unspecifiable poignancy. I seemed somehow to recognize it. I don't mean I knew who was speaking. It was the tone I recognized, the touching quality of some half-remembered and tender event, even through the static, the sonic mist.

In any case, Colorado Command resumed transmission in a matter of seconds.

"We have a deviate, Tomahawk."

"We copy. There's a voice."

"We have gross oscillation here."

"There's some interference. I have gone redundant but I'm not sure it's helping."

"We are clearing an outframe to locate source."

"Thank you, Colorado."

"It is probably just selective noise. You are negative red on the step-function quad."

"It was a voice," I told them.

"We have just received an affirm on selective noise."

"I could hear words, in English."

"We copy selective noise."

"Someone was talking, Colorado."

"What do you think selective noise is?"

"I don't know what it is."

"You are getting a spill from one of the unmanneds."

"If it's an unmanned, how could it be sending a voice?"

"It is not a voice as such, Tomahawk. It is selective noise. We have some real firm telemetry on that."

"It sounded like a voice."

"It is supposed to sound like a voice. But it is not a voice as such. It is enhanced."

"It sounded unenhanced. It sounded human in all sorts of ways."

"It is signals and they are spilling from geosynchronous orbit. This is your deviate. You are getting voice codes from twenty-two thousand miles. It is basically a weather report. We will correct, Tomahawk. In the meantime, advise you stay redundant."

About ten hours later Vollmer heard the voice. Then he heard two or three other voices. They were people speaking, people in conversation. He gestured to me as he listened, pointed to the headset, then raised his shoulders, held his hands apart to indicate surprise and bafflement. In the swarming noise (as he said later) it wasn't easy to get the drift of what people were saying. The static was frequent, the references were somewhat elusive, but Vollmer mentioned how intensely affecting these voices were, even when the signals were at their weakest. One thing he did know: it wasn't selective noise. A quality of purest, sweetest sadness issued from remote space. He wasn't sure, but he thought there was also a background noise integral to the conversation. Laughter. The sound of people laughing.

In other transmissions we've been able to recognize theme music, an announcer's introduction, wisecracks and bursts of applause, commercials for products whose long-lost brand names evoke the golden antiquity of great cities buried in sand and river silt.

Somehow we are picking up signals from radio programs of forty, fifty, sixty years ago.

Our current task is to collect imagery data on troop deployment. Vollmer surrounds his Hasselblad, engrossed in some microadjustment. There is a seaward bulge of stratocumulus. Sun glint and littoral drift. I see blooms of plankton in a blue of such Persian richness it seems an animal rapture, a color change to express some form of intuitive delight. As the surface features unfurl I list them aloud by name. It is the only game I play in space, reciting the earth names, the nomenclature of contour and structure. Glacial scour, moraine debris. Shatter-coning at the edge of a multi-ring impact site. A resurgent caldera, a mass of castellated rimrock. Over the sand seas now. Parabolic dunes, star dunes, straight dunes with radial crests. The emptier the land, the more luminous and precise the names for its features. Vollmer says the thing science does best is name the features of the world.

He has degrees in science and technology. He was a scholarship winner, an honors student, a research assistant. He ran science projects, read technical papers in the deep-pitched earnest voice that rolls off the roof of his mouth. As mission specialist (generalist), I sometimes resent his non-scientific perceptions, the glimmerings of maturity and balanced judgement. I am beginning to feel slightly preempted. I want him to stick to systems, onboard guidance, data parameters. His human insights make me nervous.

"I'm happy," he says.

These words are delivered with matter-of-fact finality, and the simple statement affects me powerfully. It frightens me, in fact. What does he mean he's happy? Isn't happiness totally outside our frame of reference? How can he think it is possible to be happy here? I want to say to him, "This is just a housekeeping arrangement, a series of more or less routine tasks. Attend to your tasks, do your testing, run through your checklists." I want to say, "Forget the measure of our vision, the sweep of things, the war itself, the terrible death. Forget the overarching night, the stars as static points, as mathematical fields. Forget the cosmic solitude, the upwelling awe and dread."

I want to say, "Happiness is not a fact of this experience, at least not to the extent that one is bold enough to speak of it."

Laser technology contains a core of foreboding and myth. It is a clean sort of lethal package we are dealing with, a well-behaved beam of photons, an engineered coherence, but we approach the weapon with our minds full of ancient warnings and fears. (There ought to be a term for this ironic condition: primitive fear of the weapons we are advanced enough to design and produce.) Maybe this is why the project managers were ordered to work out a firing procedure that depends on the coordinated actions of two men – two temperaments, two souls – operating the controls together. Fear of the power of light, the pure stuff of the universe.

A single dark mind in a moment of inspiration might think it liberating to fling a concentrated beam at some lumbering humpbacked Boeing making its commercial rounds at thirty thousand feet.

Vollmer and I approach the firing panel. The panel is designed in such a way that the joint operators must sit back to back. The reason for this, although Colorado Command never specifically said so, is to keep us from seeing each other's face. Colorado wants to be sure that weapons personnel in particular are not influenced by each other's tics and perturbations. We are back to back, therefore, harnessed in our seats, ready to begin, Vollmer in his purple and white jersey, his fleeced pad-abouts.

This is only a test.

I start the playback. At the sound of a prerecorded voice command, we each insert a modal key in its proper slot. Together we count down from five and then turn the keys one quarter left. This puts the system in what is called an open-minded mode. We count down from three. The enhanced voice says, *You are open-minded now.*

Vollmer speaks into his voice-print analyzer.

"This is code B for *bluegrass*. Request voice-identity clearance."

We count down from five and then speak into our voice-print analyzers. We say whatever comes into our heads. The point is simply to produce a voiceprint that matches the print in the memory bank. This ensures that the men at the panel are the same men authorized to be there when the system is in an open-minded mode.

This is what comes into my head: "I am standing at the corner of Fourth and Main, where thousands are dead of unknown causes, their scorched bodies piled in the street."

We count down from three. The enhanced voice says, *You are cleared to proceed to lock-in position.*

We turn our modal keys half right. I activate the logic chip and study the numbers on my screen. Vollmer disengages voiceprint and puts us in voice circuit rapport with the onboard computer's sensing mesh. We count down from five. The enhanced voice says, *You are locked in now.*

As we move from one step to the next a growing satisfaction passes through me – the pleasure of elite and secret skills, a life in which every breath is governed by specific rules, by patterns, codes, controls. I try to keep the results of the operation out of my mind, the whole point of it, the outcome of these sequences of precise and esoteric steps. But often I fail. I let the image in, I think the thought, I even say the word at times. This is confusing, of course. I feel tricked. My pleasure feels betrayed, as if it had a life of its own, a childlike or intelligent-animal existence independent of the man at the firing panel.

We count down from five. Vollmer releases the lever that unwinds the systems-purging disc. My pulse-marker shows green at three-second intervals. We count down from three. We turn the modal keys three quarters right. I activate the beam sequencer. We turn the keys one-quarter right. We count down from three. Bluegrass music plays over the squawk box. The enhanced voice says, *You are moded to fire now.*

We study our world-map kits.

"Don't you sometimes feel a power in you?" Vollmer says. "An extreme state of good health, sort of. An *arrogant* healthiness. That's it. You are feeling so good you begin thinking you're a little superior to other people. A kind of life-strength. An optimism about yourself that you generate almost at the expense of others. Don't you sometimes feel this?"

(Yes, as a matter of fact.)

"There's probably a German word for it. But the point I want to make is that this powerful feeling is so – I don't know – *delicate*. That's it. One day you feel it, the next day you are suddenly puny and doomed. A single little thing goes wrong, you feel doomed, you feel utterly weak and defeated and unable to act powerfully or even sensibly. Everyone else is lucky, you are unlucky, hapless, sad, ineffectual and doomed."

(Yes, yes.)

By chance, we are over the Missouri River now, looking toward the Red Lakes of Minnesota. I watch Vollmer go through his map kit, trying to match the two worlds. This is a deep and mysterious happiness, to confirm the accuracy of a map. He seems immensely satisfied. He keeps saying, *"That's it, that's it."*

Vollmer talks about childhood. In orbit he has begun to think about his early years for the first time. He is surprised at the power of these memories. As he speaks he keeps his head turned to the window. Minnesota is a human moment. Upper Red Lake, Lower Red Lake. He clearly feels he can see himself there.

"Kids don't take walks," he says. "They don't sunbathe or sit on the porch."

He seems to be saying that children's lives are too well supplied to accommodate the spells of reinforced being that the rest of us depend on. A deft enough thought but not to be pursued. It is time to prepare for a quantum burn.

We listen to the old radio shows. Light flares and spreads across the blue-banded edge, sunrise, sunset, the urban grids in shadow. A man and a woman trade well-timed remarks, light, pointed, bantering. There is a sweetness in the tenor voice of the young man singing, a simple vigor that time and distance and random noise have enveloped in eloquence and yearning. Every sound, every lilt of strings has this veneer of age. Vollmer says he remembers these programs, although of course he has never heard them before. What odd happenstance, what flourish or grace of the laws of physics enables us to pick up these signals? Traveled voices, chambered and dense. At times they have the detached and surreal quality of aural hallucination, voices in attic rooms, the complaints of dead relatives. But the sound effects are full of urgency and verve. Cars turn dangerous corners, crisp gunfire fills the night. It was, it is, wartime. Wartime for Duz and Grape-Nuts Flakes. Comedians make fun of the way the enemy talks. We hear hysterical mock German, moonshine Japanese. The cities are in light, the listening millions, fed, met comfortably in drowsy rooms, at war, as the night comes softly down. Vollmer says he recalls specific moments, the comic inflections, the announcer's fat-man laughter. He recalls individual voices rising from the laughter of the studio audience, the crackle of a St Louis businessman, the brassy wail of a high-shouldered blonde just arrived in California, where women wear their hair this year in aromatic bales.

Vollmer drifts across the wardroom upside down, eating an almond crunch.

He sometimes floats free of his hammock, sleeping in a fetal crouch, bumping into walls, adhering to a corner of the ceiling grid.

"Give me a minute to think of the name," he says in his sleep.

He says he dreams of vertical spaces from which he looks, as a boy, at – *something*. My dreams are the heavy kind, the kind that are hard to wake from, to rise out of. They are strong enough to pull me back down, dense enough to leave me with a heavy head, a drugged and bloated feeling. There are episodes of faceless gratification, vaguely disturbing.

"It's almost unbelievable when you think of it, how they live there in all that ice and sand and mountainous wilderness. Look at it," he says. "Huge barren deserts, huge oceans. How do they endure all those terrible things? The floods alone. The earthquakes alone make it crazy to live there. Look at those fault systems. They're so big, there's so many of them. The volcanic eruptions alone. What could be more frightening than a volcanic eruption? How do they endure avalanches, year after year, with numbing regularity? It's hard to believe people live there. The floods alone. You can see whole huge discolored areas, all flooded out, washed out. How do they survive, where do they go? Look at the cloud buildups. Look at that swirling storm center. What about the people who live in the path of a storm like that? It must be packing incredible winds. The lightning alone. People exposed on beaches, near trees and telephone poles. Look at the cities with their spangled lights spreading in all directions. Try to imagine the crime and violence. Look at the smoke pall hanging low. What does that mean in terms of respiratory disorders? It's crazy. Who would live there? The deserts, how they encroach. Every year they claim more and more arable land. How enormous those snowfields are. Look at the massive storm fronts over the ocean. There are ships down there, small craft, some of them. Try to imagine the waves, the rocking. The hurricanes alone. The tidal waves. Look at those coastal communities exposed to tidal waves. What could be more frightening than a tidal wave? But they live there, they stay there. Where could they go?'

I want to talk to him about calorie intake, the effectiveness of the earplugs and nasal decongestants. The earplugs are human moments. The apple cider and the broccoli are human moments. Vollmer himself is a human moment, never more so than when he forgets there is a war.

The close-cropped hair and longish head. The mild blue eyes that bulge slightly. The protuberant eyes of long-bodied people with stooped shoulders. The long hands and wrists. The mild face. The easy face of a handyman in a panel truck that has an extension ladder fixed to the roof and a scuffed license plate, green and white, with the state motto beneath the digits. That kind of face.

He offers to give me a haircut. What an interesting thing a haircut is, when you think of it. Before the war there were time slots reserved for such activities. Houston not only had everything scheduled well in advance but constantly monitored us for whatever meager feedback might result. We were wired, taped, scanned, diagnosed, and metered. We were men in space, objects worthy of the most scrupulous care, the deepest sentiments and anxieties.

Now there is a war. Nobody cares about my hair, what I eat, how I feel about the spacecraft's decor, and it is not Houston but Colorado we are in touch with. We are no longer delicate biological specimens adrift in an alien environment. The enemy can kill us with its photons, its mesons, its charged particles faster than any calcium deficiency or trouble of the inner ear, faster than any dusting of micrometeoroids. The emotions have changed. We've stopped being candidates for an embarrassing demise, the kind of mistake or unforeseen event that tends to make a nation grope for the appropriate response. As men in war, we can be certain, dying, that we will arouse uncomplicated sorrows, the open and dependable feelings that grateful nations count on to embellish the simplest ceremony.

A note about the universe. Vollmer is on the verge of deciding that our planet is alone in harboring intelligent life. We are an accident and we happened only once. (What a remark to make, in egg-shaped orbit, to someone who doesn't want to discuss the larger questions.) He feels this way because of the war.

The war, he says, will bring about an end to the idea that the universe swarms, as they say, with life. Other astronauts have looked past the star points and imagined infinite possibility, grape-clustered worlds teeming with higher forms. But this was before the war. Our view is changing even now, his and mine, he says, as we drift across the firmament.

Is Vollmer saying that cosmic optimism is a luxury reserved for periods between world wars? Do we project our current failure and despair out towards the star clouds, the endless night? After all, he says, where are they? If they exist, why has there been no sign, not one, not any, not a single indication that serious people might cling to, not a whisper, a radio pulse, a shadow? The war tells us it is foolish to believe.

Our dialogues with Colorado Command are beginning to sound like computer-generated teatime chat. Vollmer tolerates Colorado's jargon only to a point. He is critical of their more debased locutions and doesn't mind letting them know. Why, then, if I agree with his views on this matter, am I becoming irritated by his complaints? Is he too young to champion the language? Does he have the experience, the professional standing to scold our flight-dynamics officer, our conceptual-paradigm officer, our status consultants on waste-management systems and evasion-related zonal options? Or is it something else completely, something unrelated to

Colorado Command and our communications with them? Is it the sound of his voice? Is it just his *voice* that is driving me crazy?

———————

Vollmer has entered a strange phase. He spends all his time at the window now, looking down at the earth. He says little or nothing. He simply wants to look, do nothing but look. The oceans, the continents, the archipelagoes. We are configured in what is called a cross-orbit series and there is no repetition from one swing around the earth to the next. He sits there looking. He takes meals at the window, does checklists at the window, barely glancing at the instruction sheets as we pass over tropical storms, over grass fires and major ranges. I keep waiting for him to return to his prewar habit of using quaint phrases to describe the earth: it's a beach ball, a sun-ripened fruit. But he simply looks out of the window, eating almond crunches, the wrappers floating away. The view clearly fills his consciousness. It is powerful enough to silence him, to still the voice that rolls off the roof of his mouth, to leave him turned in the seat, twisted uncomfortably for hours at a time.

The view is endlessly fulfilling. It is like the answer to a lifetime of questions and vague cravings. It satisfies every childlike curiosity, every muted desire, whatever there is in him of the scientist, the poet, the primitive seer, the watcher of fire and shooting stars, whatever obsessions eat at the night side of his mind, whatever sweet and dreamy yearning he has ever felt for nameless places far away, whatever earth sense he possesses, the neural pulse of some wilder awareness, a sympathy for beasts, whatever belief in an immanent vital force, the Lord of Creation, whatever secret harboring of the idea of human oneness, whatever wishfulness and simple-hearted hope, whatever of too much and not enough, all at once and little by little, whatever burning urge to escape responsibility and routine, escape his own over-specialization, the circumscribed and inward-spiraling self, whatever remnants of his boyish longing to fly, his dreams of strange spaces and eerie heights, his fantasies of happy death, whatever indolent and sybaritic leanings — lotus-eater, smoker of grasses and herbs, blue-eyed gazer into space — all these are satisfied, all collected and massed in that living body, the sight he sees from the window.

'It is just so interesting,' he says at last. 'The colors and all.'

The colors and all.

H.G. WELLS

The Star
1897

It was on the first day of the New Year that the announcement was made, almost simultaneously from three observatories, that the motion of the planet Neptune, the outermost of all the planets that wheel about the sun, had become very erratic. Ogilvy had already called attention to a suspected retardation in its velocity in December. Such a piece of news was scarcely calculated to interest a world the greater portion of whose inhabitants were unaware of the existence of the planet Neptune, nor outside the astronomical profession did the subsequent discovery of a faint remote speck of light in the region of the perturbed planet cause any very great excitement. Scientific people, however, found the intelligence remarkable enough, even before it became known that the new body was rapidly growing larger and brighter, that its motion was quite different from the orderly progress of the planets, and that the deflection of Neptune and its satellite was becoming now of an unprecedented kind.

Few people without a training in science can realise the huge isolation of the solar system. The sun with its specks of planets, its dust of planetoids, and its impalpable comets, swims in a vacant immensity that almost defeats the imagination. Beyond the orbit of Neptune there is space, vacant so far as human observation has penetrated, without warmth or light or sound, blank emptiness, for twenty million times a million miles. That is the smallest estimate of the distance to be traversed before the very nearest of the stars is attained. And, saving a few comets more unsubstantial than the thinnest flame, no matter had ever to human knowledge crossed this gulf of space, until early in the twentieth century this strange wanderer appeared. A vast mass of matter it was, bulky, heavy, rushing without warning out of the black mystery of the sky into the radiance of the sun. By the second day it was clearly visible to any decent instrument, as a speck with a barely sensible diameter, in the constellation Leo near Regulus. In a little while an opera glass could attain it.

On the third day of the new year the newspaper readers of two hemispheres were made aware for the first time of the real importance of this unusual apparition in the heavens. "A Planetary Collision," one London paper headed the news, and proclaimed Duchaine's opinion that this strange new planet would probably collide with Neptune. The leader writers enlarged upon the topic; so that in most of the capitals of the world, on January 3rd, there was an expectation, however vague of some imminent phenomenon in the sky; and as the night followed the sunset round the globe, thousands of men turned their eyes skyward to see — the old familiar stars just as they had always been.

Until it was dawn in London and Pollux setting and the stars overhead grown pale. The Winter's dawn it was, a sickly filtering accumulation of daylight, and the light of gas and candles shone yellow in the windows to show where people were astir. But the yawning policeman saw the thing, the busy crowds in the markets stopped agape, workmen going to their work betimes, milkmen, the drivers of news-carts, dissipation going home jaded and pale, homeless wanderers, sentinels on their beats, and in the country, labourers trudging afield, poachers slinking home, all over the dusky quickening country it could be seen — and out at sea by seamen watching for the day — a great white star, come suddenly into the westward sky!

Brighter it was than any star in our skies; brighter than the evening star at its brightest. It still glowed out white and large, no mere twinkling spot of light, but a small round clear shining disc, an hour after the day had come. And where science has not reached, men stared and feared, telling one another of the wars and pestilences that are foreshadowed by these fiery signs in the Heavens. Sturdy Boers, dusky Hottentots, Gold Coast negroes, Frenchmen, Spaniards, Portuguese, stood in the warmth of the sunrise watching the setting of this strange new star.

And in a hundred observatories there had been suppressed excitement, rising almost to shouting pitch, as the two remote bodies had rushed together; and a hurrying to and fro, to gather photographic apparatus and spectroscope, and this appliance and that, to record this novel astonishing sight, the destruction of a world. For it was a world, a sister planet of our earth, far greater than our earth indeed, that had so suddenly flashed into flaming death. Neptune it was, had been struck, fairly and squarely, by the strange planet from outer space and the heat of the concussion had incontinently turned two solid globes into one vast mass of incandescence. Round the world that day, two hours before the dawn, went the pallid great white star, fading only as it sank westward and the sun mounted above it. Everywhere men marvelled at it, but of all those who saw it none could have marvelled more than those sailors, habitual watchers of the stars, who far away at sea had heard nothing of its advent and saw it now rise like a pigmy moon and climb zenithward and hang overhead and sink westward with the passing of the night.

And when next it rose over Europe everywhere were crowds of watchers on hilly slopes, on house-roofs, in open spaces, staring eastward for the rising of the great new star. It rose with a white glow in front of it, like the glare of a white fire, and those who had seen it come into existence the night before cried out at the sight of it. "It is larger," they cried. "It is brighter!" And, indeed the moon a quarter full and sinking in the west was in its apparent size beyond comparison, but scarcely in all its breadth had it as much brightness now as the little circle of the strange new star.

"It is brighter!" cried the people clustering in the streets. But in the dim observatories the watchers held their breath and peered at one another. *"It is nearer!"* they said. *"Nearer!"*

And voice after voice repeated, "It is nearer," and the clicking telegraph took that up, and it trembled along telephone wires, and in a thousand cities grimy compositors fingered the type. "It is nearer." Men writing in offices, struck with a strange realisation, flung down their pens, men talking in a thousand places suddenly came upon a grotesque possibility in those words, "It is nearer." It hurried along wakening streets, it was shouted down the frost-stilled ways of quiet villages; men who had read these things from the throbbing tape stood in yellow-lit doorways shouting the news to the passersby. "It is nearer." Pretty women, flushed and glittering, heard the news told jestingly between the dances, and feigned an intelligent interest they did not feel. "Nearer! Indeed. How curious! How very, very clever people must be to find out things like that!"

Lonely tramps faring through the wintry night murmured those words to comfort themselves — looking skyward. "It has need to be nearer, for the night's as cold as charity. Don't seem much warmth from it if it is nearer, all the same."

"What is a new star to me?" cried the weeping woman kneeling beside her dead.

The schoolboy, rising early for his examination work, puzzled it out for himself — with the great white star shining broad and bright through the frost-flowers of his window. "Centrifugal, centripetal," he said, with his chin on his fist. "Stop a planet in its flight, rob it of its centrifugal force, what then? Centripetal has it, and down it falls into the sun! And this —!"

"Do *we* come in the way? I wonder —"

The light of that day went the way of its brethren, and with the later watches of the frosty darkness rose the strange star again. And it was now so bright that the waxing moon seemed but a pale yellow ghost of itself, hanging huge in the sunset. In a South African City a great man had married, and the streets were alight to welcome his return with his bride. "Even the skies have illuminated," said the flatterer. Under Capricorn, two negro lovers, daring the wild beasts and evil spirits, for love of one another, crouched together in a cane brake where the fire-flies hovered. "That is our star," they whispered, and felt strangely comforted by the sweet brilliance of its light.

The master mathematician sat in his private room and pushed the papers from him. His calculations were already finished. In a small white phial there still remained a little of the drug that had kept him awake and active for four long nights. Each day, serene, explicit, patient as ever, he had given his lecture to his students, and then had come back at once to this momentous calculation. His face was grave, a little drawn and hectic from his drugged activity. For some time he seemed lost in thought. Then he went to the window, and the blind went up with a click. Half way up the sky, over the clustering roofs, chimneys and steeples of the city, hung the star.

He looked at it as one might look into the eyes of a brave enemy. "You may kill me," he said after a silence. "But I can hold you — and all the universe for that matter — in the grip of this little brain. I would not change. Even now."

He looked at the little phial. "There will be no need of sleep again," he said. The next day at noon — punctual to the minute, he entered his lecture theatre, put his hat on the end of the table as his habit was, and carefully selected a large piece of chalk. It was a joke among his students that he could not lecture without that piece of chalk to fumble in his fingers, and once he had been stricken to impotence by their hiding his supply. He came and looked under his grey eyebrows at the rising tiers of young fresh faces, and spoke with his accustomed studied commonness of phrasing.

"Circumstances have arisen — circumstances beyond my control," he said and paused, "which will debar me from completing the course I had designed. It would seem, gentlemen, if I may put the thing clearly and briefly, that — Man has lived in vain."

The students glanced at one another. Had they heard aright? Mad? Raised eyebrows and grinning lips there were, but one or two faces remained intent upon his calm grey-fringed face. "It will be interesting," he was saying, "to devote this morning to an exposition, so far as I can make it clear to you, of the calculations that have led me to this conclusion. Let us assume —"

He turned towards the blackboard, meditating a diagram in the way that was usual to him. "What was that about 'lived in vain?'" whispered one student to another. "Listen," said the other, nodding towards the lecturer.

And presently they began to understand.

That night the star rose later, for its proper eastward motion had carried it some way across Leo towards Virgo, and its brightness was so great that the sky became a luminous blue as it rose, and every star was hidden in its turn, save only Jupiter near the zenith, Capella, Aldebaran, Sirius and the pointers of the Bear. It was very white and beautiful. In many parts of the world that night a pallid halo encircled it about. It was perceptibly larger; in the clear refractive sky of the tropics it seemed as if it were nearly a quarter the size of the moon. The frost was still on the ground in England, but the world was as brightly lit as if it were midsummer moonlight. One could see to read quite ordinary print by that cold clear light, and in the cities the lamps burnt yellow and wan.

And everywhere the world was awake that night, and throughout Christendom a sombre murmur hung in the keen air over the country side like the belling of bees in the heather, and this murmurous tumult grew to a clangour in the cities. It was the tolling of the bells in a million belfry towers and steeples, summoning the people to sleep no more, to sin no more, but to gather in their churches and pray. And overhead, growing larger and brighter as the earth rolled on its way and the night passed, rose the dazzling star.

And the streets and houses were alight in all the cities, the shipyards glared, and whatever roads led to high country were lit and crowded all night long. And in all the seas about the civilised lands, ships with throbbing engines, and ships with bellying sails, crowded with men and living creatures, were standing out to ocean and the north. For already the warning of the master mathematician had been telegraphed all over the world, and translated into a hundred tongues. The new planet and Neptune, locked in a fiery embrace, were whirling headlong, ever faster and faster towards the sun. Already every second this blazing mass flew a hundred miles, and every second its terrific velocity increased. As it flew now, indeed, it must pass a hundred million of miles wide of the earth and scarcely affect it. But near its destined path, as yet only slightly perturbed, spun the mighty planet Jupiter and his moons sweeping splendid round the sun. Every moment now the attraction between the fiery star and the greatest of the planets grew stronger. And the result of that attraction? Inevitably Jupiter would be deflected from its orbit into an elliptical path, and the burning star, swung by his attraction wide of its sunward rush, would "describe a curved path" and perhaps collide with, and certainly pass very close to, our earth. "Earthquakes, volcanic outbreaks, cyclones, sea waves, floods, and a steady rise in temperature to I know not what limit" — so prophesied the master mathematician.

And overhead, to carry out his words, lonely and cold and livid, blazed the star of the coming doom.

To many who stared at it that night until their eyes ached, it seemed that it was visibly approaching. And that night, too, the weather changed, and the frost that had gripped all

Central Europe and France and England softened towards a thaw.

But you must not imagine because I have spoken of people praying through the night and people going aboard ships and people fleeing toward mountainous country that the whole world was already in a terror because of the star. As a matter of fact, use and wont still ruled the world, and save for the talk of idle moments and the splendour of the night, nine human beings out of ten were still busy at their common occupations. In all the cities the shops, save one here and there, opened and closed at their proper hours, the doctor and the undertaker plied their trades, the workers gathered in the factories, soldiers drilled, scholars studied, lovers sought one another, thieves lurked and fled, politicians planned their schemes. The presses of the newspapers roared through the night, and many a priest of this church and that would not open his holy building to further what he considered a foolish panic. The newspapers insisted on the lesson of the year 1000 — for then, too, people had anticipated the end. The star was no star — mere gas — a comet; and were it a star it could not possibly strike the earth. There was no precedent for such a thing. Common sense was sturdy everywhere, scornful, jesting, a little inclined to persecute the obdurate fearful. That night, at seven-fifteen by Greenwich time, the star would be at its nearest to Jupiter. Then the world would see the turn things would take. The master mathematician's grim warnings were treated by many as so much mere elaborate self-advertisement. Common sense at last, a little heated by argument, signified its unalterable convictions by going to bed. So, too, barbarism and savagery, already tired of the novelty, went about their nightly business, and save for a howling dog here and there, the beast world left the star unheeded.

And yet, when at last the watchers in the European States saw the star rise, an hour later it is true, but no larger than it had been the night before, there were still plenty awake to laugh at the master mathematician--to take the danger as if it had passed.

But hereafter the laughter ceased. The star grew — it grew with a terrible steadiness hour after hour, a little larger each hour, a little nearer the midnight zenith, and brighter and brighter, until it had turned night into a second day. Had it come straight to the earth instead of in a curved path, had it lost no velocity to Jupiter, it must have leapt the intervening gulf in a day, but as it was it took five days altogether to come by our planet. The next night it had become a third the size of the moon before it set to English eyes, and the thaw was assured. It rose over America near the size of the moon, but blinding white to look at, and hot; and a breath of hot wind blew now with its rising and gathering strength, and in Virginia, and Brazil, and down the St. Lawrence valley, it shone intermittently through a driving reek of thunder-clouds, flickering violet lightning, and hail unprecedented. In Manitoba was a thaw and devastating floods. And upon all the mountains of the earth the snow and ice began to melt that night, and all the rivers coming out of high country flowed thick and turbid, and soon — in their upper reaches — with swirling trees and the bodies of beasts and men. They rose steadily, steadily in the ghostly brilliance, and came trickling over their banks at last, behind the flying population of their valleys.

And along the coast of Argentina and up the South Atlantic the tides were higher than had ever been in the memory of man, and the storms drove the waters in many cases scores of miles inland, drowning whole cities. And so great grew the heat during the night that the rising of the sun was like the coming of a shadow. The earthquakes began and grew until all down America from the Arctic Circle to Cape Horn, hillsides were sliding, fissures were opening, and houses and walls crumbling to destruction. The whole side of Cotopaxi slipped out in one vast convulsion, and a tumult of lava poured out so high and broad and swift and liquid that in one day it reached the sea.

So the star, with the wan moon in its wake, marched across the Pacific, trailed the thunderstorms like the hem of a robe, and the growing tidal wave that toiled behind it, frothing and eager, poured over island and island and swept them clear of men. Until that wave came at last — in a blinding light and with the breath of a furnace, swift and terrible it came — a wall of water, fifty feet high, roaring hungrily, upon the long coasts of Asia, and swept inland across the plains of China. For a space the star, hotter now and larger and brighter than the sun in its strength, showed with pitiless brilliance the wide and populous country; towns and villages with their pagodas and trees, roads, wide cultivated fields, millions of sleepless people staring in helpless terror at the incandescent sky; and then, low and growing, came the murmur of the flood. And thus it was with millions of men that night — a flight nowhither, with limbs heavy with heat and breath fierce and scant, and the flood like a wall swift and white behind. And then death.

China was lit glowing white, but over Japan and Java and all the islands of Eastern Asia the great star was a ball of dull red fire because of the steam and smoke and ashes the volcanoes were spouting forth to salute its coming. Above was the lava, hot gases and ash, and below the seething floods, and the whole earth swayed and rumbled with the earthquake shocks. Soon the immemorial snows of Thibet and the Himalaya were melting and pouring down by ten million deepening converging channels upon the plains of Burmah and Hindostan. The tangled summits of the Indian jungles were aflame in a thousand places, and below the hurrying waters around the stems were dark objects that still struggled feebly and reflected the blood-red tongues of fire. And in a rudderless confusion a multitude of men and women fled down the broad river-ways to that one last hope of men — the open sea.

Larger grew the star, and larger, hotter, and brighter with a terrible swiftness now. The tropical ocean had lost its phosphorescence, and the whirling steam rose in ghostly wreaths from the black waves that plunged incessantly, speckled with storm-tossed ships.

And then came a wonder. It seemed to those who in Europe watched for the rising of the star that the world must have ceased its rotation. In a thousand open spaces of down and upland the people who had fled thither from the floods and the falling houses and sliding slopes of hill watched for that rising in vain. Hour followed hour through a terrible suspense, and the star rose not. Once again men set their eyes upon the old constellations they had counted lost to them forever. In England it was hot and clear overhead, though the ground quivered perpetually, but in the tropics, Sirius and Capella and Aldebaran showed through a veil of steam. And when at last the great star rose near ten hours late, the sun rose close upon it, and in the centre of its white heart was a disc of black.

Over Asia it was the star had begun to fall behind the movement of the sky, and then suddenly, as it hung over India, its light had been veiled. All the plain of India from the mouth of the Indus to the mouths of the Ganges was a shallow waste of shining water that night, out of which rose temples and palaces, mounds and hills, black with people. Every minaret was a clustering mass of people, who fell one by one into the turbid waters, as heat and terror overcame them. The whole land seemed a-wailing and suddenly there swept a shadow across that furnace of despair, and a breath of cold wind, and a gathering of clouds, out of the cooling air. Men looking up, near blinded, at the star, saw that a black disc was creeping across the light. It was the moon, coming between the star and the earth. And even as men cried to God at this respite, out of the East with a strange inexplicable swiftness sprang the sun. And then star, sun and moon rushed together across the heavens.

So it was that presently, to the European watchers, star and sun rose close upon each other, drove headlong for a space and then slower, and at last came to rest, star and sun merged into one glare of flame at the zenith of the sky. The moon no longer eclipsed the star but was lost to sight in the brilliance of the sky. And though those who were still alive regarded it for the most part with that dull stupidity that hunger, fatigue, heat and despair engender, there were still men who could perceive the meaning of these signs. Star and earth had been at their nearest, had swung about one another, and the star had passed. Already it was receding, swifter and swifter, in the last stage of its headlong journey downward into the sun.

And then the clouds gathered, blotting out the vision of the sky, the thunder and lightning wove a garment round the world; all over the earth was such a downpour of rain as men had never before seen, and where the volcanoes flared red against the cloud canopy there descended torrents of mud. Everywhere the waters were pouring off the land, leaving mud-silted ruins, and the earth littered like a storm-worn beach with all that had floated, and the dead bodies of the men and brutes, its children. For days the water streamed off the land, sweeping away soil and trees and houses in the way, and piling huge dykes and scooping out Titanic gullies over the country side. Those were the days of darkness that followed the star and the heat. All through them, and for many weeks and months, the earthquakes continued.

But the star had passed, and men, hunger-driven and gathering courage only slowly, might creep back to their ruined cities, buried granaries, and sodden fields. Such few ships as had escaped the storms of that time came stunned and shattered and sounding their way cautiously through the new marks and shoals of once familiar ports. And as the storms subsided men perceived that everywhere the days were hotter than of yore, and the sun larger, and the moon, shrunk to a third of its former size, took now fourscore days between its new and new.

But of the new brotherhood that grew presently among men, of the saving of laws and books and machines, of the strange change that had come over Iceland and Greenland and the shores of Baffin's Bay, so that the sailors coming there presently found them green and gracious, and could scarce believe their eyes, this story does not tell. Nor of the movement of mankind now that the earth was hotter, northward and southward towards the poles of the earth. It concerns itself only with the coming and the passing of the Star.

The Martian astronomers — for there are astronomers on Mars, although they are very different beings from men — were naturally profoundly interested by these things. They saw them from their own standpoint of course. "Considering the mass and temperature of the missile that was flung through our solar system into the sun," one wrote, "it is astonishing what a little damage the earth, which it missed so narrowly, has sustained. All the familiar continental markings and the masses of the seas remain intact, and indeed the only difference seems to be a shrinkage of the white discoloration (supposed to be frozen water) round either pole." Which only shows how small the vastest of human catastrophes may seem, at a distance of a few million miles.

STEVEN MILLHAUSER

The Invasion From Outer Space
2009

From the beginning we were prepared, we knew just what to do, for hadn't we seen it all a hundred times?—the good people of the town going about their business, the suddenly interrupted TV programs, the faces in the crowd looking up, the little girl pointing in the air, the mouths opening, the dog yapping, the traffic stopped, the shopping bag falling to the sidewalk, and there, in the sky, coming closer... And so, when it finally happened, because it was bound to happen, we all knew it was only a matter of time, we felt, in the midst of our curiosity and terror, a certain calm, the calm of familiarity, we knew what was expected of us, at such a moment. The story broke a little after ten in the morning. The TV anchors looked exactly the way we knew they'd look, their faces urgent, their hair neat, their shoulders tense, they were filling us with alarm but also assuring us that everything was under control, for they, too, had been prepared for this, in a sense had been waiting for it, already they were looking back at themselves during their great moment. The sighting was indisputable but, at the same time, inconclusive: something from out there had been detected, it appeared to be approaching our atmosphere at great speed, the Pentagon was monitoring the situation closely. We were urged to remain calm, to stay inside, to await further instructions. Some of us left work immediately and hurried home to our families, others stayed close to the TV, the radio, the computer, we were all talking into our cells. Through our windows we could see people at their windows, looking up at the sky. All that morning we followed the news fiercely, like children listening to a thunderstorm in the dark. Whatever was out there was still unknown, scientists had not yet been able to determine its nature, caution was advised but there was no reason for panic, our job was to stay tuned and sit tight and await further developments. And though we were anxious, though quivers of nervousness ran along our bodies like mice, we wanted to see whatever it was, we wanted to be there, since after all it was coming toward *us*, it was ours to witness, as if we were the ones they'd chosen, out there on the other side of the sky. For already it was being said that our town was the likely landing place, already the TV crews were rolling in. We wondered where it would land: between the duck pond and the seesaws in the public park, or deep in the woods at the north end of town, or maybe in the field out by the mall, where a new excavation was already under way, or maybe it would glide over the old department store on Main Street and crash through the second-floor apartments above Mangione's Pizza and Café, with a great shattering of brick and glass, maybe it would land on the thruway and we'd see eighteen-wheelers turn over, great chunks of pavement rise up at sharp angles, and car after car swerve into the guardrail and roll down the embankment.

Something appeared in the sky shortly before one o'clock. Many of us were still at lunch, others were already outside, standing motionless on the streets and sidewalks, gazing up. There were shouts and cries, arms in the air, a wildness of gesturing, pointing. And sure enough, something was glittering, up there in the sky, something was shimmering, in the blue air of summer — we saw it clearly, whatever it was. Secretaries in offices rushed to windows, storekeepers abandoned their cash registers and hurried outdoors, road workers in orange hard hats looked up from the asphalt, shaded their eyes. It must have lasted — that faraway glow, that spot of shimmer — some three or four minutes. Then it began to grow larger, until it was the size of a dime, a quarter. Suddenly the entire sky seemed to be filled with points of gold. Then it was coming down on us, like fine pollen, like yellow dust. It lay on our roof slopes, it sifted down onto our sidewalks, covered our shirtsleeves and the tops of our cars. We did not know what to make of it.

It continued to come down, that yellow dust, for nearly thirteen minutes. During that time we could not see the sky. Then it was over. The sun shone, the sky was blue. Throughout the downpour, we'd been warned to stay inside, to be careful, to avoid touching the substance from outer space, but it had happened so quickly that most of us had streaks of yellow on our clothes and in our hair. Soon after the warnings, we heard cautious reassurances: preliminary tests revealed nothing toxic, though the nature of the yellow dust remained unknown. Animals that had eaten it revealed no symptoms. We were urged to keep out of its way and await further test results. Meanwhile it lay over our lawns and sidewalks and front steps, it coated our maple trees and telephone poles. We were reminded of waking in the morning after the first snow. From our porches we watched the three-wheeled sweepers move slowly along our streets, carrying it off in big hoppers. We hosed down our grass, our front walks, our porch furniture. We looked up at the sky, we waited for more news — already we were hearing reports that the substance was composed of one-celled organisms — and through it all we could sense the swell of our disappointment.

We had wanted, we had wanted — oh, who knew what we'd been looking for? We had wanted blood, crushed bones, howls of agony. We had wanted buildings crumbling onto streets, cars bursting into flame. We had wanted monstrous versions of ourselves with enlarged heads on stalklike necks, merciless polished robots armed with death rays. We had wanted noble lords of the universe with kind, soft eyes, who would usher in a glorious new era. We had wanted terror and ecstasy — anything but this yellow dust. Had it even been an invasion? Later that afternoon, we learned that scientists all agreed: the dust was a living thing. Samples had been flown to Boston, Chicago, Washington, D.C. The single-celled organisms appeared to be harmless, though we were cautioned not to touch anything, to keep the windows shut, to wash our hands. The cells reproduced by binary fission. They appeared to do nothing but multiply.

In the morning, we woke to a world covered in yellow dust. It lay on the tops of our fences, on the crossbars of telephone poles. Black tire tracks showed in the yellow streets. Birds, shaking their wings, threw up sprays of yellow powder. Again the street sweepers came, the hoses splashed on driveways and lawns, making a yellow mist and revealing the black and the green underneath. Within an hour the driveways and lawns resembled yellow fields. Lines of yellow ran along cables and telephone wires.

According to the news, the unicellular microorganisms are rod-shaped and nourish themselves by photosynthesis. A single cell, placed in a brightly illuminated test tube, divides at such a rate that the tube will fill in about forty minutes. An entire room, in strong light, will fill in six hours. The organisms do not fit easily into our classification schemes, though in some respects they resemble blue-green algae. There is no evidence that they are harmful to human or animal life.

We have been invaded by nothing, by emptiness, by animate dust. The invader appears to have no characteristic other than the ability to reproduce rapidly. It doesn't hate us. It doesn't seek our annihilation, our subjection and humiliation. Nor does it desire to protect us from danger, to save us, to teach us the secret of immortal life. What it wishes to do is replicate. It is possible that we will find a way of limiting the spread of this primitive intruder, or of eliminating it altogether; it's also possible that we will fail and that our town will gradually disappear under a fatal accumulation. As we follow the reports from day to day, the feeling grows in us that we deserved something else, something bolder, something grander, something more thrilling, something bristling or fiery or fierce, something that might have represented a revelation or a destiny. We imagine ourselves surrounding the tilted spaceship, waiting for the door to open. We imagine ourselves protecting our children, slashing the tentacles that thrust in through the smashed cellar windows. Instead, we sweep our front walks, hose off our porches, shake out our shoes and sneakers. The invader has entered our homes. Despite our drawn shades and closed curtains, it lies in thick layers on our end tables and windowsills. It lies along the tops of our flat-screen televisions and the narrow edges of our shelved DVDs. Through our windows we can see the yellow dust covering everything, forming gentle undulations. We can almost see it rising slowly, like bread. Here and there it catches the sunlight and reminds us, for a moment, of fields of wheat.

It is really quite peaceful, in its way.

C.S. LEWIS

Forms of Things Unknown
1958

'...that what was myth in one world might always be fact in some other.' PERELANDRA

'Before the class breaks up, gentlemen,' said the instructor, 'I should like to make some reference to a fact which is known to some of you, but probably not yet to all. High Command, I need not remind you, has asked for a volunteer for yet one more attempt on the Moon. It will be the fourth. You know the history of the previous three. In each case the explorers landed unhurt; or at any rate alive. We got their messages. Every message short, some apparently interrupted. And after that never a word, gentlemen. I think the man who offers to make the fourth voyage has about as much courage as anyone I've heard of. And I can't tell you how proud it makes me that he is one of my own pupils. He is in this room at this moment. We wish him every possible good fortune. Gentlemen, I ask you to give three cheers for Lieutenant John Jenkin.'

Then the class became a cheering crowd for two minutes; after that a hurrying, talkative crowd in the corridor. The two biggest cowards exchanged the various family reasons which had deterred them from volunteering themselves. The knowing man said, 'There's something behind all this.' The vermin said, 'He always was a chap who'd do anything to get himself into the limelight.' But most just shouted out, 'Jolly good show, Jenkin,' and wished him luck.

Ward and Jenkin got away together into a pub.

'You kept this pretty dark,' said Ward. 'What's yours?'

'A pint of draught Bass,' said Jenkin.

'Do you want to talk about it?' said Ward rather awkwardly when the drinks had come. 'I mean — if you won't think I'm butting in — it's not just because of that girl, is it?'

That girl was a young woman who was thought to have treated Jenkin rather badly.

'Well,' said Jenkin, 'I don't suppose I'd be going if she had married me. But it's not a spectacular attempt at suicide or any rot of that sort. I'm not depressed. I don't feel anything particular about her. Not much interested in women at all, to tell you the truth. Not now. A bit petrified.'

'What is it then?'

'Sheer unbearable curiosity. I've read those three little messages over and over till I know them by heart. I've heard every theory there is about what interrupted them. I've —'

'Is it certain they were all interrupted? I thought one of them was supposed to be complete.'

'You mean Traill and Henderson? I think it was as incomplete as the others. First there was Stafford. He went alone, like me.'

'Must you? I'll come, if you'll have me.'

Jenkins shook his head. 'I knew you would,' he said. 'But you'll see in a moment why I don't want you to. But to go back to the messages. Stafford's was obviously cut short by something. It went: *Stafford from within fifty miles of Point X0308 on the Moon. My landing was excellent. I have* — then silence. Then come Traill and Henderson. *We have landed. We are perfectly well. The ridge M392 is straight ahead of me as I speak. Over.'*

"What do you make of *Over?'*

'Not what you do. You think it means *finis*—the message is over. But who in the world, speaking to Earth from the Moon for the first time in all history, would have so little to say—if he *could* say any more? As if he'd crossed to Calais and sent his grandmother a card to say "Arrived safely". The thing's ludicrous.'

'Well, what do *you* make of "Over"?'

'Wait a moment. The last lot were Trevor, Woodford, and Fox. It was Fox who sent the message. Remember it?'

'Probably not so accurately as you.'

'Well, it was this. *This is Fox speaking. All has gone wonderfully well. A perfect landing. You shot pretty well for I'm on Point X0308 at this moment. Ridge M392 straight ahead. On my left, far away across the crater, I see the big peaks. On my right I see the Yerkes cleft. Behind me.* Got it?'

'I don't see the point.'

'Well, Fox was cut off the moment he said *Behind me*. Supposing Traill was cut off in the middle of saying "Over my shoulder I can see" or "Over behind me", or something like that?'

'You mean —'

'All the evidence is consistent with the view that everything went well till the speaker looked behind him. Then something got him.'

'What sort of something?'

'That's what I want to find out. One idea in my head is this. Might there be something on the Moon — or something psychological about the experience of landing on the Moon — which drives men fighting mad?'

'I see. You mean Fox looked round just in time to see Trevor and Woodford preparing to knock him on the head?'

'Exactly. And Traill — for it was Traill — just in time to see Henderson a split second before Henderson murdered him. And that's why I'm not going to risk having a companion; least of all my best friend.'

'This doesn't explain Stafford.'

'No. That's why one can't rule out the other hypothesis.'

'What's it?'

'Oh, that whatever killed them all was something they found there. Something lunar.'

'You're surely not going to suggest life on the Moon at this time of day?'

'The word *life* always begs the question. Because, of course, it suggests organization as we know it on Earth — with all the chemistry which organization involves. Of course there could hardly be anything of that sort. But there might — I at any rate can't say there couldn't — be masses of matter capable of movements determined from within, determined, in fact, by intentions.'

'Oh Lord, Jenkin, that's nonsense. Animated stones, no doubt! That's mere science fiction or mythology.'

'Going to the Moon at all was once science fiction. And as for mythology, haven't they found the Cretan labyrinth?'

'And all it really comes down to,' said Ward, 'is that no one has ever come back from the Moon, and no one, so far as we know, ever survived there for more than a few minutes. Damn the whole thing.' He stared gloomily into his tankard.

'Well,' said Jenkin cheerily, 'somebody's got to go. The whole human race isn't going to be licked by any blasted satellite.'

'I might have known that was your real reason,' said Ward.

'Have another pint and don't look so glum,' said Jenkin. 'Anyway, there's loads of time. I don't suppose they'll get me off for another six months at the earliest.'

But there was hardly any time. Like any man in the modern world on whom tragedy has descended or who has undertaken a high enterprise, he lived for the next few months a life not unlike that of a hunted animal. The Press, with all their cameras and notebooks, were after him. They did not care in the least whether he was allowed to eat or sleep or whether they made a nervous wreck of him before he took off. 'Flesh-flies,' he called them. When forced to address them, he always said, 'I wish I could take you all with me.' But he reflected also that a Saturn's ring of dead (and burnt) reporters circling round his spaceship might get on his nerves. They would hardly make 'the silence of those eternal spaces' any more homelike.

The take-off when it came was a relief. But the voyage was worse than he had ever anticipated. Not physically — on that side it was nothing worse than uncomfortable — but in the emotional experience. He had dreamed all his life, with mingled terror and longing, of those eternal spaces; of being utterly 'outside', in the sky. He had wondered if the agoraphobia of the roofless and bottomless vacuity would overthrow his reason. But the moment he had been shut into his ship there descended upon him the suffocating knowledge that the real danger of space-travel is claustrophobia. You have been put in a little metal container; somewhat like a cupboard, very like a coffin. You can't see out; you can see things only on the screen. Space and the stars are just as remote as they were on the Earth. Where you are is always your world. The sky is never where you are. All you have done is to exchange a large world of earth and rock and water and clouds for a tiny world of metal.

This frustration of a life-long desire bit deeply into his mind as the cramped hours passed. Then he became conscious of another motive which, unnoticed, had been at work on him when he volunteered. That affair with the girl had indeed frozen him stiff; petrified him, you might say. He wanted to feel again, to be flesh, not stone. To feel anything, even terror. Well, on this trip there would be terrors enough before all was done. He'd be wakened, never fear. That part of his destiny at least he felt he could shake off.

The landing was not without terror, but there were so many gimmicks to look after, so much skill to be exercised, that it did not amount to very much. But his heart was beating a little more noticeably than usual as he put the finishing touches to his space-suit and climbed out. He was carrying the transmission apparatus with him. It felt, as he had expected, as light as a loaf. But he was not going to send any message in a hurry. That might be where all the others had gone wrong. Anyway, the longer he waited the longer those pressmen would be kept out of their beds waiting for the story. Do 'em good.

The first thing that struck him was that his helmet had been too lightly tinted. It was painful to look at all in the direction of the sun. Even the rock — it was, after all, rock not dust (which disposed of one hypothesis) — was dazzling. He put down the apparatus; tried to take in the scene.

The surprising thing was how small it looked. He thought he could account for this. The lack of atmosphere forbade nearly all the effect that distance has on Earth. The serrated boundary of the crater was, he knew, about twenty-five miles away. It looked as if you could have touched it. The peaks looked as if they were a few feet high. The black sky, with its inconceivable multitude and ferocity of stars, was like a cap forced down upon the crater; the stars only just out of his reach. The impression of a stage-set in a toy theatre, therefore of something arranged, therefore of something waiting for him, was at once disappointing and oppressive. Whatever terrors there might be, here too agoraphobia would not be one of them.

He took his bearings and the result was easy enough. He was, like Fox and his friends, almost exactly on Point X0308. But there was no trace of human remains.

If he could find any, he might have some clue as to how they died. He began to hunt. He went in each circle further from the ship. There was no danger of losing it in a place like this.

Then he got his first real shock of fear. Worse still, he could not tell what was frightening him. He only knew that he was engulfed in sickening unreality; seemed neither to be where he was nor to be doing what he did. It was also somehow connected with an experience long ago. It was something that had happened in a cave. Yes; he remembered now. He had been walking along supposing himself alone and then noticed that there was always a sound of other feet following him. Then in a flash he realized what was wrong. This was the exact reverse of the experience in the cave. Then there had been too many footfalls. Now there were too few. He walked on hard rock as silently as a ghost. He swore at himself for a fool — as if every child didn't know that a world without air would be a world without noise. But the silence, though explained, became none the less terrifying.

He had now been alone on the Moon for perhaps thirty-five minutes. It was then that he noticed the three strange things.

The sun's rays were roughly at right angles to his line of sight, so that each of the things had a bright side and a dark side; for each dark side a shadow like Indian ink lay out on the rock. He thought they looked like Belisha beacons. Then he thought they looked like huge apes. They were about the height of a man. They were indeed like clumsily shaped men. Except — he resisted an impulse to vomit — they had no heads.

They had something instead. They were (roughly) human up to their shoulders. Then, where the head should have been, there was utter monstrosity — a huge spherical block; opaque, featureless. And every one of them looked as if it had that moment stopped moving or were at that moment about to move.

Ward's phrase about 'animated stones' darted up hideously from his memory. And hadn't he himself talked of something that we couldn't call life, not in our sense, something that could nevertheless produce locomotion and have intentions? Something which, at any rate, shared with life life's tendency to kill? If there were such creatures — mineral equivalents to organisms — they could probably stand perfectly still for a hundred years without feeling any strain.

Were they aware of him? What had they for senses? The opaque globes on their shoulders gave no hint.

There comes a moment in nightmare, or sometimes in real battle, when fear and courage both dictate the same course: to rush, planless, upon the thing you are afraid of. Jenkins sprang upon the nearest of the three abominations and rapped his gloved knuckles against its globular top.

Ach! — he'd forgotten. No noise. All the bombs in the world might burst here and make no noise. Ears are useless on the Moon.

He recoiled a step and next moment found himself sprawling on the ground. 'This is how they all died,' he thought.

But he was wrong. The figure above him had not stirred. He was quite undamaged. He got up again and saw what he had tripped over.

It was a purely terrestrial object. It was, in fact, a transmission set. Not exactly like his own, but an earlier and supposedly inferior model — the sort Fox would have had.

As the truth dawned on him an excitement very different from that of terror seized him. He looked at their misshaped bodies; then down at his own limbs. Of course; that was what one looked like in a space-suit. On his own head there was a similar monstrous globe, but fortunately not an opaque one. He was looking at three statues of spacemen: at statues of Trevor, Woodford, and Fox.

But then the Moon must have inhabitants; and rational inhabitants; more than that, artists.

And what artists! You might quarrel with their taste, for no line anywhere in any of the three statues had any beauty. You could not say a word against their skill. Except for the head and face inside each headpiece, which obviously could not be attempted in such a medium, they were perfect. Photographic accuracy had never reached such a point on earth. And though they were faceless you could see from the set of their shoulders, and indeed of their whole bodies, that a momentary pose had been exactly seized. Each was the statue of a man turning to look behind him. Months of work had doubtless gone to the carving of each; it caught that instantaneous gesture like a stone snapshot.

Jenkin's idea was now to send his message at once. Before anything happened to himself, Earth must hear this amazing news. He set off in great strides, and presently in leaps—now first enjoying lunar gravitation—for his ship and his own set. He was happy now. He *had* escaped his destiny. Petrified, eh? No more feelings? Feelings enough to last him for ever.

He fixed the set so that he could stand with his back to the sun. He worked the gimmicks. 'Jenkin, speaking from the Moon,' he began.

His own huge black shadow lay out before him. There is no noise on the Moon. Up from behind the shoulders of his own shadow another shadow pushed its way along the dazzling rock. It was that of a human head. And what a head of hair. It was all rising, writhing — swaying in the wind perhaps. Very thick the hairs looked. Then, as he turned in terror, there flashed through his mind the thought, 'But there's no wind. No air. It can't be *blowing* about.' His eyes met hers.

JOHN UPDIKE

Conjunction
1987

Geoffrey Parrish, approaching sixty, had long enjoyed an uneasy relationship with the stars. In childhood, when we assume the world to have been elaborately arrayed for our own benefit, with a virtual eternity allowed for inspection of its many large and mysterious parts, he had taken the stars, like the clouds overhead, for granted. His mother knew the Big Dipper, and Orion, and on a summer evening might point out, in a voice of unaccountable excitement, Venus – a white shining puncture in the blue that was deepening above the gory sunset. For a moment or two at night, he might become aware, as a skater is suddenly aware of the dark water he skims across, of the speckled heavens, a dust of distant worlds, between the massy silhouettes of black treetops. But in his back yard, where such revelations would find him, he was generally intent upon catching fireflies or feeling the throb of his breath and heartbeat as he ran, late for his bedtime, toward the tall lit windows of the house.

Wynken, Blynken, and Nod, illustrated by Vernon Grant, had been one of the big thin books, smelling like the oilcloth on the kitchen table, that his mother would read to him at bedtime, and somehow it seemed to be taking place among the stars:

> The little stars were the herring fish
> That lived in the beautiful sea....

The images upset him, conveying a seethe of activity that went on without him, all night:

> All night long their nets they threw
> To the stars in the twinkling foam....

Wynken and Blynken turned out to be his, the listener's, two little eyes, and Nod his little head. It was a hideous thought, like two eggs and a cabbage bouncing around in this glimmering soup, and in merciful escape from the unthinkable he let himself be lulled by his mother's enclosing voice as it read aloud, in a grave voice sweetened by the approach of the end:

> So shut your eyes while mother sings
> Of wonderful sights that be,
> And you shall see the beautiful things
> As you rock in the misty sea....

High School and college brought him word of what the stars really were, how senselessly large and distant and numerous, but such intellectual shocks were cushioned by the distractions of co-education — the female bodies with their supple heft, their powdered and perfumed auras, their fuzzy sweaters and silken blouses, and the glimpses, at the edges, of elastic underwear. Why do girls wear skirts, with their strange nether openness and vulnerability, while boys get to wear trousers? And why do girls like to talk so much, and what do they say to each other all the time? Such questions, and courtship, and marriage, eclipsed the stars, which yet seemed to hang waiting for Geoffrey to get to know them. One summer, while renting a seaside place with a long deck, he had purchased a pocket guide to the heavens and (with difficulty, for the blazing points strewn across the black dome overhead made a poor match with the little diagrams picked out by dying flashlight) taught himself the summer triangle of bright stars, Deneb and Altair and Vega, and a few prominent constellations — Andromeda's flying V, and cruciform Cygnus, and boxy little Lyra, and Cepheus, shaped like a house in a child's drawing.

In these decipherings — the planks of the deck rough beneath his bare feet, the shingled house alive with lights and the voices of his wife and children talking to one another — Parrish felt united with ancient generations. Man no sooner had attained erect posture than he began to try to unriddle the stars, to name them after gods and animals, and then to construct huge rings and pyramids of stone as if to demonstrate a placatory harmony with the cycles of the heavenly machine. Who was the first man — a creature scarcely more than ape — who realized that the frozen spatter above turned through the night like an off-center disk? And who were those wakeful wise men who first noticed the planets, the wanderers keeping their own slow looping paths across the surface of this disk? The stars were the fathers of speculation, of philosophy. Under Parrish's gaze, as if he were suspended by his heels above an abysmal bowl, the stars seemed to sing, to scream in chorus. In actuality, he heard lonely sounds from the deck — the sea breaking on a distant beach, a bell buoy rocking outside the harbor, crickets droning in the high grass. He would become dizzy, staring up. His neck would begin to hurt. His patience and his sense of spatial relationships were limited, and, having satisfied himself with a few chronic identifications, or having, out of the corner of his eye, seemed to see a meteor fall, he would leave the deck to go back into the house, into the womanly warmth, the electric light.

And then the summer was over, the heavens mostly unlearned, and a new season of constellations sent to bewilder the eyes. Decades went by in which his acquaintance with the stars failed to advance. He read about them now and then in the newspapers — eclipses, meteor showers, astronomical discoveries of huge vacancies in the web of galaxies and of a mysterious apparent arc millions of light-years in length. Scanning the comic strips one day, while his wife tried to make breakfast conversation, he noticed a small article, with an illustration, stating that Jupiter and Mars were to undergo, this winter, a rare conjunction.

That evening, in spite of the cold, he took the torn-out illustration into his side yard, and there, above treetops that by coincidence closely matched the schematic ones in the drawing, shone the conjunction just as diagrammed — Jupiter bright and bluish, Mars smaller and red-tinged, a bit lower and to the right. He had studied the stars but had not knowingly looked at a planet since the summer evenings, a half-century ago — could it be that long? — when his mother would dramatically gesture toward Venus. As he gazed, the stars surrounding the two conjoined planets swarmed into his vision, more and more of them as he looked, as if he were film in a developing pan; but he had no trouble finding the two planets again, their close pairing distinctive as a signature. The redness of Mars was lodged in its twinkle, a perhaps hallucinatory spark, whereas Jupiter's blue glow appeared cool and steady. Parrish's eyesight had deteriorated over the years. Without his glasses, near things blurred and far ones looked double. He needed a telescope. He began by suggesting to his wife that she might want to get him one for Christmas.

"Why don't you get it for yourself?" Berenice asked. "I might get the wrong kind."

"You're as much an expert as I am," he told her. "It's like everything else — you go by the money. The more it costs, the better it probably is."

"It would feel like a test you're setting me. I'd be scared to get any except the most expensive, and then you'll say I spent too much money."

He wondered if this were just. True, everything she did lately seemed to him slightly excessive or insufficient, a bit too determined and rigid or else irritatingly casual and heedless; yet he imagined his irritation to be invisible within the vast context of their decades together, their children and now grandchildren, their ever-expanding, circumambient troth. They had met at college and married in a wave of passion; she was still a junior and he was a poor graduate student. Aeons later, it turned out that she had resented truncating her education and sitting home mired in pregnancy and motherhood while he paraded off in a business suit to a glamorous world of credit-card lunches and smartly dressed young female lackeys. Well, he could not help feeling in response, he didn't make the world, and he didn't ask to be born a male, with a male's responsibilities and prerogatives. Their children grew and went away, their automobiles became foreign and expensive, their houses increased in price and suburban remove, and at the center of all this centrifugal movement the cinder of her resentment remained, paired with his resentment of her resentment. He had laid his life at her feet, and all she cared about was gender politics.

She went on, "Everybody says how financially timid women are, the ones that aren't extravagant, but look at the figures: your firm charges two hundred dollars an hour for your time and mine is absolutely worthless; I have to go give it away in volunteer work."

"Or else stay in bed," he said, "while I'm having a great time fighting the tunnel traffic."

———

Parrish bought himself the telescope, wrapping and putting it beneath the tree with a card saying "Love, Berenice." The children and the grandchildren were impressed, and greedily took turns with it spying on their neighbors' windows and bringing closer the distant skyscrapers of Boston. But in fact it was not a very expensive telescope; his wife's uncertainties over the proper price to pay had infected him and made him cautious. Also, the very expensive ones looked too complicated. What he wanted was a tube that he would look into at one end and that would deliver reality, enlarged, at the other. This was not as easy as he had hoped. His own tremor jiggled the image, and the plastic eyepiece clicked against his glasses. A boat far from shore, a mere hyphen in the grey water, would reveal, in sudden focus, amazing detail — railings, and a pilothouse that needed paint, and a man in a watch cap and dark slicker standing on the forward deck within an eerie windless silence, an eerie ignorance of being seen. There was a bubble around things thus captured, a hermetic breathlessness and a pressure that squeezed the perspective flat.

On a clear night early in the new year, Parrish took the tripod and the telescope outdoors, and set it up on the snowy driveway, and aimed it at the conjunction. Through even this weak telescope the stars multiplied confusingly; Mars and Jupiter, though obvious to his naked eye, took a lot of calibrated groping to center in the lens. Tremors, not just his own but those of invisible events within the transparent atmosphere, beset the planets. Mars, at the maximum enlargement, remained disappointing — no canals, no red deserts, no polar ice caps, not even the impression of a sphere. Just a stubborn small hole, spitting red, in space. But Jupiter, that big smear of pallor nearby, did, unmistakably, thrillingly, resolve into a disk, a world calling out with its solemn white roundness across the deeps of space. He could not make out the churning stripes or the big oblong spot so vivid in Voyager photographs, but there *was* something unexpected — off to the side, four bright dots in a curving line, a kind of plume lifted upward, to the left. Could these be the famous moons, whose observation by Galileo marked the end of Ptolemaic astronomy? Parrish would not have expected them to extend so far out from the body of the mother globe, or to be so distinct, and organized in so smooth an arc. When he lifted his head and looked with the naked eye, Jupiter was still there but they were gone; when he peered again through the telescope, they had returned, in their unexpected pattern and vividness — a small school of the herring fish that lived in that beautiful sea.

His face and fingers and feet ached with the cold; tears in his eyes now added to the difficulties of vision. He took his equipment back into the house, keen to share the triumph of discovery; but his wife had already drifted into sleep. Though he did not again trouble to set up the telescope outdoors, all winter he would glance toward that section of sky he had explored and watch twinkling red Mars slowly climb level with coolly glowing Jupiter, and then imperceptibly, inexorably pull away, as if tracing some movement of titanic gears. The gap between them, once less than the moon's breadth, opened as the smaller planet ascended, yet Parrish had no trouble keeping track of these specks of light. He had worn a small comfortable place in the spangled void where his gaze could rest as he stepped from the car, home from a party, a meeting, a trip.

He and Berenice had the habit, as spring approached, of travelling to a warm island for several weeks, to reward themselves for having endured another New England winter; even though she was now afraid of skin cancer, and stayed in their cabaña while he went to the beach, they still made the trip, with its flavor of honeymoon. The tropical stars were different — the few constellations he knew sprawled crazily at one side of the sky, distended by their new relation to the horizon. Yet the air was familiar, the humid fraught air of summer. Sitting after dinner on the hotel terrace while a steel band played beneath the stars, Parrish suddenly again saw, as if an inner telescope had zoomed, his wife and himself, before they married, on the flat pebbled roof of the Cambridge row house where he had lived as a graduate student. Rules had been numerous in that dark age, and she had come to him illegally, lying to her housemother so that she could spend the night. The sudden May heat was so great in his airless room they took blankets up to the pebbled roof, close to the stars, which their luminous bodies seemed to join; the spine of the galaxy bent above them like an immense torn pale rainbow. Wherever his eyes travelled on her body, splendor glimmered.

He asked Berenice to dance.

"To this music? We don't know how."

"You just shuffle, from the look of it."

"Let the young people do it, Geoff. Don't put me to the test."

The test? Her face, white on the dim starlit terrace, while the black band poured forth its practiced jubilation, did not look old to him, but somehow closed, too firmly knit, as if her life, her life with him, were a wound that had nearly healed at last. Behind her, the warm dark sea, struck by the light of a full moon, seemed to lift in a bulge toward the other heavenly body's cold brightness.

Back home, where the snow had all melted, Parrish stepped from the car and glanced toward the sky, and could find neither Mars nor Jupiter. They had parted and lost themselves among the less wandering stars. He could not believe it, and searched for minutes. His wife had taken the keys and gone into the house, turning on the switches, filling window after window with artificial light. Conscious of his breath, conscious of his heartbeat, he followed her in.

HANS CHRISTIAN ANDERSON

Translation from *Aunt Judy's Christmas Volume, 6-7 for Young People*

The Comet

1872

And the comet came — shone with its core of fire and threatened with its rod. They were looking at it from the rich palace and from the poor cottage; the crowd upon the street were looking at it, and the solitary wanderer, as he went his way over the pathless heath. Each one had his own thoughts about it.

"Come and look at the sign in the heavens! Come and see the splendid sight!" they said; and everybody hastened to look.

But in a low room there still sat a boy and his mother. The tallow candle was burning, and mother fancied there was a winding-sheet in the candle; the tallow rose in a point and curled over; that betokened, in her belief, that the little boy was destined soon to die; you see the winding-sheet turned towards him.

It was an old superstition, and she had it.

The little boy was really going to live many years upon the earth — live and see the comet, when, after more than sixty years, it appeared again.

The little boy did not see the winding-sheet in the candle, nor was he thinking about the comet that for the first time in his life was shining in the sky. He was sitting with a slop-basin before him, that had been mended with a rivet: in it were some soapsuds, and into these he was now dipping the bowl of a little clay pipe; then he put the pipe to his mouth and blew soap bubbles, great and small. They trembled and floated in the air with the most lovely colors, changing from yellow to red and lilac and blue; and then they turned green, like the leaves of the forest when the sun shines through them.

"God grant thee as many years here upon the earth as the bubbles thou art blowing!"

"Oh, there will be so many, so many!" cried the child. "The soapsuds will never be all used up!" And the little fellow blew bubble after bubble.

"*There* goes a year! *There* goes a year! See how they fly!" said he, as each bubble got free and flew away. One or two went right into his eyes; they smarted and burnt, and the tears ran down his cheeks. In every bubble he saw a vision of the future, bright and glittering.

"Now you can see the comet!" cried the neighbors. "Come out! Don't stay in there!"

And mother took the little one by the hand; he was obliged to put by the clay pipe, and part from his plaything, soap-bubbles and all — the comet was there.

And the little fellow saw the gleaming ball of fire with its radiant tail. Some said that it was three yards long, others that it was millions of yards; — people see so differently.

"Children and children's children may be dead before it appears again!" people said.

And the most of those that said so were really dead and gone when it again appeared; but the little boy for whom the winding-sheet curled in the candle, and of whom his mother believed "he will soon die!" — he was still living and was an old man with white hairs. "White hairs are flowers of old age!" says the proverb, and he had many of these flowers.

The school children used to say that he was very clever, and knew ever so much; that he knew history, and geography, and all about the heavenly bodies. "Everything comes round again," he used to say; "all persons and all events — only take note of them, and you will find that they always come round again, in another dress, in another country."

The schoolmaster had just been telling them about William Tell, who had to shoot an apple from his son's head; but before he shot off the arrow, he hid in his bosom another arrow to shoot the wicked Gesler in the heart with. That happened in Switzerland; but many years before the same thing happened in Denmark with Palnatoka: he also had to shoot an apple from his son's head, and like Tell hid an arrow to avenge himself with; and more than a thousand years further back still the same story was recorded as having taken place in Egypt: the same thing comes round again, just like the comets; they pass away, disappear, and come again.

And he talked about the comet that was expected — the comet he had seen when a little boy. "Schoolmaster," you know, knew all about the heavenly bodies, and reflect upon them; but for all that did not forget history and geography.

He had laid out his garden in the form of the map of Denmark. The plants and flowers were there placed according as they flourished best in different regions of the country. "Fetch me some peas!" he said, and they went to the bed that represented Lapland. "Fetch me some buckwheat!" and then they went to Langeland. The lovely blue gentian and sweet-willow were to be found up at the Skaw, the glistening hollow over Silkebourg. The towns themselves were marked by wooden emblems. There stood St. Canute, with the dragon, that signified Odense. Absalon with his crozier stood for Soro; the little ship with its anchor was a sign that here lay the town of Aarbus. From the schoolmaster's garden you could learn the map of Denmark famously; but then of course you had first to be instructed by him, and that was very amusing.

Now the comet was expected, and he told them all about it, and what people in old times, when it was last here, had said and decided. "The comet year is a good wine year," said he; "you may dilute the wine with water, it will not be noticed." The wine merchants ought to be very fond of comet-years.

Clouds covered the sky for a whole fortnight night and day: the comet could not be seen, but it was there.

The old schoolmaster sat in his chamber close up by the schoolroom. The Bornholm clock handed down from his parents' time stood in the corner; the heavy leaden weights neither rose nor sank; the pendulum did not move; the little cuckoo that in old times used to come forward and announce the hour of the day had for several years remained silent behind the closed door. All was mute and still in there; the clock did not go any more. But the old harpsichord close by, also handed down from his parents' time, still had life; the strings could make music and play, though certainly a little hoarsely, the tunes of a whole generation. By help of this the old man was calling to mind many, many things, both joyous and sad, that had happened in the long course of years, from the time when he as a child saw the comet till now when it was here again. He remembered what mother had said about the winding-sheet in the candle; he remembered the lovely soap bubbles he blew; each was a year of life, he had said — how bright, how radiant with colours! He had seen in them all that was beautiful and joyous, the sports of childhood and the pleasures of youth, the whole wide world lying open in sunshine — and out into the world he was to go! They were the bubbles of Futurity. Now, an old man, he heard from the strings of the harpsichord melodies from the days that were no more — bubbles of Recollection, with the hues of old memories. *That* was the tune his grandmother used to sing when she knitted stockings:

"Believe me maids,' twas never a shrew
That first warm hosen wove."

That was the ditty their old servant sang to him when he was a child.

"'Tis a path of dangers,
'Tis a vale of woe;
Out among the dangers

My little one must go."

Now there were tunes from his first ball, a minuet and a Molinaski; now came soft, melancholy tunes, so that tears came to the old man's eyes; now rattled along a war march; now it was psalmody; and now gay, spritely music — bubble after bubble, just as then, when a little boy, he blew them from the soapsuds.

His clouds were fixed upon the window; a cloud out there upon the sky glided away, and he saw in the clear air the comet, its shining core, its glittering, misty tail.

It was as if he had seen it only yesterday evening, and yet there lay a whole rich life between that time and now; then he was a child and looked into the bubbles *forward*; now the bubbles opened the view *backwards*. He felt with the heart of a child, and the faith of a child; his eye gleamed bright, and his hand fell down upon the keys of the harpsichord; — there was a clang, as if a string was broken.

"Come and see, the comet is here!" cried the neighbors. "The sky is beautifully clear! Come out and see it properly!"

The schoolmaster did not answer, he was gone to see it properly; his soul was gone upon a greater path, in a wider space, than the comet traverses in it flight. And so once more they were looking at the comet — the people at the rich palace and the poor cottage, the crowd upon the street and the solitary wanderer over the pathless heath. But his soul was looked upon by God, and by the dear ones who had gone before; these were they he had longed after.

STEPHEN BAXTER

Last Contact
2007

March 15th

Caitlin walked into the garden through the little gate from the drive. Maureen was working on the lawn.

Just at that moment Maureen's phone pinged. She took off her gardening gloves, dug the phone out of the deep pocket of her old quilted coat and looked at the screen. "Another contact," she called to her daughter.

Caitlin looked cold in her thin jacket; she wrapped her arms around her body. "Another super-civilization discovered, off in space. We live in strange times, Mum."

"That's the fifteenth this year. And I did my bit to help discover it. Good for me," Maureen said, smiling. "Hello, love." She leaned forward for a kiss on the cheek.

She knew why Caitlin was here, of course. Caitlin had always hinted she would come and deliver the news about the Big Rip in person, one way or the other. Maureen guessed what that news was from her daughter's hollow, stressed eyes. But Caitlin was looking around the garden, and Maureen decided to let her tell it all in her own time.

She asked, "How're the kids?"

"Fine. at school. Bill's at home, baking bread." Caitlin smiled. "Why do stay-at-home fathers always bake bread? But he's starting at Webster's next month."

"That's the engineers in Oxford?"

"That's right. Not that it makes much difference now. We won't run out of money before, well, before it doesn't matter." Caitlin considered the garden. It was just a scrap of lawn really, with a quite nicely stocked border, behind a cottage that was a little more than a hundred years old, in this village on the outskirts of Oxford. "It's the first time I've seen this properly."

"Well, it's the first bright day we've had. My first spring here." They walked around the lawn. "It's not bad. It's been let to run to seed a bit by Mrs. Murdoch. Who was another lonely old widow," Maureen said.

"You mustn't think like that."

"Well, it's true. This little house is fine for someone on their own, like me, or her. I suppose I'd pass it on to somebody else in the same boat, when I'm done."

Caitlin was silent at that, silent at the mention of the future.

Maureen showed her patches where the lawn had dried out last summer and would need reseeding. And there was a little brass plaque fixed to the wall of the house to show the level reached by the Thames floods of two years ago. "The lawn is all right. I do like this time of year when you sort of wake it up from the winter. The grass needs raking and scarifying, of course. I'll reseed bits of it, and see how it grows during the summer. I might think about getting some of it relaid. Now the weather's so different, the drainage might not be right anymore."

"You're enjoying getting back in the saddle, aren't you, Mum?"

Maureen shrugged. "Well, the last couple of years weren't much fun. Nursing your dad, and then getting rid of the house. It's nice to get this old thing back on again." She raised her arms and looked down at her quilted gardening coat.

Caitlin wrinkled her nose. "I always hated that stupid old coat. You really should get yourself something better, Mum. These modern fabrics are very good."

"This will see me out," Maureen said firmly.

They walked around the verge, looking at the plants, the weeds, the autumn leaves that hadn't been swept up and were now rotting in place.

Caitlin said, "I'm going to be on the radio later. BBC Radio 4. There's to be a government statement on the Rip, and I'll be in the follow-up discussion. It starts at nine, and I should be on about nine-thirty."

"I'll listen to it. Do you want me to tape it for you?"

"No. Bill will get it. Besides, you can listen to all these things on the websites these days."

Maureen said carefully, "I take it the news is what you expected, then."

"Pretty much. The Hawaii observatories confirmed it. I've seen the new Hubble images, deep sky fields. Empty, save for the foreground objects. All the galaxies beyond the local group have gone. Eerie, really, seeing your predictions come true like that. That's couch grass, isn't it?"

"Yes. I stuck a fork in it. Nothing but root mass underneath. It will be a devil to get up. I'll have a go, and then put down some bin liners for a few weeks, and see if that kills it off. Then there are these roses that should have been pruned by now. I think I'll plant some gladioli in this corner —"

"Mum, it's October." Caitlin blurted that out. She looked thin, pale, and tense, a real office worker, but then Maureen had always thought that about her daughter, that she worked too hard. Now she was thirty- five, and her moderately pretty face was lined at the eyes and around her mouth, the first wistful signs of age. "October 14th, at about four in the afternoon. I say 'about.' I could give you the time down to the attosecond if you wanted."

Maureen took her hands. "It's all right, love. It's about when you thought it would be, isn't it?"

"Not that it does us any good, knowing. There's nothing we can do about it."

They walked on. They came to a corner on the south side of the little garden. "This ought to catch the sun," Maureen said. "I'm thinking of putting in a seat here. A pergola maybe. Somewhere to sit. I'll see how the sun goes around later in the year."

"Dad would have liked a pergola," Caitlin said. "He always did say a garden was a place to sit in, not to work."

"Yes. It does feel odd that your father died, so soon before all this. I'd have liked him to see it out. It seems a waste somehow."

Caitlin looked up at the sky. "Funny thing, Mum. It's all quite invisible to the naked eye still. You can see the Andromeda Galaxy, just, but that's bound to the Milky Way by gravity. So the expansion hasn't reached down to the scale of the visible, not yet. It's still all instruments, telescopes. But it's real all right."

"I suppose you'll have to explain it all on Radio 4."

"That's why I'm there. We'll probably have to keep saying it over and over, trying to find ways of saying it that people can understand. *You* know, don't you, Mum? It's all to do with dark energy. It's like an antigravity field that permeates the universe. Just as gravity pulls everything together, the dark energy is pulling the universe apart, taking more and more of it so far away that its light can't reach us anymore. It started at the level of the largest structures in the universe, superclusters of galaxies. But in the end it will fold down to the smallest scales. Every bound structure will be pulled apart. Even atoms, even subatomic particles. The Big Rip.

"We've known about this stuff for years. What we didn't expect was that the expansion would accelerate as it has. We thought we had trillions of years. Then the forecast was billions. And now —"

"Yes."

"It's funny for me being involved in this stuff, Mum. Being on the radio. I've never been a people person. I became an astrophysicist, for God's sake. I always thought that what I studied would have absolutely no effect on anybody's life.

How wrong I was. Actually there's been a lot of debate about whether to announce it or not."

"I think people will behave pretty well," Maureen said. "They usually do. It might get trickier toward the end, I suppose. But people have a right to know, don't you think?"

"They're putting it on after nine, so people can decide what to tell their kids."

"After the watershed! Well, that's considerate. Will you tell your two?"

"I think we'll have to. Everybody at school will know. They'll probably get bullied about it if they don't know. Imagine that. Besides, the little beggars will probably have googled it on their mobiles by one minute past nine."

Maureen laughed. "There is that."

"It will be like when I told them Dad had died," Caitlin said. "Or like when Billy started asking hard questions about Santa Claus."

"No more Christmases," Maureen said suddenly. "If it's all over in October."

"No more birthdays for my two either," Caitlin said. "November and January."

"Yes. It's funny, in the lab, when the date came up, that was the first thing I thought of."

Maureen's phone pinged again. "Another signal. Quite different in nature from the last, according to this."

"I wonder if we'll get any of those signals decoded in time."

Maureen waggled her phone. "It won't be for want of trying, me and a billion other search-for-ET-at-home enthusiasts. Would you like some tea, love?"

"It's all right. I'll let you get on. I told Bill I'd get the shopping in, before I have to go back to the studios in Oxford this evening."

They walked toward the back door into the house, strolling, inspecting the plants and the scrappy lawn.

June 5th

It was about lunchtime when Caitlin arrived from the garden center with the pieces of the pergola. Maureen helped her unload them from the back of a white van, and carry them through the gate from the drive. They were mostly just prefabricated wooden panels and beams that they could manage between the two of them, though the big iron spikes that would be driven into the ground to support the uprights were heavier. They got the pieces stacked upon the lawn.

"I should be able to set it up myself," Maureen said. "Joe next door said he'd lay the concrete base for me, and help me lift on the roof section. There's some nailing to be done, and creosoting, but I can do all that."

"Joe, eh?" Caitlin grinned.

"Oh, shut up, he's just a neighbor. Where did you get the van? Did you have to hire it?"

"No, the garden center loaned it to me. They can't deliver. They are still getting stock in, but they can't rely on the staff. They just quit, without any notice. In the end it sort of gets to you, I suppose."

"Well, you can't blame people for wanting to be at home."

"No. Actually Bill's packed it in. I meant to tell you. He didn't even finish his induction at Webster's. But the project he was working on would never have got finished anyway."

"I'm sure the kids are glad to have him home."

"Well, they're finishing the school year. At least I think they will, the teachers still seem keen to carry on."

"It's probably best for them."

"Yes. We can always decide what to do after the summer, if the schools open again."

Maureen had prepared some sandwiches, and some iced elderflower cordial. They sat in the shade of the house and ate their lunch and looked out over the garden.

Caitlin said, "Your lawn's looking good."

"It's come up quite well. I'm still thinking of relaying that patch over there."

"And you put in a lot of vegetables in the end," Caitlin said.

"I thought I should. I've planted courgettes and French beans and carrots, and a few outdoor tomatoes. I could do with a greenhouse, but I haven't really room for one. It seemed a good idea, rather than flowers, this year."

"Yes. You can't rely on the shops."

Things had kept working, mostly, as people stuck to their jobs. But there were always gaps on the supermarket shelves, as supply chains broke down. There was talk of rationing some essentials, and there were already coupons for petrol.

"I don't approve of how tatty the streets are getting in town," Maureen said sternly.

Caitlin sighed. "I suppose you can't blame people for packing in a job like street-sweeping. It is a bit tricky getting around town though. We need some work done on the roof, we're missing a couple of tiles. It's just as well we won't have to get through another winter," she said, a bit darkly. "But you can't get a builder for love or money."

"Well, you never could."

They both laughed.

Maureen said, "I told you people would cope. People do just get on with things."

"We haven't got to the end game yet," Caitlin said. "I went into London the other day. That isn't too friendly, Mum. It's not all like this, you know."

Maureen's phone pinged, and she checked the screen. "Four or five a day now," she said. "New contacts, lighting up all over the sky."

"But that's down from the peak, isn't it?"

"Oh, we had a dozen a day at one time. But now we've lost half the stars, haven't we?"

"Well, that's true, now the Rip has folded down into the galaxy. I haven't really been following it, Mum. Nobody's been able to decode any of the signals, have they?"

"But some of them aren't the sort of signal you can decode anyhow. In one case somebody picked up an artificial element in the spectrum of a star. Something that was manufactured, and then just chucked in to burn up, like a flare."

Caitlin considered. "That can't say anything but 'here we are,' I suppose."

"Maybe that's enough."

"Yes."

It had really been Harry who had been interested in wild speculations about alien life and so forth. Joining the phone network of home observers of ET, helping to analyze possible signals from the stars in a network of millions of others, had been Harry's hobby, not Maureen's. It was one of Harry's things she had kept up after he had died, like his weather monitoring and his football pools. It would have felt odd just to have stopped it all.

But she did understand how remarkable it was that the sky had suddenly lit up with messages like a Christmas tree, after more than half a century of dogged, fruitless, frustrating listening. Harry would have loved to see it.

"Caitlin, I don't really understand how all these signals can be arriving just now. I mean, it takes years for light to travel between the stars, doesn't it? We only knew about the phantom energy a few months ago."

"But others might have detected it long before, with better technology than we've got. That would give you time to send something. Maybe the signals have been timed to get here, just before the end, aimed just at us."

"That's a nice thought."

"Some of us hoped that there would be an answer to the dark energy in all those messages."

"What answer could there be?"

Caitlin shrugged. "If we can't decode the messages we'll never know. And I suppose if there was anything to be done, it would have been done by now."

"I don't think the messages need decoding," Maureen said.

Caitlin looked at her curiously, but didn't pursue it. "Listen, Mum. Some of us are going to try to do something. You understand that the Rip works down the scales, so that larger structures break up first. The galaxy, then the solar system, then planets like Earth. And then the human body."

Maureen considered. "So people will outlive the Earth."

"Well, they could. For maybe about thirty minutes, until atomic structures get pulled apart. There's talk of establishing a sort of shelter in Oxford that could survive the end of the Earth. Like a submarine, I suppose. And if you wore a pressure suit you might last a bit longer even than that. The design goal is to make it through to the last microsecond. You could gather another thirty minutes of data that way. They've asked me to go in there."

"Will you?"

"I haven't decided. It will depend on how we feel about the kids, and — you know."

Maureen considered. "You must do what makes you happy, I suppose."

"Yes. But it's hard to know what that is, isn't it?" Caitlin looked up at the sky. "It's going to be a hot day."

"Yes. And a long one. I think I'm glad about that. The night sky looks odd now the Milky Way has gone."

"And the stars are flying off one by one," Caitlin murmured. "I suppose the constellations will look funny by the autumn."

"Do you want some more sandwiches?"

"I'll have a bit more of that cordial. It's very good, Mum."

"It's elderflower. I collect the blossoms from that bush down the road. I'll give you the recipe if you like."

"Shall we see if your Joe fancies laying a bit of concrete this afternoon? I could do with meeting your new beau."

"Oh, shut up," Maureen said, and she went inside to make a fresh jug of cordial.

October 14th

That morning Maureen got up early. She was pleased that it was a bright morning, after the rain of the last few days. It was a lovely autumn day. She had breakfast listening to the last-ever episode of *The Archers*, but her radio battery failed before the end.

She went to work in the garden, hoping to get everything done before the light went. There was plenty of work, leaves to rake up, the roses and the clematis to prune. She had decided to plant a row of daffodil bulbs around the base of the new pergola.

She noticed a little band of goldfinches, plundering a clump of Michaelmas daisies for seed. She sat back on her heels to watch. The colorful little birds had always been her favorites.

Then the light went, just like that, darkening as if somebody was throwing a dimmer switch. Maureen looked up. The sun was rushing away, and sucking all the light out of the sky with it. It was a remarkable sight, and she wished she had a camera. As the light turned gray, and then charcoal, and then utterly black, she heard the goldfinches fly off in a clatter, confused. It had only taken a few minutes.

Maureen was prepared. She dug a little torch out of the pocket of her old quilted coat. She had been hoarding the batteries; you hadn't been able to buy them for weeks. The torch got her as far as the pergola, where she lit some rush torches that she'd fixed to canes.

Then she sat in the pergola, in the dark, with her garden lit up by her rush torches, and waited. She wished she had thought to bring out her book. She didn't suppose there would be time to finish it now. Anyhow, the flickering firelight would be bad for her eyes.

"Mum?"

The soft voice made her jump. It was Caitlin, threading her way across the garden with a torch of her own.

"I'm in here, love."

Caitlin joined her mother in the pergola, and they sat on the wooden benches, on the thin cushions Maureen had been able to buy. Caitlin shut down her torch to conserve the battery.

Maureen said, "The sun went, right on cue."

"Oh, it's all working out, bang on time."

Somewhere there was shouting, whooping, a tinkle of broken glass.

"Someone's having fun," Maureen said.

"It's a bit like an eclipse," Caitlin said. "Like in Cornwall, do you remember? The sky was cloudy, and we couldn't see a bit of the eclipse. But at that moment when the sky went dark, everybody got excited. Something primeval, I suppose."

"Would you like a drink? I've got a flask of tea. The milk's a bit off, I'm afraid."

"I'm fine, thanks."

"I got up early and managed to get my bulbs in. I didn't have time to trim that clematis, though. I got it all ready for the winter, I think."

"I'm glad."

"I'd rather be out here than indoors, wouldn't you?"

"Oh, yes."

"I thought about bringing blankets. I didn't know if it would get cold."

"Not much. The air will keep its heat for a bit. There won't be time to get very cold."

"I was going to fix up some electric lights out here. But the power's been off for days."

"The rushes are better, anyway. I would have been here earlier. There was a jam by the church. All the churches are packed, I imagine. And then I ran out of petrol a couple of miles back. We haven't been able to fill up for weeks."

"It's all right. I'm glad to see you. I didn't expect you at all. I couldn't ring." Even the phone networks had been down for days. In the end everything had slowly broken down, as people simply gave up their jobs and went home. Maureen asked carefully, "So how's Bill and the kids?"

"We had an early Christmas," Caitlin said. "They'll both miss their birthdays, but we didn't think they should be cheated out of Christmas too. We did it all this morning. Stockings, a tree, the decorations and the lights down from the loft, presents, the lot. And then we had a big lunch. I couldn't find a turkey but I'd been saving a chicken. After lunch the kids went for their nap. Bill put their pills in their lemonade."

Maureen knew she meant the little blue pills the NHS had given out to every household.

"Bill lay down with them. He said he was going to wait with them until he was sure — you know. That they wouldn't wake up, and be distressed. Then he was going to take his own pill."

Maureen took her hand. "You didn't stay with them?"

"I didn't want to take the pill." There was some bitterness in her voice. "I always wanted to see it through to the end. I suppose it's the scientist in me. We argued about it. We fought, I suppose. In the end we decided this way was the best."

Maureen thought that on some level Caitlin couldn't really believe her children were gone, or she couldn't keep functioning like this. "Well, I'm glad you're here with me. And I never fancied those pills either. Although — will it hurt?"

"Only briefly. When the Earth's crust gives way. It will be like sitting on top of an erupting volcano."

"You had an early Christmas. Now we're going to have an early Bonfire Night."

"It looks like it. I wanted to see it through," Caitlin said again. "After all I was in at the start — those supernova studies."

"You mustn't think it's somehow your fault."

"I do, a bit," Caitlin confessed. "Stupid, isn't it?"

"But you decided not to go to the shelter in Oxford with the others?"

"I'd rather be here. With you. Oh, but I brought this." She dug into her coat pocket and produced a sphere, about the size of a tennis ball.

Maureen took it. It was heavy, with a smooth black surface.

Caitlin said, "It's the stuff they make space shuttle heatshield tiles out of. It can soak up a lot of heat."

"So it will survive the Earth breaking up."

"That's the idea."

"Are there instruments inside?"

"Yes. It should keep working, keep recording until the expansion gets down to the centimeter scale, and the Rip cracks the sphere open. Then it will release a cloud of even finer sensor units, motes we call them. It's nanotechnology, Mum, machines the size of molecules. They will keep gathering data until the expansion reaches molecular scales."

"How long will that take after the big sphere breaks up?"

"Oh, a microsecond or so. There's nothing we could come up with that could keep data-gathering after that."

Maureen hefted the little device. "What a wonderful little gadget. It's a shame nobody will be able to use its data."

"Well, you never know," Caitlin said. "Some of the cosmologists say this is just a transition, rather than an end. The universe has passed through transitions before, for instance from an age dominated by radiation to one dominated by matter — our age. Maybe there will be life of some kind in a new era dominated by the dark energy."

"But nothing like us."

"I'm afraid not."

Maureen stood and put the sphere down in the middle of the lawn. The grass was just faintly moist, with dew, as the air cooled. "Will it be all right here?"

"I should think so."

The ground shuddered, and there was a sound like a door slamming, deep in the ground. Alarms went off, from cars and houses, distant wails. Maureen hurried back to the pergola. She sat with Caitlin, and they wrapped their arms around each other.

Caitlin raised her wrist to peer at her watch, then gave it up. "I don't suppose we need a countdown."

The ground shook more violently, and there was an odd sound, like waves rushing over pebbles on a beach. Maureen peered out of the pergola. Remarkably, one wall of her house had given way, just like that, and the bricks had tumbled into a heap.

"You'll never get a builder out now," Caitlin said, but her voice was edgy.

"We'd better get out of here."

"All right."

They got out of the pergola and stood side by side on the lawn, over the little sphere of instruments, holding onto each other. There was another tremor, and Maureen's roof tiles slid to the ground, smashing and tinkling.

"Mum, there's one thing."

"Yes, love."

"You said you didn't think all those alien signals needed to be decoded."

"Why, no. I always thought it was obvious what all the signals were saying."

"What?"

Maureen tried to reply.

The ground burst open. The scrap of dewy lawn flung itself into the air, and Maureen was thrown down, her face pressed against the grass. She glimpsed houses and trees and people, all flying in the air, underlit by a furnace-red glow from beneath.

But she was still holding Caitlin. Caitlin's eyes were squeezed tight shut. "Goodbye," Maureen yelled. "They were just saying goodbye." But she couldn't tell if Caitlin could hear.

REGINALD MCKNIGHT

Uncle Moustapha's Eclipse
1988

Idi, my very best friend here in Senegal, was suffering from a very strange eye malady. He didn't know precisely what had caused his usually quick, pebble eyes to swell, yellow, tear, and itch so. He'd gone to both doctors and marabous and they didn't know either. "All that I can say," said Idi, "is that my eye sickness remind me very much of my Uncle Moustapha's eye sickness." And at that he proceeded to tell me the story of his Uncle Moustapha M'Baye's eye "sickness":

"This was a long, long time ago, Marcus. Before I even was born. My uncle live in a small, small village along the Gambian river near to Bassi Santa Su, call Sakaam. It is too, too hot there. You would not believe it, my friend. The sunshine is so heavy there that a man can reach his hand into the hot air and squeeze the sunshine like wet clay. The mosquito there can only walk and the baboons move like old men, in Sakaam.

"It was there my Uncle Moustapha live and work with his three wives and seven children. He, it is say, was the finest peanut farmer in his whole village. He hardly never had a bad crop. When even there was too much rain, his crop was fair, and other farmers' much worse. And when the rains were thin, Uncle Moustapha always have plenty of rice for he save from the good years. This mean he was a very careful man. He was a hard worker, and very lucky. He had strong juju and was also a good Muslim.

"His only problem in life was that always, always he think about Death. He always think about Death most deeply on the night before his birthday. Now, you must understand, Marcus, that even when I was born thirty years ago, people did not know their birthdays. But Uncle Moustapha was very fond of many things in white culture. He like chocolate and watches, books and French bread. He like birthdays too, because my father tell me, he was a proud man and like the idea of having a personal day of celebration. So he begin keeping a birthday from the day his seventh child was born. He begin at the age of forty, and every year for twenty years, he keep the day of June seven as his birthday. This only add to his worry, for as we say here, Marcus, Death is birth and birth is Death.

"So on the eve night of his sixtieth birthday, he think about his death and he could not sleep. He lay in his hot room and no sound came to his ears. He wait with a numb heart for Death to enter any minute. He focus on nothing but the door, knowing that his final moments were upon him. He expect that soon, soon, a long, white hand would push the door open with no sound; that Death's face would be reveal to him and that he would be taken. He was not really afraid to die. Only he was very worry that his lazy brothers would not take good care of his wives and children. 'The moment I see this door open,' he say, 'I shall light a cigarette and smile at the old fool.' He feel for his cigarette and his matches. Upon coming into contact with both, he let his hand rest on them and say in a loud voice, 'How do you do, Death? Do you care for a smoke? No, no we have time, you and I; have one... yes, yes, of course. I have plenty left. Have one with me. .. indeed, master, sit anywhere.... So how are you? Been busy lately?' This make him laugh, you see, but only for a brief moment. He choke back his laughter when he notice that he cause his wife to wake. 'Why do you wake me?' she say.

"'I wait for Death,' he say, 'as always. My birthday is tomorrow, you remember.'

"'Ah, you crazy man,' my Auntie say. 'These whiteman ways make you too, too silly. To talk and laugh with yourself is madness. Madness, you hear? If you have no birthday, you have no fear of Death.'

" 'I do not have.. .'

" 'First it is chocolate which make you sick always. Then it is watch which make your wrist turn green. Then it is birthday which make you fear Death and ignore the courage that Allah give you. Then it is foolishness about sun...'

" 'It is eclipse, you old'ooman. Eclipse. And it is true. There are a thousand of white men in Bassi Santa Su who wait for it. They say the sun shall disappear and I believe them. It will be tomorrow on my birthday. You shall see.'

"'Dugga doff tropp,' she say, which mean my Uncle Mousse was a very crazy man. Auntie Fatima was my uncle's favorite wife, but not because she was always sweet to him, but because she always tell him the truth. His other wives always would smile at all his curious doings and hold out their hands for the xallis. Fatima love him the most, and she did not care for a man with a lot of *xallis*. She say when he was first having birthdays she did not mind much. She used to even sit up with him each night before his birthday and humor him. But through the many years, as you say, Marcus, no dice. It make her angry.

"So she say, 'Dugga doff tropp,' to him and turn away to sleep. Uncle Moustapha only shrug, get up from bed and cross the room to where his clothes were. He reach into the pocket of his boubou and remove his watch. It was some minutes after midnight. He lay the watch on the floor and then say his prayers, thanking Allah with all his heart.

"'Get up, old man' say Auntie Fatima. 'Get up, I say.' It was morning. Uncle Moustapha open his eyes, but seem to see nothing as he always did in the mornings. His old bones were sore. He look about himself with his blind eyes and say, 'Fatima, it is dark, yet. Why do you wake me?' Auntie Fatima look at him and say, '*Wyyo*! Did you not ask me to wake you at cock-crow? It is you who ask me to do this so that you may see this Sun foolishness.'

"'Where did I put my watch?'

"'I do not know where is this watch,' say Auntie and she leave the room.

"Uncle Moustapha leap from his bed and find his watch. It was six o'clock and some minutes in the morning. There was still plenty of time for him to get to Bassi Santa Su before the eclipse. He wash his body, had a breakfast of bread and bitter black coffee, and put on his best boubou. 'Fati! ' he say. Auntie Fatima return to the bedroom. 'Fatima,' he say, 'I will take my lunch in town today.'

"'There is someone to see you, Mousse,' say Auntie.

'"Why did you say nothing to me?'

"'He came only this moment.'

"'Who is this who comes here?' say my uncle, very angry. You see, he want no one to interfere with his trip to town on this most important day. 'It is a white man' my Auntie say, 'with many strange machines.'

"'The name is Madison,' say the white man. And it seem he was a scientist interested in renting some of Uncle Moustapha's land to set up his machines and telescopes on. Uncle Mousse's land is green, green and beautiful as heaven. It is call the jewel of Sakaam, and I would not be surprise if Madison the white man want to stay at there because of its beauty, but he say instead that it was the perfect scientific place for him to view the eclipse because of all these scientific reasons. 'How much may I give you, Mr. M'Baye?' say Madison. And he reach to his pocket for some money. Uncle Moustapha stop the white man's hand and say, 'Wait, wait, wait! I want no money from you.' This shock Madison to make his green eyes stick out and his face turn red, red.

"'But your land is perfect,' he say. 'I need it. I will pay you any price.' Uncle Moutapha say no. This make Madison even more shock for he have never seen a black man refuse money, you see. 'But I do not want this money,' say Uncle Mousse.

'Please allow kindly, Mr. Madison, for me to view the eclipse with your machines.' Uncle Moustapha explain, that because it was his birthday, he must be allow to see this very special gift from Allah. Madison only shake my uncle's hand and smile a big, big smile.

"Time move slow, slow for the two men. The eclipse begin at eight o'clock and some minutes in the morning, and all the land and sky change to a mysterious, curious haze. Like a pearl. Many people stay in their homes because this cloudless sky was becoming darker and darker. Uncle Mousse was singing and dancing inside himself because it was his personal day and a very strange important thing was happening. But like a true Wolof man, he was quiet and serious outside. He help Madison the white man assemble his equipment as Madison explain to him many things about telescopes, eclipses, etcetera. The sky grew darker. It became empty of birds and the land was quiet and golden green.

"Every few moments Uncle Mousse would turn his eyes up to the sky of haze to look at the Sun, but when Madison one time saw this, he say, 'Mr. M'Baye, you must not look at the Sun. It is too dangerous. One could go blind from such a thing.' Uncle Moustapha say nothing, but he did as Madison say.

"When the machinery was prepare, my uncle and the white man take turns viewing the sun. Uncle Moustapha was astonish. Never did he see something like this in his life. Finally, the sky was as dark as early evening. 'Happy birthday, Mr. M'Baye,' say Mr. Madison. My uncle was overjoy. This was his gift from Allah, a present from his ancestors. He shake Madison's hand and walk away very quickly to his home with the memory of the orange-black moonsun deep in his mind. 'Fati, ' he yell, 'Fati! You must come go with me to our baobab tree.' This shock and surprise Auntie because Uncle Mousse never had interest in baobab tree or in the spirits of the old ones, though he respect them.

"So, anyway, he take Auntie Fatima and tell her all he saw and all what Madison had say him. They walk in the semidark to the great baobab tree of the M'Baye family. The baobab tree, as you must know, Marcus, is the great and huge upside-down tree in which, it is say, live the spirits of the village. The tree that belong to Sakaam (perhap you have seen it when we were there together) sits on the great knoll on the edge of the village very close to the river. It stands alone there; more alone than any tree or shrub or twig in the entire environs. The most remarkable thing about this baobab is the curious way it bows to the east. It resembles a faithful servant of Allah.

"Uncle move as if he were pull to the tree. He ran the last few meters, pulling Auntie along with him. Then he let go of her hand and threw himself at the base of the tree. He say a silent prayer to himself and with his hands, grasp the enormous roots. Auntie Fati say it is as if the very touch of the tree make him feel a sudden power of the spirit, and cleaning of his heart and mind. He seem to empty his heart on the red soil under him as he begin to sing the ancient song of our ancestors.

Oh fathers. Oh Mother

> *Welcome to our hearts*
> *You will bring us comfort*
> *At the setting of the Sun.*

"Of course, this strange behavior in my uncle did not too much surprise my Auntie Fatima because, as I say, she love him so much. She fall to her knees and say a prayer too. Then she rise when Uncle Moustapha rise and kiss him and say to him in English, 'Fine birthday to you, crazy old man.'

'"Ahh and then, Marcus, my uncle's senses at this moment became strongly, powerfully alive. His ears heard like a bat. He smelt the river and the earth and the rustling grass, the sweet, hot air. The smells about him were as strong as the smells of the ocean or a steaming bowl of *tjebugin*. His eyes took in everything — everything. He view each individual stock of yellow-green grass, every twig, every pebble that sat on the ground. The twigs had made the earth look like to be an enormous patchwork boubou. The soft air touch him delicately as a smile. He turn slowly around — seeing, smelling, hearing everything no matter how small, small or subtle or obscure. And with not one moment of hesitation, he lift his face to the sky and stare directly into the eclipse with his both eyes wide open. He stand staring, unblinking, unflinching.

"He saw it all in supreme detail, as if his eye beams were like Madison's telescopes. He watch the burning moonsun, his birthday present from Allah, and Auntie Fatima watch his eyes knowing somehow that she must not disturb him. Uncle Mousse could see the eclipse more clearly, he later say to

Auntie, than he could see them in Madison's machines. It was, you see, his eclipse. His eclipse!

"'Mousse,' say Auntie to him. 'Hey! Mousse. You say the white man say it is dangerous to look at this thing. Hey, Mousse. This is too dangerous. ' She lead him to the bottom of the knoll. 'Mousse,' say Auntie, 'are you fine?' Uncle Moustapha's eyes were close. He sense that it would be unwise to open them straightaway, though he knew that he could still see. The image of the eclipse was yet in his eyes. It became a lemon, now an emerald, now a circle of evening sky—deep blue, now a violet, a rose and then it fade into darkness. 'Did you see it? 'he whisper. 'Did you see my eclipse?'

"'No' say Auntie. 'You tell me on the way here to not look at it. Anyway, it is your gift, you crazy old man. Are you fine? Can you see?'

'"What does it matter? I saw it. My own eclipse.'

"'We must go, old man. You are hungry.'

"So, Marcus, they walk away from the hill. They did not look back. Soon, Moustapha open his eyes and look about him. The whole world was more beautiful to him than ever before. He tell his wife of all that he have seen before, during, and after the eclipse as they walk home. He was happy that he did not obey Madison.

"When they get to the family compound they saw Madison packing his equipment into his suitcases and Auntie ran to him and speak very fast, but he did not understand. He spoke no Wolof, you see. 'Don't worry about my 'ooman, Mr.

Madison,' say Uncle Mousse. 'She is afraid for I look into the eclipse.' Madison almost pull out his hairs when my uncle say this for, as you know, my friend, it was dangerous. 'You crazy man!' say Madison, 'I say not to do this, but you do this. Why?'

"'But I am not blind, Mr. Madison.'

"'One does not have any difficulty seeing after looking directly at an eclipse for a few hours, or even days. You must go see a doctor.' But Uncle Mousse smile only and light a cigarette. He spoke to Madison in the manner of a great imam. 'I will,' he say, 'see today, tomorrow, and always. I have seen what no other living soul have seen today. No, Mr. Madison, no doctor for me.' So Madison finish packing his things, slip some money to Auntie Fatima and went away.

"'What did he say to you?' ask my aunt.

"'He say foolishness,' say Uncle Mousse. 'He tell me to go to the doctor, but I will not. No, I do not care to —' But he stop short. 'Did you,' he say to Auntie Fatima, 'see a big, black thing fly by to the left of us?'

"'No,' say Auntie.

"'I thought I saw a black shadow fly by us.'

"'Mousse, Mousse, you are going blind. Oyo! Oyo! Ndeysahn. I think I must —.'

"'Fati, stop this. I know what you will say. You old 'ooman, you… . 'But he was silence again by the dark spot that fly by his vision. It move slower this time and he turn quick to the left to see it, but was gone. 'You saw it again, didn't you, Mousse?' my aunt say with almost crying in her voice.

"'Yes, old 'ooman. Perhap I have make myself blind, indeed. Perhap I should see a doctor.' Auntie insist that Uncle Mousse go to see one of our own marabous because it was the white magic that put him in this situation. Of course, my friend, as you have perhap already guess, Uncle Mousse decide to see a European doctor. He got on the bus to Bassis Santa Su.

"The doctor find Mousse's story incredulous, for he find nothing wrong at all with my uncle's eyes. Nevertheless, Mousse saw the black constantly almost. It flick on and off, on and off in the corner of his left eye. At first it irritate him almost to vexation, but he soon got use to it. The doctor say to him over and over, 'This I don't believe. Your eyesight is excellent except for a slight asti'matism on your left eye.'

"'This I have for years, Doctor Blake. This you already have tell me. Listen, I do not know why I see this little black spot out the corner of my eye; I can still see as before.' He would have say more, but he notice that Dr. Blake was beginning to become too red and his lips look like the lips of a baboon. Very thin and tight. My uncle look at the doctor's eye chart for a moment and then he say, 'Must I return to you?'

"'Yes,' say the doctor. 'I will see you two times more. Come on the tenth and the twentieth, please.'

"'Very good,' say Uncle Moustapha, and he went away.

"Upon arriving to home, Uncle Mousse explain to his wife what the doctor say and ate his lunch with a satisfy smile. Then he retire to his room for his nap. The little black spot follow him to his room like an English lady's dog follow her through town. The room was too warm so he open the window. With the door close and his reading lamp on (my uncle was the first in Sakaam to have electricity and running water in his house), he spread out his mat on the floor and take his Koran to begin his prayer and study before the nap. Everything was silent and still. His heart must have been at peace.

"As he begin to read, he notice that the dark spot no longer flash on and off, but it remain there, hanging in the air. It begin to grow. He was afraid to notice this growing blackness, because he fear it would disappear before he could turn. Or worse yet, would take completely his sight. A sudden chill touch him as the spot grew larger. He spin around violently. His heart pound as he fix his eyes on the giant, black image before him. Without thinking he fumble in his pocket for his cigarettes, offer one to the white hand of his guest, light his own and say to him, 'Been busy lately?'"

"Quite a story," I said to my friend Idi. "And you say it's true?"

"Who knows?" said Idi, lighting a Craven. "You must keep an eye on story-telling Africans."

RAY BRADBURY

Kaleidoscope
1951

The first concussion cut the rocket up the side with a giant can opener. The men were thrown into space like a dozen wriggling silverfish. They were scattered into a dark sea; and the ship, in a million pieces, went on, a meteor swarm seeking a lost sun.

"Barkley, Barkley, where are you?"

The sound of voices calling like lost children on a cold night.

"Woode, Woode!"

"Captain!"

"Hollis, Hollis, this is Stone."

"Stone, this is Hollis. Where are you?"

"I don't know. How can I? Which way is up? I'm falling. Good God, I'm falling."

They fell. They fell as pebbles fall down wells. They were scattered as jack-stones are scattered from a gigantic throw. And now instead of men there were only voices — all kinds of voices, disembodied and impassioned, in varying degrees of terror and resignation.

"We're going away from each other."

This was true. Hollis, swinging head over heels, knew this was true. He knew it with a vague acceptance. They were parting to go their separate ways, and nothing could bring them back. They were wearing their sealed- tight space suits with the glass tubes over their pale faces, but they hadn't had time to lock on their force units. With them they could be small lifeboats in space, saving themselves, saving others, collecting together, finding each other until they were an island of men with some plan. But without the force units snapped to their shoulders they were meteors, senseless, each going to a separate and irrevocable fate.

A period of perhaps ten minutes elapsed while the first terror died and a metallic calm took its place. Space began to weave its strange voices in and out, on a great dark loom, crossing, recrossing, making a final pattern.

"Stone to Hollis. How long can we talk by phone?"

"It depends on how fast you're going your way and I'm going mine."

"An hour, I make it."

"That should do it," said Hollis, abstracted and quiet.

"What happened?" asked Hollis a minute later.

"The rocket blew up, that's all. Rockets do blow up."

"Which way are you going?"

"It looks like I'll hit the Moon."

"It's Earth for me. Back to old Mother Earth at ten thousand miles per hour. I'll burn like a match." Hollis thought of it with a queer abstraction of mind. He seemed to be removed from his body, watching it fall down and down through space, as objective as he had been in regard to the first falling snowflakes of a winter season long gone.

The others were silent, thinking of the destiny that had brought them to this, falling, falling, and nothing they could do to change it. Even the captain was quiet, for there was no command or plan he knew that could put things back together again.

"Oh, it's a long way down. Oh, it's a long way down, a long, long, long way down," said a voice. "I don't want to die, I don't want to die, it's a long way down."

"Who's that?"

"I don't know."

"Stimson, I think. Stimson, is that you?"

"It's a long, long way and I don't like it. Oh, God, I don't like it."

"Stimson, this is Hollis. Stimson, you hear me?"

A pause while they fell separate from one another.

"Stimson?"

"Yes." He replied at last.

"Stimson, take it easy; we're all in the same fix."

"I don't want to be here. I want to be somewhere else."

"There's a chance we'll be found."

"I must be, I must be," said Stimson. "I don't believe this; I don't believe any of this is happening."

"It's a bad dream," said someone.

"Shut up!" said Hollis.

"Come and make me," said the voice. It was Applegate. He laughed easily, with a similar objectivity. "Come and shut me up."

Hollis for the first time felt the impossibility of his position. A great anger filled him, for he wanted more than anything at this moment to be able to do something to Applegate. He had wanted for many years to do something and now it was too late. Applegate was only a telephonic voice.

Falling, falling, falling...

Now, as if they had discovered the horror, two of the men began to scream. In a nightmare Hollis saw one of them float by, very near, screaming and screaming.

"Stop it!" The man was almost at his fingertips, screaming insanely. He would never stop. He would go on screaming for a million miles, as long as he was in radio range, disturbing all of them, making it impossible for them to talk to one another.

Hollis reached out. It was best this way. He made the extra effort and touched the man. He grasped the man's ankle and pulled himself up along the body until he reached the head. The man screamed and clawed frantically, like a drowning swimmer. The screaming filled the universe.

One way or the other, thought Hollis. The Moon or Earth or meteors will kill him, so why not now?

He smashed the man's glass mask with his iron fist. The screaming stopped. He pushed off from the body and let it spin away on its own course, falling.

Falling, falling down space Hollis and the rest of them went in the long, endless dropping and whirling of silence.

"Hollis, you still there?"

Hollis did not speak, but felt the rush of heat in his face.

"This is Applegate again."

"All right, Applegate."

"Let's talk. We haven't anything else to do."

The captain cut in. "That's enough of that. We've got to figure a way out of this."

"Captain, why don't you shut up?" said Applegate.

"What!"

"You heard me, Captain. Don't pull your rank on me, you're ten thousand miles away by now, and let's not kid ourselves. As Stimson puts it, it's a long way down."

"See here, Applegate!"

"Can it. This is a mutiny of one. I haven't a damn thing to lose. Your ship was a bad ship and you were a bad captain and I hope you break when you hit the Moon."

"I'm ordering you to stop!"

"Go on, order me again." Applegate smiled across ten thousand miles. The captain was silent. Applegate continued, "Where were we, Hollis? Oh yes, I remember. I hate you too. But you know that. You've known it for a long time."

Hollis clenched his fists, helplessly.

"I want to tell you something," said Applegate. "Make you happy. I was the one who blackballed you with the Rocket Company five years ago."

A meteor flashed by. Hollis looked down and his left hand was gone. Blood spurted. Suddenly there was no air in his suit. He had enough air in his lungs to move his right hand over and twist a knob at his left elbow, tightening the joint and sealing the leak. It had happened so quickly that he was not surprised. Nothing surprised him any more. The air in the suit came back to normal in an instant now that the leak was sealed. And the blood that had flowed so swiftly was pressured as he fastened the knob yet tighter, until it made a tourniquet.

All of this took place in a terrible silence on his part. And the other men chatted. That one man, Lespere, went on and on with his talk about his wife on Mars, his wife on Venus, his wife on Jupiter, his money, his wondrous times, his drunkenness, his gambling, his happiness. On and on, while they all fell. Lespere reminisced on the past, happy, while he fell to his death.

It was so very odd. Space, thousands of miles of space, and these voices vibrating in the center of it. No one visible at all, and only the radio waves quivering and trying to quicken other men into emotion.

"Are you angry, Hollis?"

"No." And he was not. The abstraction had returned and he was a thing of dull concrete, forever falling nowhere.

"You wanted to get to the top all your life, Hollis. You always wondered what happened. I put the black mark on you just before I was tossed out myself."

"That isn't important," said Hollis. And it was not. It was gone. When life is over it is like a flicker of bright film, an instant on the screen, all of its prejudices and passions condensed and illumined for an instant on space, and before you could cry out, "There was a happy day, there a bad one, there an evil face, there a good one," the film burned to a cinder, the screen went dark.

From this outer edge of his life, looking back, there was only one remorse, and that was only that he wished to go on living. Did all dying people feel this way, as if they had never lived? Did life seem that short, indeed, over and done before you took a breath? Did it seem this abrupt and impossible to everyone, or only to himself, here, now, with a few hours left to him for thought and deliberation?

One of the other men, Lespere, was talking. "Well, I had me a good time: I had a wife on Mars, Venus, and Jupiter. Each of them had money and treated me swell. I got drunk and once I gambled away twenty thousand dollars."

But you're here now, thought Hollis. I didn't have any of those things. When I was living I was jealous of you, Lespere; when I had another day ahead of me I envied you your women and your good times. Women frightened me and I went into space, always wanting them and jealous of you for having them, and money, and as much happiness as you could have in your own wild way. But now, falling here, with everything over, I'm not jealous of you any more, because it's over for you as it is for me, and right now it's like it never was. Hollis craned his face forward and shouted into the telephone.

"It's all over, Lespere!"

Silence.

"It's just as if it never was, Lespere!"

"Who's that?" Lespere's faltering voice.

"This is Hollis."

He was being mean. He felt the meanness, the senseless meanness of dying. Applegate had hurt him; now he wanted to hurt another. Applegate and space had both wounded him.

"You're out here, Lespere. It's all over. It's just as if it had never happened, isn't it?"

"No."

"When anything's over, it's just like it never happened. Where's your life any better than mine, now? Now is what counts. Is it any better? Is it?"

"Yes, it's better!"

"How!"

"Because I got my thoughts, I remember!" cried Lespere, far away indignant, holding his memories to his chest with both hands.

And he was right. With a feeling of cold water rushing through his head and body, Hollis knew he was right. There were differences between memories and dreams. He had only dreams of things he had wanted to do, while Lespere had memories of things done and accomplished. And this knowledge began to pull Hollis apart, with a slow, quivering precision.

"What good does it do you?" he cried to Lespere. "Now?" When a thing's over it's not good any more. You're no better off than I."

"I'm resting easy," said Lespere. "I've had my turn. I'm not getting mean at the end, like you."

"Mean?" Hollis turned the word on his tongue. He had never been mean, as long as he could remember, in his life. He had never dared to be mean. He must have saved it all of these years for such a time as this. "Mean." He rolled the word into the back of his mind. He felt tears start into his eyes and roll down his face. Someone must have heard his gasping voice.

"Take it easy, Hollis."

It was, of course, ridiculous. Only a minute before he had been giving advice to others, to Stimson; he had felt a braveness which he had thought to be the genuine thing, and now he knew that it had been nothing but shock and the objectivity possible in shock. Now he was trying to pack a lifetime of suppressed emotion into an interval of minutes.

"I know how you feel, Hollis," said Lespere, now twenty thousand miles away, his voice fading. "I don't take it personally."

But aren't we equal? he wondered. Lespere and I? Here, now? If a thing's over, it's done, and what good is it? You die anyway. But he knew he was rationalizing, for it was like trying to tell the difference between a live man and a corpse.

There was a spark in one, and not in the other — an aura, a mysterious element.

So it was with Lespere and himself; Lespere had lived a good full life, and it made him a different man now, and he, Hollis, had been as good as dead for many years. They came to death by separate paths and, in all likelihood, if there were kinds of death, their kinds would be as different as night from day. The quality of death, like that of life, must be of an infinite variety, and if one has already died once, then what was there to look for in dying for good and all, as he was now?

It was a second later that he discovered his right foot was cut sheer away. It almost made him laugh. The air was gone from his suit again. He bent quickly, and there was blood, and the meteor had taken flesh and suit away to the ankle. Oh, death in space was most humorous. It cut you away, piece by piece, like a black and invisible butcher. He tightened the valve at the knee, his head whirling into pain, fighting to remain aware, and with the valve tightened, the blood retained, the air kept, he straightened up and went on falling, falling, for that was all there was left to do.

"Hollis?"

Hollis nodded sleepily, tired of waiting for death.

"This is Applegate again," said the voice.

"Yes."

"I've had time to think. I listened to you. This isn't good. It makes us bad. This is a bad way to die. It brings all the bile out. You listening, Hollis?"

"Yes."

"I lied. A minute ago. I lied. I didn't blackball you. I don't know why I said that. Guess I wanted to hurt you. You seemed the one to hurt. We've always fought. Guess I'm getting old fast and repenting fast. I guess listening to you be mean made me ashamed. Whatever the reason, I want you to know I was an idiot too. There's not an ounce of truth in what I said. To hell with you."

Hollis felt his heart begin to work again. It seemed as if it hadn't worked for five minutes, but now all of his limbs began to take color and warmth. The shock was over, and the successive shocks of anger and terror and loneliness were passing. He felt like a man emerging from a cold shower in the morning, ready for breakfast and a new day.

"Thanks, Applegate."

"Don't mention it. Up your nose, you bastard."

"Hey," said Stone.

"What?" Hollis called across space; for Stone, of all of them, was a good friend.

"I've got myself into a meteor swarm, some little asteroids."

"Meteors?"

"I think it's the Myrmidone cluster that goes out past Mars and in toward Earth once every five years. I'm right in the middle. It's like a big kaleidoscope. You get all kinds of colors and shapes and sizes. God, it's beautiful, all that metal."

Silence.

"I'm going with them," said Stone. "They're taking me off with them. I'll be damned." He laughed.

Hollis looked to see, but saw nothing. There were only the great diamonds and sapphires and emerald mists and velvet inks of space, with God's voice mingling among the crystal fires. There was a kind of wonder and imagination in the thought of Stone going off in the meteor swarm, out past Mars for years and coming in toward Earth every five years, passing in and out of the planet's ken for the next million centuries. Stone and the Myrmidone cluster eternal and unending, shifting and shaping like the kaleidoscope colors when you were a child and held the long tube to the sun and gave it a twirl.

"So long, Hollis." Stone's voice, very faint now. "So long."

"Good luck," shouted Hollis across thirty thousand miles.

"Don't be funny," said Stone, and was gone.

The stars closed in.

Now all the voices were fading, each on his own trajectory, some to Mars, others into farthest space. And Hollis himself... He looked down. He, of all the others, was going back to Earth alone.

"So long."

"Take it easy."

"So long, Hollis." That was Applegate.

The many good-bys. The short farewells. And now the great loose brain was disintegrating. The components of the brain which had worked so beautifully and efficiently in the skull case of the rocket ship firing through space were dying one by one; the meaning of their life together was falling apart. And as a body dies when the brain ceases functioning, so the spirit of the ship and their long time together and what they meant to one another was dying. Applegate was now no more than a finger blown from the parent body, no longer to be despised and worked against. The brain was exploded, and the senseless, useless fragments of it were far scattered. The voices faded and now all of space was silent. Hollis was alone, falling.

They were all alone. Their voices had died like echoes of the words of God spoken and vibrating in the starred deep. There went the captain to the Moon; there Stone with the meteor swarm; there Stimson; there Applegate toward Pluto; there Smith and Turner and Underwood and all the rest, the shards of the kaleidoscope that had formed a thinking pattern for so long, hurled apart.

And I? thought Hollis. What can I do? Is there anything I can do now to make up for a terrible and empty life? If only I could do one good thing to make up for the meanness I collected all these years and didn't even know was in me! But there's no one here but myself and how can you do good all alone? You can't. Tomorrow night I'll hit Earth's atmosphere.

I'll burn, he thought, and be scattered in ashes all over the continental lands. I'll be put to use. Just a little bit, but ashes are ashes and they'll add to the land.

He fell swiftly, like a bullet, like a pebble, like an iron weight, objective, objective all of the time now, not sad or happy or anything, but only wishing he could do a good thing now that everything was gone, a good thing for just himself to know about.

When I hit the atmosphere, I'll burn like a meteor. "I wonder," he said, "if anyone'll see me?"

The small boy on the country road looked up and screamed. "Look, Mom, look! A falling star!"
The blazing white star fell down the sky of dusk in Illinois.
"Make a wish," said his mother. "Make a wish."

MARGARET ATWOOD

Homelanding
1990

1.

Where should I begin? After all, you have never been there; or if you have, you may not have understood the significance of what you saw, or thought you saw. A window is a window, but there is looking out and looking in. The native you glimpsed, disappearing behind the curtain, or into the bushes, or down the manhole in the main street — my people are shy — may have been only your reflection in the glass. My country specializes in such illusions.

2.

Let me propose myself as typical. I walk upright on two legs, and have in addition two arms, with ten appendages, that is to say, five at the end of each. On the top of my head, but not on the front, there is an odd growth, like a species of seaweed. Some think this is a kind of fur, others consider it modified feathers, evolved perhaps from scales like those of lizards. It serves no functional purpose and is probably decorative.

My eyes are situated in my head, which also possess two small holes for the entrance and exit of air, the invisible fluid we swim in, and one larger hole, equipped with bony protuberances called teeth, by means of which I destroy and assimilate certain parts of my surroundings and change them into myself. This is called eating. The things I eat include roots, berries, nuts, fruits, leaves, and the muscle tissues of various animals and fish. Sometimes I eat their brains and glands as well. I do not as a rule eat insects, grubs, eyeballs or the snouts of pigs, though these are eaten with relish in other countries.

3.

Some of my people have a pointed but boneless external appendage, in the front, below the navel or midpoint. Others do not. Debate about whether the possession of such a thing is an advantage or disadvantage is still going on. If this item is lacking, and in its place there is a pocket or inner cavern in which fresh members of our community are grown, it is considered impolite to mention it openly to strangers. I tell you this because it is the breach of etiquette most commonly made by tourists.

In some of our more private gatherings, the absence of cavern or prong is politely overlooked, like club feet or blindness. But sometimes a prong and a cavern will collaborate in a dance, or illusion, using mirrors and water, which is always absorbing for the performers but frequently grotesque for the observers. I notice that you have similar customs.

Whole conventions and a great deal of time have recently been devoted to discussions of this state of affairs. The prong people tell the cavern people that the latter are not people at all and are in reality more akin to dogs or potatoes, and the cavern people abuse the prong people for their obsession with images of poking, thrusting, probing and stabbing. Any long object with a hole at the end, out of which various projectiles can be shot, delights them.

I myself-I am a cavern person-find it a relief not to have to worry about climbing over barbed wire fences or getting caught in zippers.

But that is enough about our bodily form.

4.

As for the country itself, let me begin with the sunsets, which are long and red, resonant, splendid and melancholy, symphonic you might almost say; as opposed to the short boring sunsets of other countries, no more interesting than a lightswitch. We pride ourselves on our sunsets. "Come and see the sunset," we say to one another. This causes everyone to rush outdoors or over to the window.

Our country is large in extent, small in population, which accounts for our fear of large empty spaces, and also our need for them. Much of it is covered in water, which accounts for our interest in reflections, sudden vanishings, the dissolution of one thing into another. Much of it, however, is rock, which accounts for our belief in Fate.

In summer we lie about in the blazing sun, almost naked, covering our skins with fat and attempting to turn red. But when the sun is low in the sky and faint, even at noon, the water we are so fond of changes to something hard and white and cold and covers up the ground. Then we cocoon ourselves, become lethargic, and spend much of our time hiding in crevices. Our mouths shrink and we say little.

Before this happens, the leaves on many of our trees turn blood red or lurid yellow, much brighter and more exotic than the interminable green of jungles. We find this change beautiful. "Come and see the leaves," we say, and jump into our moving vehicles and drive up and down past the forest of sanguinary trees, pressing our eyes to the glass.

We are a nation of metamorphs.

Anything red compels us.

5.

Sometimes we lie still and do not move. If air is still going in and out of our breathing holes, this is called sleep. If not, it is called death. When a person has achieved death a kind of picnic is held, with music, flowers and food. The person so honored, if in one piece, and not, for instance, in shreds or falling apart, as they do if exploded or a long time drowned, is dressed in becoming clothes and lowered into a hole in the ground, or else burned up.

These customs are among the most difficult to explain to strangers. Some of our visitors, especially the young ones, have never heard of death and are bewildered. They think that death is simply one more of our illusions, our mirror tricks; they cannot understand why, with so much food and music, the people are sad.

But you will understand. You too must have death among you. I can see it in your eyes.

6.

I can see it in your eyes. If it weren't for this I would have stopped trying long ago, to communicate with you in this halfway language which is so difficult for both of us, which exhausts the throat and fills the mouth with sand; if weren't for this I would have gone away, gone back. It's this knowledge of death, which we share, where we overlap. Death is our common ground. Together, on it, we can walk forward.

By now you must have guessed: I come from another planet. But I will never say to you, take me to your leaders. Even I — unused to your ways though I am — would never make that mistake. We ourselves have such beings among us, made of cogs, pieces of paper, small disks of shiny metal, scraps of colored cloth. I do not need to encounter more of them.

Instead I will say, take me to your trees. Take me to your breakfasts, your sunsets, your bad dreams, your shoes, your nouns. Take me to your fingers; take me to your deaths.

These are worth it. These are what I have come for.

J.G. BALLARD

The Message From Mars
1992

The successful conclusion of NASA's Mars mission in 2008, signalled by the safe touch-down of the Zeus IV space vehicle at Edwards Air Force Base in California, marked an immense triumph for the agency. During the 1990s after the failure of the Shuttle project, NASA's entire future was in jeopardy. The American public's lack of interest in the space programme, coupled with unsettling political events in the former Soviet bloc, led Congress to cut back its funding of astronautics. Successive US Presidents were distracted by the task of balancing the national budget, and their scientific advisors had long insisted that the exploration of the solar system could be achieved far more economically by unmanned vehicles.

But NASA's directors had always known that the scientific exploration of space was a small part of the agency's claim to existence. Manned flights alone could touch the public imagination and guarantee the huge funds needed to achieve them. The triumph of the Apollo landing on the moon in 1969 had shown that the road to the spiritual heart of America could be paved with dollar bills, but by the year 2000 that road seemed permanently closed. Struggling to keep the agency alive, the NASA chiefs found themselves reduced to the satellite mapping of mid-western drought areas, and were faced with the prospect of being absorbed into the Department of Agriculture.

However, at the last hour the agency was saved, and given the funds to embark on its greatest mission. The announcement in Peking on January 1, 2001, that a Chinese spacecraft had landed on the moon sent an uneasy tremor through the American nation. True, the Stars and Stripes had been planted on the moon more than thirty years earlier, but that event lay in a past millennium. Was the next millennium to be dominated by the peoples on the Asian side of the Pacific rim, spending their huge trade surpluses on spectacular projects that would seize the planet's imagination for the next century?

As the pictures of Chinese astronauts, posing beside their pagoda-shaped space vehicle, The Temple of Lightness, were relayed to the world's TV screens, news came that an Indonesian space crew and an unmanned Korean probe would soon land next to the Chinese.

Galvanised by all this, a no longer somnolent President Quayle addressed both houses of Congress. Within weeks, NASA was assigned a multi-billion-dollar emergency fund and ordered to launch a crash programme that would leap-frog the moon and land an American on Mars before the end of the decade.

NASA, as always, rose bravely to the challenge of the tax-dollar. Armies of elderly space-engineers were recruited from their Florida retirement homes. Fifty civilian and military test pilots were pressed into astronaut training. Within two years Zeus I, the unmanned prototype of the vast space vehicle that would later carry a five-man crew, had roared away from Cape Canaveral on a six-month reconnaissance voyage. It circled the Red Planet a dozen times and surveyed the likely landing zone, before returning successfully to Earth.

After two more unmanned flights, in 2005 and 2006, Zeus IV set off in November, 2007, guaranteeing President Quayle's third-term electoral landslide, which the five astronauts saluted from the flight-deck of the spacecraft. By now the Chinese, Indonesian and Korean lunar programmes had been forgotten. The world's eyes were fixed on the Zeus IV, and its five crew-members were soon more famous than any Hollywood superstar.

Wisely, NASA had selected an international crew, led by Colonel Dean Irwin of the USAF. Captain Clifford Horner and Commander John Merritt were former US Army and Navy test pilots, but the team was completed by a Russian doctor, Colonel Valentina Tsarev, and a Japanese computer specialist, Professor Hiroshi Kawahito.

During the two-month voyage to Mars the quirks and personalities of the five astronauts became as familiar as any face across a breakfast table. The Zeus IV was the largest spacecraft ever launched, and had the dimensions of a nuclear submarine. Its wide control rooms and observation decks, its crew facilities and non-denominational chapel (if a marriage was arranged, Colonel Irwin was authorised to conduct it) happily reminded TV viewers of the Starship Enterprise in the *Star Trek* TV series, still endlessly broadcast on a hundred networks. Everyone responded to the calm and dignified presence of Colonel Irwin, the deadpan humour of Captain Horner, the chirpy computer-speak of the mercurial Japanese, and the mothering but sometimes flirtatious eye of Dr. Valentina. Millions of viewers rallied to their aid when the Zeus IV passed through an unexpected meteor storm, but the ultra-hard carbon fibre and ceramic hull, a byproduct of the most advanced tank armour, proved even more resilient than the designers had hoped. The inspection space-walks seemed like gracefully choreographed ballets — which of course they were, like every other activity shown to the TV audience- and confirmed that mankind had at last entered the second Space Age.

Two months to the day after leaving Cape Canaveral, the Zeus IV landed on Mars, whose somber presence had loomed ever more threateningly for the previous weeks. Signals blackouts caused by the planet's magnetic field added their own thrills and panics, skillfully orchestrated by NASA's PR specialists. But the landing was a triumph, celebrated by the hoisting of the Stars and Stripes and, behind it, the flag of the United Nations. Within an hour the crew of the Zeus IV was standing on Martian soil beside the spacecraft, intoning their carefully rehearsed 'Hymn to the Space Age'. From that moment no Congressman dared to deny the NASA chiefs anything that they demanded.

For the next six weeks public interest in the Mars mission remained high, sustained by NASA's careful attention to the emotional needs of the worldwide audience. Life within the spacecraft was presented as a cross between a TV sitcom and a classroom course in elementary astronautics. The crew tolerantly went along with these charades. Dr. Valentina was seen replacing a filling in Commander Merritt's mouth, and Professor Kawahito, the heart-throb of a billion Asian viewers, won a hard-fought chess tournament against the Zeus IV's combined on-board computers. Romance was in the air as Dr. Valentina's cabin door remained tantalizingly ajar. The TV cameras followed the crew as they drove in their excursion vehicles across the fossil Martian seas, collecting rock samples and analysing the local atmosphere.

At the halfway stage of their mission the crew revealed a mild impatience with the media roles imposed on them, which NASA psychologists attributed to a greater maturity brought on by a sense of planetary awe. To remind them of earth, the astronauts were urged to watch episodes of *Dallas*, *Dynasty* and *The Flintstones*, and to take part in a series of Oval Office interviews with President Quayle. But their spirits lifted as the day of departure drew near. When the Zeus IV rose at last from the Martian surface the entire crew burst spontaneously into an unscripted cheer, in which some observers detected a small note of irony.

Ignoring this impromptu levity, NASA planned a lavish reception at Edwards Air Force Base, where the Zeus IV would land. Every Congressman and Governor in the United States would be present, along with President Quayle, the heads of thirty countries and a host of entertainment celebrities. An unending programme of media appearances awaited the astronauts — there would be triumphal parades through a dozen major cities, followed by a worldwide tour lasting a full six months. NASA had already appointed firms of literary agents and public relations experts to look after the commercial interests of the astronauts. There were sports sponsorships, book contracts and highly paid consultancies. The news of these deals was transmitted to the home-coming crew, who seemed gratified by the interest in their achievement, unaware that whenever they appeared on screen their images were accompanied by the cash totals now committed to them. Two days before Zeus IV landed, NASA announced that three major Hollywood studios would collaborate on the most expensive film of all time, in which the astronauts would play themselves in a faithful recreation of the Martian voyage.

So, at 3.35 pm on April 29th, 2008, the Zeus IV appeared in the California sky. Accompanied by six chase planes, the spacecraft swept down to a perfect landing, guided by its on-board computers to within 50 metres of President Quayle's reception podium. The stunned silence was broken by an immense cheer when two of the astronauts were glimpsed in the observation windows. The crowd surged forward, waiting for the hatches to open as soon as the landing checks were over.

Despite the warmth of this welcome, the astronauts were surprisingly reluctant to emerge from their craft. The decontamination teams were poised by the airlocks, ready to board the spaceship and evacuate its atmosphere for laboratory analysis. But the crew had overridden the computerized sequences and made no reply over the radio link to the urgent queries of the ground controllers. They had switched off the television cameras inside the craft, but could be seen through the observation windows, apparently tidying their cabins and changing into overalls. Dr Valentina was spotted in the galley, apparently sterilizing her surgical instruments. A rumour swept the review stands, where President Quayle, the Congress and invited heads of state sweltered in the sun, that one of the crew had been injured on re-entry, but it soon transpired that Dr Valentina was merely making soup. Even more strangely, Professor Kawahito was seen setting out six parallel chessboards, as if preparing for another tournament.

At this point, an hour after their arrival, the crew became irritated by the grimacing faces pressed against the observation windows, and the interior shutters abruptly closed. This dismissive gesture made the crowd even more restive, and the ground staff tried to force the main hatch. When they failed, the head of NASA's crash recovery team began to pound on the locks with a baseball bat borrowed from a youngster seated on his father's shoulders. The first whistles and jeers rose from the crowd, who jostled the scaffolding towers on which the impatient TV crews were waiting. A cameraman lost his footing and fell through the roof of a parked bus. Loud-speakers blared meaninglessly across the million or more spectators sitting on their cars around the perimeter of the airfield. The heads of state, diplomats and generals consulted their watches, while President Quayle, making involuntary putting movements with the portable microphone in his hands, beckoned in an unsettling way to his military aide carrying the briefcase of nuclear launch codes. The boos of the crowd were only drowned when a squadron of jet planes flew low over the field, releasing streams of red, white and blue smoke. Ordered away by the frantic control tower, the victory flight broke up in confusion as the pilots returned to their muster points in the sky, leaving a delirium of crazed smoke over the Zeus IV.

At last calm was restored when a company of military police took up positions around the spacecraft, forcing the crowds behind the VIP stand. Led by President Quayle, the dignitaries shuffled from their seats and hurried along the lines of red carpet to the refreshment tents. The TV cameras trained their lenses on the Zeus IV, watching for the smallest sign of movement.

As evening fell, the spectators beyond the airfield perimeter began to disperse. Powerful arc-lights bathed the spacecraft, and during the night a fresh attempt was made to contact the crew. But the messages in morse code tapped on the hull, like the laser beams shone at the darkened observation windows, failed to draw any response. No sound could be heard from the interior of the craft, as if the crew had settled in for the night, and a hundred theories began to circulate among the NASA chiefs and the teams of doctors and psychiatrists summoned to their aid.

Were the astronauts in the last stages of a fatal contagious disease? Had their brains been invaded by an alien parasite? Were they too emotionally exhausted by their voyage to face the reception awaiting them, or gripped by so strong a sense of humility that they longed only for silence and anonymity? Had an unexpected consequence of time dilation returned them psychologically hours or days after their physical arrival? Had they, perhaps, died in a spiritual sense, or were they, for inexplicable reasons of their own, staging a mutiny?

Surrounded by the deserted stands and the silent bunting, the NASA chiefs made their decision. An hour before dawn, two thermal lances played their fiery hoses against the heat-resistant plates of the spacecraft. But the carbon-ceramic hull of the Zeus IV had been forged in temperatures far beyond those of a thermal lance.

A controlled explosion was the only solution, despite the danger to the crew within. But as the demolition squad placed their charges against the ventral hatchway, the shutter of an observation window opened for the first time. Captured on film, the faces of Colonel Irwin and Commander Merritt looked down at the limpet mines, the detonators and fuse wire. They gazed calmly at the NASA officials and engineers gesticulating at them, and shook their heads, rejecting the world with a brief wave before closing the shutter for the last time.

Needless to say, NASA allowed nothing of this to leak to the public at large, and claimed that the crew had alerted their ground controllers to the possible dangers of a virulent interplanetary disease. NASA spokesmen confirmed that they had ordered the crew to isolate themselves until this mystery virus could be identified and destroyed. The Zeus IV was hitched to its tractor and moved to an empty hangar on a remote corner of the airbase, safe from the TV cameras and the thousands still camped around the perimeter fence.

Here, over the next weeks and months, teams of engineers and psychologists, astrophysicists and churchmen tried to free the crew from their self-imposed prison. Right from the start, as the doors of the hangar sealed the Zeus IV from the world, it was taken for granted that the astronauts' immolation was entirely voluntary. Nonetheless, an armed guard, backed by electronic security devises, kept careful watch on the craft. Sets of aircraft scales were manoeuvred under the landing wheels, so that the weight of the Zeus IV could be measured at all times, and instantly expose any attempt at escape.

As it happened, the spaceship's weight remained constant, never fluctuating by more than the accumulated dust on its hull. In all senses the Zeus IV constituted a sealed world, immune to any pressures from within and without. A controlled explosion strong enough to split the hull would also rupture the engines and disperse the craft's nuclear fuel supply, provoking a worldwide political outcry that would doom NASA forever. There was no way of starving the crew out — to deal with the possibility of the Zeus IV missing its rendezvous with Mars and stranding itself forever in deep space, a 200-ton stock of food had been placed aboard, enough to last the crew for 40 years. Its air, water and human waste were recycled, and there were enough episodes of *Dallas* in the video-library to amuse astronauts for all eternity.

The Zeus, in fact, no longer needed the Earth, and the NASA officials accepted that only psychological means would ever persuade the crew to leave their craft. They assumed that a profound spiritual crisis had afflicted the astronauts, and that until this resolved itself the rescuers main task was to establish a channel of communication.

So began a long period of ruses, pleas and stratagems. The puzzled entreaties of relatives, whose tearful faces were projected onto the hangar roof, the prayers of churchmen, the offers of huge cash bribes, the calls to patriotism and even the threat of imprisonment, failed to prompt a single response. After two months, when public curiosity was still at fever pitch, the NASA teams admitted to themselves that the crew of the Zeus IV had probably not even heard these threats and promises.

Meanwhile, an impatient President Quayle, aware that he was the butt of cartoonists and TV comedians, demanded firmer action. He ordered that pop music be played at full blast against the spacecraft's hull and, further, that the huge ship be rocked violently from side to side until the crew came to their senses. This regime was tried but discontinued after two hours, partly for its sheer ludicrousness, and partly for fear of damaging the nuclear reactors.

More thoughtful opinion was aware that the crisis afflicting the Zeus crew merited careful study in its own right, if mankind were ever to live permanently in space. A prominent theologian was invited to the Edwards airbase, and surveyed the claustrophobic hangar in which the Zeus was now entombed, draped like Gulliver in its cables and acoustic sensors. He wondered why the crew had bothered to return to Earth at all, knowing what they probably faced, when they might have stayed forever on the vast and empty landscapes of Mars. By returning at all, he ventured, they were making an important point, and acknowledged that they still saw their place among the human race.

So a patient vigil began. Concealed cameras watched for any signs of internal movement and electronic gauges mapped the smallest activities of the crew. After a further three months, the daily pattern of life within the Zeus IV had been well established. The crew never spoke to each other except when carrying out the daily maintenance checks of the spacecraft systems. All took regular exercise in the gymnasium, but otherwise stayed in their own quarters. No music was played and they never listened to radio or television. For all that anyone knew, they passed the days in sleep, meditation and prayer. The temperature remained at a steady 68°F, and the only constant sound was that of the circulation of air.

After six months the NASA psychiatrists concluded that the crew of the Zeus IV had suffered a traumatic mental collapse, probably brought on by oxygen starvation, and were now in a vegetative state. Relatives protested, but public interest began to wane. Congress refused to allocate funds for further Zeus missions, and NASA reluctantly committed itself to a future of instrumented spaceflights.

A year passed, and a second. A small guard and communications crew, including a duty psychologist and a clergyman, still maintained a vigil over the Zeus. The monitors recorded the faint movements of the crew, and the patterns of daily life which they had established within a few hours of their landing. A computerized analysis of their foot-treads identified each of the astronauts and revealed that they kept to their own quarters and seldom met, though they all took part in the maintenance drills.

So the astronauts anguished in their twilight world. A new President and the unfolding decades of peace led the public to forget about the Zeus IV, and its crew, if remembered at all, were assumed to be convalescing at a secret institution. In 2016, eight years after their return, there a flurry of activity when a deranged security officer lit a large fire under the spacecraft, in an attempt to smoke out the crew. Four years later, a Hollywood telepathist claimed to be in contact with the astronauts, reporting that they had met God on Mars and had been sworn to silence about the tragic future in store for the human race.

In 2025 the NASA headquarters in Houston were alerted to a small but sudden fall in the overall weight of the Zeus — 170 pounds, had been wiped from the scales. Was the spacecraft preparing for take-off, perhaps employing an anti-gravity device which the crew had been constructing in the seventeen years since their return? However, the tread-pattern analysis confirmed that only four astronauts were now aboard the craft. Colonel Irwin was missing, and an exhaustive hunt began of the Edward's airbase. But the organic sediments in the trapped gases released from the discharge vent revealed what some engineers had already suspected. Colonel Irwin had died at the age of 62, and his remains had been vapourized and returned to the atmosphere. Four years later he was followed by the Japanese, Professor Kawahito, and the Zeus was lighter by a further 132 pounds. The food stocks aboard the Zeus would now last well beyond the deaths of the three astronauts still alive.

In 2035 NASA was dissolved, and its functions assigned to the immensely wealthy universities which ran their own scientific space programmes. The Zeus IV was offered to the Smithsonian Institute in Washington, but the director declined, on the grounds that the museum could not accept exhibits that contained living organisms. The USAF had long wished to close the Edwards airbase, and responsibility for this huge desert expanse passed to the National Parks Bureau, which was eager to oversee one of the few areas of California not yet covered with tract housing. The armed guards around the Zeus IV had long gone, and two field officers supervised the elderly instruments that still kept watch over the spacecraft.

Captain Horner died in 2040, but the event was not noticed until the following year when a bored repair man catalogued the accumulated acoustic tapes and ran a computer analysis of tread-patterns and overall weight.

The news of this death, mentioned only in the National Parks Bureau's annual report, came to the attention of a Las Vegas entrepreneur who had opened the former Nevada atomic proving grounds to the tourist trade, mounting simulated A-bomb explosions. He leased the Zeus hangar from the Parks Bureau, and small parties of tourists trooped around the spacecraft, watching bemused as the rare tread-patterns crossed the sonar screens in the monitor room.

After three years of poor attendance the tours were discontinued, but a decade later a Tijuana circus proprietor sub-leased the site for his winter season. He demolished the now derelict hangar and constructed an inflatable astro-dome with a huge arena floor. Helium-filled latex 'spacecraft' circled the Zeus IV, and the performance ended with a mass ascent of the huge vehicle by a team of topless women acrobats.

When the dome was removed the Zeus IV sat under the stars, attached to a small shack where a single technician of the Parks Bureau kept a desultory watch on the computer screens for an hour each day. The spaceship was now covered with graffiti and obscene slogans, and the initials of thousands of long-vanished tourists. With its undercarriage embedded in the desert sand, it resembled a steam locomotive of the 19th century, which many passers-by assumed it to be. Tramps and hippies sheltered under its fins, and at one time the craft was incorporated into a small shanty village. In later years a desert preacher attracted a modest following, claiming that the Messiah had made his second coming and was trapped inside the Zeus. Another cultist claimed that the devil had taken up residence in the ancient structure. The tract housing drew ever closer, and eventually surrounded the Zeus, which briefly served as an illuminated landmark advertising an unsuccessful fast-food franchise.

In 2070, sixty-two years after its return from Mars, a young graduate student at Reno University erected a steel frame around the Zeus and attached a set of high-intensity magnetic probes to its hull. The computerized imaging equipment — later confiscated by the US government — revealed the silent and eerie interior of the spacecraft, its empty flight decks and corridors.

An aged couple, Commander John Merritt and Dr Valentina Tsarev, now in their late eighties, sat in their small cabins, hands folded on their laps. There were no books or ornaments beside their simple beds. Despite their extreme age they were clearly alert, tidy and reasonably well nourished. Most mysteriously, across their eyes moved the continuous play of a keen and amused intelligence.

STANISLAW LEM
Translated from the Polish by MICHAEL KANDEL

The Seventh Voyage

1964

It was on a Monday, April second — I was cruising in the vicinity of Betelgeuse — when a meteor no larger than a lima bean pierced the hull, shattered the drive regulator and part of the rudder, as a result of which the rocket lost all maneuverability. I put on my spacesuit, went outside and tried to fix the mechanism, but found I couldn't possibly attach the spare rudder — which I'd had the foresight to bring along — without the help of another man. The constructors had foolishly designed the rocket in such a way, that it took one person to hold the head of the bolt in place with a wrench, and another to tighten the nut. I didn't realize this at first and spent several hours trying to grip the wrench with my feet while using both hands to screw on the nut at the other end. But I was getting nowhere, and had already missed lunch. Then finally, just as I almost succeeded, the wrench popped out from under my feet and went flying off into space. So not only had I accomplished nothing, but lost a valuable tool besides; I watched helplessly as it sailed away, growing smaller and smaller against the starry sky. After a while the wrench returned in an elongated ellipse, but though it had now become a satellite of the rocket, it never got close enough for me to retrieve it. I went back inside and, sitting down to a modest supper, considered how best to extricate myself from this stupid situation. Meanwhile the ship flew on, straight ahead, its velocity steadily increasing, since my drive regulator too had been knocked out by that blasted meteor. It's true there were no heavenly bodies on course, but this headlong flight could hardly continue indefinitely.

For a while I contained my anger, but then discovered, when starting to wash the dinner dishes, that the now-overheated atomic pile had ruined my very best cut of sirloin (I'd been keeping it in the freezer for Sunday). I momentarily lost my usually level head, burst into a volley of the vilest oaths and smashed a few plates. This did give me a certain satisfaction, but was hardly practical. In addition, the sirloin which I threw overboard, instead of drifting off into the void, didn't seem to want to leave the rocket and revolved about it, a second artificial satellite, which produced a brief eclipse of the sun every eleven minutes and four seconds. To calm my nerves I calculated till evening the components of its trajectory, as well as the orbital perturbation caused by the presence of the lost wrench. I figured out that for the next six million years the sirloin, rotating about the ship in a circular path, would lead the wrench, then catch up with it from behind and pass it again. Finally, exhausted by these computations, I went to bed. In the middle of the night I had the feeling someone was shaking me by the shoulder. I opened my eyes and saw a man standing over the bed; his face was strangely familiar, though I hadn't the faintest idea who this could be.

"Get up," he said, "and take the pliers, we're going out and screwing on the rudder bolts..."

"First of all, your manner is somewhat unceremonious, and we haven't even been introduced," I replied, "and secondly, I know for a fact that you aren't there. I'm alone on this rocket, and have been now for two years, en route from Earth to the constellation of the Ram. Therefore you are a dream and nothing more."

However he continued to shake me, repeating that I should go with him at once and get the tools.

"This is idiotic," I said, growing annoyed, because this dream argument could very well wake me up, and I knew from experience the difficulty I would have getting back to sleep.

"Look, I'm not going anywhere, there's no point in it. A bolt tightened in a dream won't change things as they are in the sober light of day. Now kindly stop pestering me and evaporate or leave in some other fashion, otherwise I might awake."

"But you are awake, word of honor!" cried the stubborn apparition.

"Don't you recognize me? Look here!"

And saying this, he pointed to the two warts, big as strawberries, on his left cheek. Instinctively I clutched my own face, for yes, I had two warts, exactly the same, and in that very place. Suddenly I realized why this phantom reminded me of someone I knew: he was the spitting image of myself.

"Leave me alone, for heaven's sake!" I cried, shutting my eyes, anxious to stay asleep. "If you are me, then fine, we needn't stand on ceremony, but it only proves you don't exist!"

With which I turned on my other side and pulled the covers up over my head. I could hear him saying something about utter nonsense; then finally, when I didn't respond, he shouted: "You'll regret this, knucklehead! And you'll find out, too late, that this was not a dream!"

But I didn't budge. In the morning I opened my eyes and immediately recalled that curious nocturnal episode. Sitting up in bed, I thought about what strange tricks the mind can play: for here, without a single fellow creature on board and confronted with an emergency of the most pressing kind, I had — as it were — split myself in two, in that dream fantasy, to answer the needs of the situation.

After breakfast, discovering that the rocket had acquired an additional chunk of acceleration during the night, I took to leafing through the ship's library, searching the textbooks for some way out of this predicament. But I didn't find a thing. So I spread my star map out on the table and in the light of nearby Betelgeuse, obscured every so often by the orbiting sirloin, examined the area in which I was located for the seat of some cosmic civilization that might possibly come to my aid. But unfortunately this was a complete stellar wilderness, avoided by all vessels as a region unusually dangerous, for in it lay gravitational vortices, as formidable as they were mysterious, one hundred and forty-seven of them in all, whose existence was explained by six astrophysical theories, each theory saying something different.

The cosmonautical almanac warned of them, in view of the incalculable relativistic effects that passage through a vortex could bring about - particularly when traveling at high velocities. Yet there was little I could do. According to my calculations I would be making contact with the edge of the first vortex at around eleven, and therefore hurriedly prepared lunch, not wanting to face the danger on an empty stomach. I had barely finished drying the last saucer when the rocket began to pitch and heave in every direction, till all the objects not adequately tied down went flying from wall to wall like hail. With difficulty I crawled over to the armchair, and after I'd lashed myself to it, as the ship tossed about with ever increasing violence, I noticed a sort of pale lilac haze forming on the opposite side of the cabin, and in the middle of it, between the sink and the stove, a misty human shape, which had on an apron and was pouring omelet batter into a frying pan. The shape looked at me with interest, but without surprise, then shimmered and was gone. I rubbed my eyes. I was obviously alone, so attributed the vision to a momentary aberration.

As I continued to sit in — or rather, jump along with — the armchair, it suddenly hit me, like a dazzling revelation, that this hadn't been a hallucination at all. A thick volume of the General Theory of Relativity came whirling past my chair and I grabbed for it, finally catching it on the fourth pass. Turning the pages of that heavy tome wasn't easy under the circumstances - awesome forces hurled the rocket this way and that, it reeled like a drunken thing - but at last I found the right chapter. It spoke of the manifestation of the "time loop," that is, the bending of the direction of the flow of time in the presence of gravitational fields of great intensity, which phenomenon might even on occasion lead to the complete reversal of time and the "duplication of the present." The vortex I had just entered was not one of the most powerful. I knew that if I could turn the ship's bow, even if only a little, towards the Galactic Pole, it would intersect the so-called Vortex Gravitatiosus Pinckenbachii, in which had been observed more than once the duplication, even the triplication, of the present.

True, the controls were out, but I went down to the engine room and fiddled with the instruments so long, that I actually managed to produce a slight deflection of the rocket towards the Galactic Pole. This took several hours. The results were beyond my expectations. The ship fell into the center of the vortex at around midnight, its girders shook and groaned until I began to fear for its safety; but it emerged from this ordeal whole and once again was wrapped in the lifeless arms of cosmic silence, whereupon I left the engine room, only to see myself sound asleep in bed. I realized at once that this was I of the previous day, that is, from Monday night. Without reflecting on the philosophical side of this rather singular event, I ran over and shook the sleeper by the shoulder, shouting for him to get up, since I had no idea how long his Monday existence would last in my Tuesday one, therefore it was imperative we go outside and fix the rudder as quickly as possible, together.

But the sleeper merely opened one eye and told me that not only was I rude, but didn't exist, being a figment of his dream and nothing more. I tugged at him in vain, losing patience, and even attempted to drag him bodily from the bed. He wouldn't budge, stubbornly repeating that it was all a dream; I began to curse, but he pointed out logically that bolts tightened in dreams wouldn't hold on rudders in the sober light of day. I gave my word of honor that he was mistaken, I pleaded and swore in turn, to no avail — even the warts did not convince him. He turned his back to me and started snoring.

I sat down in the armchair to collect my thoughts and take stock of the situation. I'd lived through it twice now, first as that sleeper, on Monday, and then as the one trying to wake him, unsuccessfully, on Tuesday. The Monday me hadn't believed in the reality of the duplication, while the Tuesday me already knew it to be a fact. Here was a perfectly ordinary time loop. What then should be done in order to get the rudder fixed? Since the Monday me slept on — I remembered that on that night I had slept through to the morning undisturbed — I saw the futility of any further efforts to rouse him. The map indicated a number of other large gravitational vortices up ahead, therefore I could count on the duplication of the present within the next few days. I decided to write myself a letter and pin it to the pillow, enabling the Monday me, when he awoke, to see for himself that the dream had been no dream.

But no sooner did I sit at the table with pen and paper than something started rattling in the engines, so I hurried there and poured water on the overheated atomic pile till dawn, while the Monday me slept soundly, licking his lips from time to time, which galled me no end. Hungry and bleary-eyed, for I hadn't slept a wink, I set about making breakfast, and was just wiping the dishes when the rocket fell into the next gravitational vortex. I saw my Monday self staring at me dumbfounded, lashed to the armchair, while Tuesday I fried an omelet. Then a lurch knocked me off balance, everything grew dark, and down I went. I came to on the floor among bits of broken china; near my face were the shoes of a man standing over me.

"Get up," he said, lifting me. "Are you all right?"

"I think so," I answered, keeping my hands on the floor, for my head was still spinning. "From what day of the week are you?"

"Wednesday," he said. "Come on, let's get that rudder fixed while we have the chance!"

"But where's the Monday me?" I asked.

"Gone. Which means, I suppose, that you are he."

"How is that?"

"Well, the Monday me on Monday night became, Tuesday morning, the Tuesday me, and so on."

"I don't understand."

"Doesn't matter — you'll get the hang of it. But hurry up, we're wasting time!"

"Just a minute," I replied, remaining on the floor. "Today is Tuesday. Now if you are the Wednesday me, and if by that time on Wednesday the rudder still hasn't been fixed, then it follows that something will prevent us from fixing it, since otherwise you, on Wednesday, would not now, on Tuesday, be asking me to help you fix it. Wouldn't it be best, then, for us not to risk going outside?"

"Nonsense!" he exclaimed. "Look, I'm the Wednesday me and you're the Tuesday me, and as for the rocket, well, my guess is that its existence is patched, which means that in places it's Tuesday, in places Wednesday, and here and there perhaps there's even a bit of Thursday. Time has simply become shuffled up in passing through these vortices, but why should that concern us, when together we are two and therefore have a chance to fix the rudder?!"

"No, you're wrong!" I said. "If on Wednesday, where you already are, having lived through all of Tuesday, so that now Tuesday is behind you, if on Wednesday — I repeat — the rudder isn't fixed, then one can only conclude that it didn't get fixed on Tuesday, since it's Tuesday now and if we were to go and fix the rudder right away, that right away would be your yesterday and there would now be nothing to fix. And consequently..."

"And consequently you're as stubborn as a mule!" he growled. "You'll regret this! And my only consolation is that you too will be infuriated by your own pigheadedness, just as I am now — when you yourself reach Wednesday!!"

"Ah, wait," I cried, "do you mean that on Wednesday, I, being you, will try to convince the Tuesday me, just as you are doing here, except that everything will be reversed, in other words you will be me and I you? But of course! That's what makes a time loop! Hold on, I'm coming, yes, it makes sense now..."

But before I could get up off the floor we fell into a new vortex and the terrible acceleration flattened us against the ceiling. The dreadful pitching and heaving didn't let up once throughout that night from Tuesday to Wednesday. Then, when things had finally quieted down a little, the volume of the General Theory of Relativity came flying across the cabin and hit me on the forehead with such force, that I lost consciousness. When I opened my eyes I saw broken dishes and a man sprawled among them. I immediately jumped to my feet and lifted him, shouting: "Get up! Are you all right?"

"I think so," he replied, blinking. "From what day of the week are you?"

"Wednesday," I said, "come on, let's get that rudder fixed while we have the chance."

"But where's the Monday me?" he asked, sitting up. He had a black eye.

"Gone," I said, "which means that you are he."

"How is that?"

"Well, the Monday me on Monday night became, Tuesday morning, the Tuesday me, and so on."

"I don't understand."

"Doesn't matter — you'll get the hang of it. But hurry up, we're wasting time!"

Saying this, I was already looking around for the tools.

"Just a minute," he drawled, not budging an inch. "Today is Tuesday. Now, if you are the Wednesday me, and if by that time on Wednesday the rudder still hasn't been fixed, then it follows that something will prevent us from fixing it, since otherwise you, on Wednesday, would not be asking me now, on Tuesday, to help you fix it. Wouldn't it be best, then, for us not to risk going outside?"

"Nonsense!!" I yelled, losing my temper. "Look, I'm the Wednesday me, you're the Tuesday me..."

And so we quarreled, in opposite roles, during which he did in fact drive me into a positive fury, for he persistently refused to help me fix the rudder and it did no good calling him pigheaded and a stubborn mule. And when at last I managed to convince him, we plunged into the next gravitational vortex. I was in a cold sweat, for the thought occurred to me that we might now go around and around in this time loop, repeating ourselves for all eternity, but luckily that didn't happen. By the time the acceleration had slackened enough for me to stand, I was alone once more in the cabin. Apparently the localized existence of Tuesday, which until now had persisted in the vicinity of the sink, had vanished, becoming a part of the irretrievable past. I rushed over to the map, to find some nice vortex into which I could send the rocket, so as to bring about still another warp of time and in that way obtain a helping hand.

There was in fact one vortex, quite promising too, and by manipulating the engines with great difficulty, I aimed the rocket to intersect it at the very center. True, the configuration of that vortex was, according to the map, rather unusual — it had two foci, side by side. But by now I was too desperate to concern myself with this anomaly.

After several hours of bustling about in the engine room my hands were filthy, so I went to wash them, seeing as there was plenty of time yet before I would be entering the vortex. The bathroom was locked. From inside came the sounds of someone gargling.

"Who's there?!" I hollered, taken aback.

"Me," replied a voice.

"Which me is that?!"

"Ijon Tichy."

"From what day?"

"Friday. What do you want?"

"I wanted to wash my hands..." I said mechanically, thinking meanwhile with the greatest intensity: it was Wednesday evening, and he came from Friday, therefore the gravitational vortex into which the ship was to fall would bend time from Friday to Wednesday, but as for what then would take place within the vortex, that I could in no way picture. Particularly intriguing was the question of where Thursday might be. In the meantime the Friday me still wasn't letting me into the bathroom, taking his sweet time, though I pounded on the door insistently.

"Stop that gargling!" I roared, out of patience. "Every second is precious — come out at once, we have to fix the rudder!"

"For that you don't need me," he said phlegmatically from behind the door. "The Thursday me must be around here somewhere, go with him..."

"What Thursday me? That's not possible..."

"I ought to know whether it's possible or not, considering that I'm already in Friday and consequently have lived through your Wednesday as well as his Thursday..."

Feeling dizzy, I jumped back from the door, for yes, I did hear some commotion in the cabin: a man was standing there, pulling the toolbag out from under the bed.

"You're the Thursday me?!" I cried, running into the room.

"Right," he said. "Here, give me a hand..."

"Will we be able to fix the rudder this time?" I asked as together we pulled out the heavy satchel.

"I don't know, it wasn't fixed on Thursday, ask the Friday me..." That hadn't crossed my mind! I quickly ran back to the bathroom door.

"Hey there, Friday me! Has the rudder been fixed?"

"Not on Friday," he replied.

"Why not?"

"This is why not," he said, opening the door. His head was wrapped in a towel, and he pressed the flat of a knife to his forehead, trying in this manner to reduce the swelling of a lump the size of an egg. The Thursday me meanwhile approached with the tools and stood beside me, calmly scrutinizing the me with the lump, who with his free hand was putting back on the shelf a siphon of seltzer. So it was its gurgle I had taken for his gargle.

"What gave you that?" I asked sympathetically.

"Not what, who," he replied. "It. was the Sunday me."

"The Sunday me? But why...that can't be!" I cried.

"Well it's a long story..."

"Makes no difference! Quick, let's go outside, we might just make it!" said the Thursday me, turning to the me that was I.

"But the rocket will fall into the vortex any minute now," I replied. "The shock could throw us off into space, and that would be the end of us..."

"Use your head, stupid," snapped the Thursday me. "If the Friday me's alive, nothing can happen to us. Today is only Thursday."

"It's Wednesday," I objected.

"It makes no difference, in either case I'll be alive on Friday, and so will you."

"Yes, but there really aren't two of us, it only looks that way," I observed. "Actually there is one me, just from different days of the week..."

"Fine, fine, now open the hatch..."

But it turned out here that we had only one spacesuit between us. Therefore we could not both leave the rocket at the same time, and therefore our plan to fix the rudder was completely ruined.

"Blast!" I cried, angrily throwing down the toolbag. "What I should have done is put on the spacesuit to begin with and kept it on. I just didn't think of it — but you, as the Thursday me, you ought to have remembered!"

"I had the spacesuit, but the Friday me took it," he said.

"When? Why?"

"Eh, it's not worth going into," he shrugged and, turning around, went back to the cabin. The Friday me wasn't there; I looked in the bathroom, but it was empty too.

"Where's the Friday me?" I asked, returning. The Thursday me methodically cracked an egg with a knife and poured its contents onto the sizzling fat.

"Somewhere in the neighborhood of Saturday, no doubt," he replied, indifferent, quickly scrambling the egg.

"Excuse me," I protested, "but you already had your meals on Wednesday — what makes you think you can go and eat a second Wednesday supper?"

"These rations are mine just as much as they are yours," he said, calmly lifting the browned edge of the egg with his knife. "I am you, you are me, so it makes no difference..."

"What sophistry! Wait, that's too much butter! Are you crazy? I don't have enough food for this many people!"

The skillet flew out of his hand, and I went crashing into a wall: we had fallen into a new vortex. Once again the ship shook as if in a fever, but my only thought was get to the corridor where the spacesuit was hanging and put it on. For in that way (I reasoned) when Wednesday became Thursday, I, as the Thursday me, would be wearing that spacesuit, and if only I didn't take it off for a single minute (and I was determined not to) then I would obviously be wearing it on Friday also. And therefore the me on Thursday and the me on Friday would both be in our spacesuits, so that when we came together in the same present it would finally be possible to fix that miserable rudder.

The increasing thrust of gravity made my head swim, and when I opened my eyes I noticed that I was lying to the right of the Thursday me, and not to the left, as I had been a few moments before. Now while it had been easy enough for me to develop this plan about the spacesuit, it was considerably more difficult to put it into action, since with the growing gravitation I could hardly move. When it weakened just a little, I began to inch my way across the floor — in the direction of the door that led to the corridor. Meanwhile I noticed that the Thursday me was likewise heading for the door, crawling on his belly towards the corridor. At last, after about an hour, when the vortex had reached its widest point, we met at the threshold, both flattened to the floor. Then I thought, why should I have to strain myself to reach the handle? Let the Thursday me do it. Yet at the same time I began to recall certain things which clearly indicated that it was I now who was the Thursday me, and not he.

"What day of the week are you?" I asked, to make sure. With my chin pressed to the floor I looked him in the eye. Struggling, he opened his mouth.

"Thurs — day — me," he groaned. Now that was odd. Could it be that, in spite of everything, I was still the Wednesday me? Calling to mind all my recollections of the recent past, I had to conclude that this was out of the question. So he must have been the Friday me. For if he had preceded me by a day before, then he was surely a day ahead now. I waited for him to open the door, but apparently he expected the same of me. The gravitation had now subsided noticeably, so I got up and ran to the corridor. Just as I grabbed the spacesuit, he tripped me, pulling it out of my hands, and I fell flat on my face.

"You dog!" I cried. "Tricking your own self — that's really low!" He ignored me, stepping calmly into the spacesuit. The shamelessness of it was appalling. Suddenly a strange force threw him from the suit — as it turned out, someone was already inside. For a moment I wavered, no longer knowing who was who.

"You, Wednesday!" called the one in the spacesuit. "Hold back Thursday, help me!"

For the Thursday me was indeed trying to tear the spacesuit off him.

"Give me the spacesuit!" bellowed the Thursday me as he wrestled with the other.

"Get off! What are you trying to do? Don't you realize I'm the one who should have it, and not you?!" howled the other.

"And why is that, pray?"

"For the reason, fool, that I'm closer to Saturday than you, and by Saturday there will be two of us in suits!"

"But that's ridiculous," I said, getting into their argument, "at best you'll be alone in the suit on Saturday, like an absolute idiot, and won't be able to do a thing. Let me have the suit: if I put it on now, then you'll be wearing it on Friday as the Friday me, and I will also on Saturday as the Saturday me, and so you see there will then be two of us, and with two suits... Come on, Thursday, give me a hand!!"

"Wait," protested the Friday me when I had forcibly yanked the spacesuit off his back. "In the first place, there is no one here for you to call 'Thursday,' since midnight has passed and you are now the Thursday me, and in the second place, it'll be better if I stay in the spacesuit. The spacesuit won't do you a bit of good."

"Why not? If I put it on today, I'll have it on tomorrow too."

"You'll see for yourself... after all, I was already you, on Thursday, and my Thursday has passed, so I ought to know..."

"Enough talk. Let go of it this instant!" I snarled. But he grabbed it from me and I chased him, first through the engine room and then into the cabin. It somehow worked out that there were only two of us now. Suddenly I understood why the Thursday me, when we were standing at the hatch with the tools, had told me that the Friday me took the spacesuit from him: for in the meantime I myself had become the Thursday me, and here the Friday me was in fact taking it. But I had no intention of giving in that easily. Just you wait, I thought, I'll take care of you, and out I ran into the corridor, and from there to the engine room, where before — during the chase — I had noticed a heavy pipe lying on the floor, which served to stoke the atomic pile, and I picked it up and — thus armed — dashed back to the cabin.

The other me was already in the spacesuit, he had pulled on everything but the helmet.

"Out of the spacesuit!" I snapped, clenching my pipe in a threatening manner.

"Not a chance."

"Out, I say!!"

Then I wondered whether or not I should hit him. It was a little disconcerting, the fact that he had neither a black eye nor a bump on his head, like the other Friday me, the one I'd found in the bathroom, but all at once I realized that this was the way it had to be. That Friday me by now was the Saturday me, yes, and perhaps even was knocking about somewhere in the vicinity of Sunday, while this Friday me inside the spacesuit had only recently been the Thursday me, into which same Thursday me I myself had been transformed at midnight. Thus I was moving along the sloping curve of the time loop towards that place in which the Friday me before the beating would change into the Friday me already beaten. Still, he did say, back then, that it had been the Sunday me who did it, and there was no trace, as yet, of him. We stood alone in the cabin, he and I. Then suddenly I had a brainstorm.

"Out of that spacesuit!" I growled.

"Keep off, Thursday!" he yelled.

"I'm not Thursday, I'm the SUNDAY ME!" I shrieked, closing in for the kill. He tried to kick me, but spacesuit boots are very heavy and before he could raise his leg, I let him have it over the head. Not too hard, of course, since I had grown sufficiently familiar with all of this to know that I in turn, when eventually I went from the Thursday to the Friday me, would be on the receiving end, and I wasn't particularly set on fracturing my own skull. The Friday me fell with a groan, holding his head, and I brutally tore the spacesuit off him. While he made for the bath room on wobbly legs, muttering, "Where's the cotton... where's the seltzer," I quickly began to don the suit that we had struggled over, until I noticed — sticking out from under the bed — a human foot. I took a closer look, kneeling. Under the bed lay a man; trying to muffle the sound of his chewing, he was hurriedly bolting down the last bar of the milk chocolate I had stored away in the suitcase for a rainy sidereal day. The bastard was in such a hurry that he ate the chocolate along with bits of tin foil, which glittered on his lips. "Leave that chocolate alone!" I yelled, pulling at his foot. "Who are you anyway? The Thursday me?..." I added in a lower voice, seized by a sudden doubt, for the thought occurred that maybe I already was the Friday me, and would soon have to collect what I had dished out earlier to the same.

"The Sunday me," he mumbled, his mouth full. I felt weak. Now either he was lying, in which case there was nothing to worry about, or telling the truth, and if he was, I faced a clobbering for sure, because the Sunday me — after all

— was the one who had hit the Friday me, the Friday me told me so himself before it happened, and then later I, impersonating the Sunday me, had let him have it with the pipe. But on the other hand, I said to myself, even if he's lying and not the Sunday me, it's still quite possible that he's a later me than me, and if he is a later me, he remembers everything that I do, therefore already knows that I lied to the Friday me, and so could deceive me in a similar manner, since what had been a spur of-the-moment stratagem on my part was for him — by now — simply a memory, a memory he could easily make use of. Meanwhile, as I remained in uncertainty, he had eaten the rest of the chocolate and crawled out from under the bed.

"If you're the Sunday me, where's your spacesuit?!" I cried, struck by a new thought.

"I'll have it in a minute," he said calmly, and then I noticed the pipe in his hand... The next thing I saw was a bright flash, like a few dozen supernovas going off at once, after which I lost consciousness.

I came to, sitting on the floor of the bathroom; someone was banging on the door. I began to attend to my bruises and bumps, but he kept pounding away; it turned out to be the Wednesday me. After a while I showed him my battered head, he went with the Thursday me for the tools, then there was a lot of running around and yanking off of spacesuits, this too in one way or another I managed to live through, and on Saturday morning crawled under the bed to see if there wasn't some chocolate left in the suitcase. Someone started pulling at my foot as I ate the last bar, which I'd found underneath the shirts; I no longer knew just who this was, but hit him over the head anyhow, pulled the spacesuit off him and was going to put it on - when the rocket fell into the next vortex.

When I regained consciousness, the cabin was packed with people. There was barely elbowroom. As it turned out, they were all of them me, from different days, weeks, months, and one - so he said - was even from the following year. There were plenty with bruises and black eyes, and five among those present had on spacesuits. But instead of immediately going out through the hatch and repairing the damage, they began to quarrel, argue, bicker and debate. The problem was, who had hit whom, and when. The situation was complicated by the fact that there now had appeared morning me's and afternoon me's — I feared that if things went on like this, I would soon be broken into minutes and seconds - and then too, the majority of the me's present were lying like mad, so that to this day I'm not altogether sure whom I hit and who hit me when that whole business took place, triangularly, between the Thursday, the Friday and the Wednesday me's, all of whom I was in turn. My impression is that because I had lied to the Friday me, pretending to be the Sunday me, I ended up with one blow more than I should have, going by the calendar. But I would prefer not to dwell any longer on these unpleasant memories; a man who for an entire week does nothing but hit himself over the head has little reason to be proud. Meanwhile the arguments continued. The sight of such inaction, such wasting of precious time, drove me to despair, while the rocket rushed blindly on, straight ahead, plunging every now and then into another gravitational vortex. At last the ones wearing spacesuits started slugging it out with the ones who were not. I tried to introduce some sort of order into that absolute chaos and finally, after superhuman efforts, succeeded in organizing something that resembled a meeting, in which the one from next year — having seniority — was elected chairman by acclamation.

We then appointed an elective committee, a nominating committee, and a committee for new business, and four of us from next month were made sergeants at arms. But in the mean time we had passed through a negative vortex, which cut our number in half, so that on the very first ballot we lacked a quorum, and had to change the bylaws before proceeding to vote on the candidates for rudder-repairer. The map indicated the approach of still other vortices, and these undid all that we had accomplished so far: first the candidates already chosen disappeared, and then the Tuesday me showed up with the Friday me, who had his head wrapped in a towel, and they created a shameful scene. Upon passage through a particularly strong positive vortex we hardly fit in the cabin and corridor, and opening the hatch was out of the question — there simply wasn't room. But the worst of it was, these time displacements were increasing in amplitude, a few grayhaired me's had already appeared, and here and there I even caught a glimpse of the close-cropped heads of children, that is of myself, of course — or rather — myselves from the halcyon days of boyhood.

I really can't recall whether I was still the Sunday me, or had already turned into the Monday me. Not that it made any difference. The children sobbed that they were being squashed in the crowd, and called for their mommy; the chairman — the Tichy from next year — let out a string of curses, because the Wednesday me, who had crawled under the bed in a futile search for chocolate, bit him in the leg when he accidentally stepped on the latter's finger. I saw that all this would end badly, particularly now as here and there gray beards were turning up. Between the 142nd and 143rd vortices I passed around an attendance sheet, but afterwards it came to light that a large number of those present were cheating. Supplying false vital statistics, God knows why. Perhaps the prevailing atmosphere had muddled their wits. The noise and confusion were such that you could make yourself understood only by screaming at the top of your lungs.

But then one of last year's Ijons hit upon what seemed to be an excellent idea, namely, that the oldest among us tell the story of his life; in that way we would learn just who was supposed to fix the rudder. For obviously the oldest me contained within his past experience the lives of all the others there from their various months, days and years. So we turned, in this matter, to a hoary old gentleman who, slightly palsied, was standing idly in the corner. When questioned, he began to speak at great length of his children and grandchildren, then passed to his cosmic voyages, and he had embarked upon no end of these in the course of his ninety-some years. Of the one now taking place — the only one of interest to us — the old man had no recollection whatever, owing to his generally sclerotic and overexcited condition, however he was far too proud to admit this and went on evasively, obstinately, time and again returning to his high connections, decorations and grandchildren, till finally we shouted him down and ordered him to hold his tongue.

The next two vortices cruelly thinned our ranks. After the third, not only was there more room, but all of those in spacesuits had disappeared as well. One empty suit remained; we voted to hang it up in the corridor, then went back to our deliberations. Then, following another scuffle for the possession of that precious garment, a new vortex came along and suddenly the place was deserted. I was sitting on the floor, puffy-eyed, in my strangely spacious cabin, surrounded by broken furniture, strips of clothing, ripped up books. The floor was strewn with ballots. According to the map, I had now passed through the entire zone of gravitational vortices. No longer able to count on duplication, and thus no longer able to correct the damage, I fell into numb despair.

About an hour later I looked out in the corridor and discovered, to my great surprise, that the spacesuit was missing. But then I vaguely remembered — yes — right before that last vortex two little boys sneaked out into the corridor. Could they have possibly, both of them, put on the one spacesuit?!

Struck by a sudden thought, I ran to the controls. The rudder worked! So then, those little tykes had fixed it after all, while we adults were stuck in endless disagreements. I imagine that one of them placed his arms in the sleeves of the suit, and the other — in the pants; that way, they could have tightened the nut and bolt with wrenches at the same time, working on either side of the rudder. The empty spacesuit I found in the air lock, behind the hatch. I carried it inside the rocket like a sacred relic, my heart full of boundless gratitude for those brave lads I had been so long ago! And thus concluded what was surely one of my most unusual adventures. I reached my destination safely, thanks to the courage and resourcefulness I had displayed when only two children.

It was said afterwards that I invented the whole thing, and those more malicious even went so far as to insinuate that I had a weakness for alcohol, carefully concealed on Earth but freely indulged during those long and lonely cosmic flights. Lord only knows what other gossip has been circulating on the subject. But that is how people are; they'll willingly give credence to the most far-fetched drivel, but not to the simple truth, which is precisely what I have presented here.

VIRGINIA WOOLF

The Searchlight
1944

The mansion of the eighteenth century Earl had been changed in the twentieth century into a Club. And it was pleasant, after dining in the great room with the pillars and the chandeliers under a glare of light to go out on to the balcony overlooking the Park. The trees were in full leaf, and had there been a moon, one could have seen the pink and cream coloured cockades on the chestnut trees. But it was a moonless night; very warm, after a fine summer's day.

Mr. and Mrs. Ivimey's party were drinking coffee and smoking on the balcony. As if to relieve them from the need of talking, to entertain them without any effort on their part, rods of light wheeled across the sky. It was peace then; the air force was practising; searching for enemy aircraft in the sky. After pausing to prod some suspected spot, the light wheeled, like the wings of a windmill, or again like the antennae of some prodigious insect and revealed here a cadaverous stone front; here a chestnut tree with all its blossoms riding; and then suddenly the light struck straight at the balcony, and for a second a bright disc shone — perhaps it was a mirror in a ladies' hand-bag.

"Look!" Mrs. Ivimey exclaimed.

The light passed. They were in darkness again

"You'll never guess what *that* made me see!" she added. Naturally, they guessed.

"No, no, no," she protested. Nobody could guess; only she knew; only she could know, because she was the great-granddaughter of the man himself. He had told her the story. What story? If they liked, she would try to tell it. There was still time before the play.

"But where do I begin?" she pondered. "In the year 1820?... It must have been about then that my great grandfather was a boy. I'm not young myself" — no, but she was very well set up and handsome —"and he was a very old man when I was a child — when he told me the story. A very handsome old man, with a shock of white hair, and blue eyes. He must have been a beautiful boy. But queer... That was only natural," she explained, "seeing how they lived. The name was Comber. They'd come down in the world. They'd been gentlefolk; they'd owned land up in Yorkshire. But when he was a boy only the tower was left. The house was nothing but a little farmhouse, standing in the middle of fields. We saw it ten years ago and went over it. We had to leave the car and walk across the fields. There isn't any road to the house. It stands all alone, the grass grows right up to the gate... there were chickens pecking about, running in and out of the rooms. All gone to rack and ruin. I remember a stone fell from the tower suddenly." She paused. "There they lived," she went on, "the old man, the woman and the boy. She wasn't his wife, or the boy's mother. She was just a farm hand, a girl the old man had taken to live with him when his wife died. Another reason perhaps why nobody visited them — why the whole place was gone to rack and ruin. But I remember a coat of arms over the door; and books, old books, gone mouldy. He taught himself all he knew from books. He read and read, he told me, old books, books with maps hanging out from the pages. He dragged them up to the top of the tower — the rope's still there and the broken steps. There's a chair still in the window with the bottom fallen out; and the window swinging open, and the panes broken, and a view for miles and miles across the moors."

She paused as if she were up in the tower looking from the window that swung open.

"But we couldn't," she said, "find the telescope." In the dining-room behind them the clatter of plates grew louder. But Mrs. Ivimey, on the balcony, seemed puzzled, because she could not find the telescope.

"Why a telescope?" someone asked her.

"Why? Because if there hadn't been a telescope," she laughed, "I shouldn't be sitting here now."

And certainly she was sitting there now, a well set-up, middle-aged woman, with something blue over her shoulders.

"It must have been there," she resumed, "because, he told me, every night when the old people had gone to bed he sat at the window looking through the telescope at the stars. Jupiter, Aldebaran, Cassiopeia." She waved her hand at the stars that were beginning to show over the trees. It was growing darker. And the searchlight seemed brighter, sweeping across the sky, pausing here and there to stare at the stars.

"There they were," she went on, "the stars. And he asked himself, my great-grandfather — that boy: 'What are they? Why are they? And who am I?' as one does, sitting alone, with no one to talk to, looking at the stars."

She was silent. They all looked at the stars that were coming out in the darkness over the trees. The stars seemed very permanent, very unchanging. The roar of London sank away. A hundred years seemed nothing. They felt that the boy was looking at the stars with them. They seemed to be with him, in the tower, looking out over the moors at the stars.

Then a voice behind them said:

"Right you are. Friday."

They all turned, shifted, felt dropped down on to the balcony again.

"Ah, but there was nobody to say that to him," she murmured. The couple rose and walked away.

"*He* was alone," she resumed. "It was a fine summer's day. A June day. One of those perfect summer days when everything seems to stand still in the heat. There were the chickens pecking in the farm-yard; the old horse stamping in the stable; the old man dozing over his glass. The woman scouring pails in the scullery. Perhaps a stone fell from the tower. It seemed as if the day would never end. And he had no one to talk to — nothing whatever to do. The whole world stretched before him. The moor rising and falling; the sky meeting the moor; green and blue, green and blue, for ever and ever."

In the half light, they could see that Mrs. Ivimey was leaning over the balcony, with her chin propped on her hands, as if she were looking out over the moors from the top of a tower.

"Nothing but moor and sky, moor and sky, for ever and ever," she murmured.

Then she made a movement, as if she swung something into position.

"But what did the earth look like through the telescope?" she asked.

She made another quick little movement with her fingers as if she were twirling something.

"He focussed it," she said. "He focussed it upon the earth. He focussed it upon a dark mass of wood upon the horizon. He focussed it so that he could see ... each tree ... each tree separate ... and the birds ... rising and falling ... and a stem of smoke ... there... in the midst of the trees. ... And then... lower ... lower ... (she lowered her eyes) ... there was a house ... a house among the trees ... a farmhouse ... every brick showed ... and the tubs on either side of the door... with flowers in them blue, pink, hydrangeas, perhaps. ..." She paused ... "And then a girl came out of the house ... wearing something blue upon her head ... and stood there ... feeding birds ... pigeons... they came fluttering round her. ... And then ... look. ... A man.

... A man! He came round the corner. He seized her in his arms! They kissed ... they kissed."

Mrs. Ivimey opened her arms and closed them as if she were kissing someone.

"It was the first time he had seen a man kiss a woman — in his telescope — miles and miles away across the moors!"

She thrust something from her — the telescope presumably. She sat upright.

"So he ran down the stairs. He ran through the fields. He ran down lanes, out upon the high road, through woods. He ran for miles and miles, and just when the stars were showing above the trees he reached the house ... covered with dust, streaming with sweat...."

She stopped, as if she saw him.

"And then, and then ... what did he do then? What did he say? And the girl ..." they pressed her.

A shaft of light fell upon Mrs. Ivimey as if someone had focussed the lens of a telescope upon her. (It was the air force, looking for enemy air craft.) She had risen. She had something blue on her head. She had raised her hand, as if she stood in a doorway, amazed.

"Oh the girl. ... She was my —" she hesitated, as if she were about to say "myself." But she remembered; and corrected herself. "She was my great-grandmother," she said.

She turned to look for her cloak. It was on a chair behind her.

"But tell us — what about the other man, the man who came round the corner?" they asked.

"That man? Oh, that man," Mrs. Ivimey murmured, stooping to fumble with her cloak (the searchlight had left the balcony), "he, I suppose, vanished."

"The light," she added, gathering her things about her, "only falls here and there."

The searchlight had passed on. It was now focussed on the plain expanse of Buckingham Palace. And it was time they went on to the play.

JAMES FENNIMORE COOPER

The Eclipse
1836

The eclipse of the sun, which you have requested me to describe, occurred in the summer of 1806, on Monday, the 16th of June. Its greatest depth of shadow fell upon the American continent, somewhere about the latitude of 42 deg. I was then on a visit to my parents, at the home of my family, among the Highlands of Otsego, in that part of the country where the eclipse was most impressive. My recollections of the great event, and the incidents of the day, are as vivid as if they had occurred but yesterday.

Lake Otsego, the headwaters of the Susquehanna, lies as nearly as possible in latitude 42 deg. The village, which is the home of my family, is beautifully situated at the foot of the lake, in a valley lying between two nearly parallel ranges of heights, quite mountainous in character. The Susquehanna, a clear and rapid stream, flowing from the southeastern shore of the lake, is crossed by a high wooden bridge, which divides the main street of the little town from the lawns and meadows on the eastern bank of the river. Here were all the materials that could be desired, lake, river, mountain, wood, and the dwellings of man, to give full effect to the varied movement of light and shadow through that impressive day.

Throughout the belt of country to be darkened by the eclipse, the whole population were in a state of almost anxious expectation for weeks before the event. On the eve of the 16th of June, our family circle could think or talk of little else. I had then a father and four brothers living, and as we paced the broad hall of the house, or sat about the family board, our conversation turned almost entirely upon the movements of planets and comets, occultations and eclipses. We were all exulting in the feeling that a grand and extraordinary spectacle awaited us — a spectacle which millions then living could never behold. There may have been a tinge of selfishness in the feeling that we were thus favored beyond others, and yet, I think, the emotion was too intellectual in its character to have been altogether unworthy.

Many were the prophecies regarding the weather, the hopes and fears expressed by different individuals, on this important point, as evening drew near. A passing cloud might veil the grand vision from our sight; rain or mist would sadly impair the sublimity of the hour. I was not myself among the desponding. The great barometer in the hall — one of the very few then found in the State, west of Albany — was carefully consulted. It was propitious. It gave promise of dry weather. Our last looks that night, before sleep fell on us, were turned toward the starlit heavens.

And the first movement in the morning was to the open window — again to examine the sky. When I rose from my bed, in the early morning, I found the heavens serene, and cloudless. Day had dawned, but the shadows of night were still lingering over the valley. For a moment, my eye rested on the familiar view — the limpid lake, with its setting of luxuriant woods and farms, its graceful bay and varied points, the hills where every cliff and cave and glen had been trodden a thousand times by my boyish feet — all this was dear to me as the face of a friend. And it appeared as if the landscape, then lovely in summer beauty, were about to assume something of dignity hitherto unknown — were not the shadows of a grand eclipse to fall upon every wave and branch within a few hours! There was one object in the landscape which a stranger would probably have overlooked, or might perhaps have called unsightly, but it was familiar to every eye in the village, and endowed by our people with the honors of an ancient landmark — the tall gray trunk of a dead and branchless pine, which had been standing on the crest of the eastern hill, at the time of the foundation of the village, and which was still erect, though rocked since then by a thousand storms. To my childish fancy, it had seemed an imaginary flag-staff, or, in rustic parlance, the "liberty pole" of some former generation; but now, as I traced the familiar line of the tall trunk, in its peculiar shade of silvery gray, it became to the eye of the young sailor the mast of some phantom ship. I remember greeting it with a smile, as this was the first glance of recognition given to the old ruin of the forest since my return.

But an object of far higher interest suddenly attracted my eye. I discovered a star — a solitary star — twinkling dimly in a sky which had now changed its hue to a pale grayish twilight, while vivid touches of coloring were beginning to flush the eastern sky. There was absolutely no other object visible in the heavens — cloud there was none, not even the lightest vapor. That lonely star excited a vivid interest in my mind. I continued at the window gazing, and losing myself in a sort of day-dream. That star was a heavenly body, it was known to be a planet, and my mind was filling itself with images of planets and suns. My brain was confusing itself with vague ideas of magnitude and distance, and of the time required by light to pierce the apparently illimitable void that lay between us — of the beings who might inhabit an orb like that, with life, feeling, spirit, and aspirations like my own.

Soon the sun himself rose into view. I caught a glimpse of fiery light glowing among the branches of the forest, on the eastern mountain. I watched, as I had done a hundred times before, the flushing of the skies, the gradual illuminations of the different hills, crowned with an undulating and ragged outline of pines, nearly two hundred feet in height, the golden light gliding silently down the breast of the western mountains, and opening clearer views of grove and field, until lake, valley, and village lay smiling in one cheerful glow of warm sunshine.

Our family party assembled early. We were soon joined by friends and connections, all eager and excited, and each provided with a colored glass for the occasion. By nine o'clock the cool air, which is peculiar to the summer nights in the Highlands, had left us, and the heat of midsummer filled the valley. The heavens were still absolutely cloudless, and a more brilliant day never shone in our own bright climate. There was not a breath of air, and we could see the rays of heat quivering here and there on the smooth surface of the lake. There was every appearance of a hot and sultry noontide.

We left the house, and passed beyond the grounds into the broad and grassy street which lay between the gates and the lake. Here there were no overhanging branches to obstruct the view; the heavens, the wooded mountains, and the limpid sheet of water before us, were all distinctly seen. As the hour for the eclipse drew near, our eagerness and excitement increased to an almost boyish impatience. The elders of the party were discussing the details of some previous eclipse: leaving them to revive their recollections, I strolled away, glass in hand, through the principal streets of the village. Scarce a dwelling, or a face, in the little town, that was not familiar to me, and it gave additional zest to the pleasure of a holiday at home, to meet one's townsfolk under the excitement of an approaching eclipse. As yet there was no great agitation, although things wore a rather unusual aspect for the busy hours of a summer's day. Many were busy with their usual tasks, women and children were coming and going with pails of water, the broom and the needle were not yet laid aside, the blacksmith's hammer and the carpenter's plane were heard in passing their shops. Loaded teams, and travellers in waggons, were moving through the streets; the usual quiet traffic at the village counters had not yet ceased. A farm-waggon, heavily laden with hay, was just crossing the bridge, coming in from the fields, the driver looking drowsy with sleep, wholly unconscious of the movement in the heavens. The good people in general, however, were on the alert; at every house some one seemed to be watching, and many groups were passed, whose eager up-turned faces and excited conversation spoke the liveliest interest. It was said, that there were not wanting one or two philosophers of the skeptical school, among our people, who did not choose to commit themselves to the belief in a total eclipse of the sun -- simply because they had never seen one. Seeing is believing, we are told, though the axiom admits of dispute. But what these worthy neighbors of ours had not seen, no powers of reasoning, or fulness of evidence, could induce them to credit. Here was the dignity of human reason! Here was private judgment taking a high stand! Anxious to witness the conversion of one of these worthies, with boyish love of fun I went in quest of him. He had left the village, however, on business. But, true to his principles, before mounting his horse that morning, he had declared to his wife that "he was not running away from that eclipse;" nay, more, with noble candor, he averred that if the eclipse did overtake him, in the course of his day's journey, "he would not be above acknowledging it!" This was highly encouraging.

I had scarcely returned to the family party, left on the watch, when one of my brothers, more vigilant, or with clearer sight than his companions, exclaimed that he clearly saw a dark line, drawn on the western margin of the sun's disc! All faces were instantly turned upwards, and through the glasses we could indeed now see a dusky, but distinct object, darkening the sun's light. An exclamation of delight, almost triumphant, burst involuntarily from the lips of all. We were not to be disappointed, no cloud was there to veil the grand spectacle; the vision, almost unearthly in its sublime dignity, was about to be revealed to us. In an incredibly short time, the oval formation of the moon was discerned. Another joyous burst of delight followed, as one after another declared that he beheld with distinctness the dark oval outline, drawn against the flood of golden light. Gradually, and at first quite imperceptibly to our sight, that dark and mysterious sphere gained upon the light, while a feeling of watchful stillness, verging upon reverence, fell upon our excited spirits.

As yet there was no change perceptible in the sunlight falling upon lake and mountain; the familiar scene wore its usual smiling aspect, bright and glowing as on other days of June. The people, however, were now crowding into the streets — their usual labors were abandoned — forgotten for the moment — and all faces were turned upward. So little, however, was the change in the power of the light, that to a careless observer it seemed more the gaze of faith, than positive perception, which turned the faces of all upward. Gradually a fifth, and even a fourth, of the sun's disc became obscured, and still the unguarded eye could not endure the flood of light — it was only with the colored glass that we could note the progress of the phenomenon. The noon-day heat, however, began to lessen, and something of the coolness of early morning returned to the valley.

I was looking upward, intently watching for the first moment where the dark outline of the moon should be visible to the naked eye, when an acquaintance passed. "Come with me!" he said quietly, at the same moment drawing his arm within my own, and leading me away. He was a man of few words, and there was an expression in his face which induced me to accompany him without hesitation. He led me to the Court House, and from thence into an adjoining building, and into a room then occupied by two persons. At a window, looking upward at the heavens, stood a figure which instantly riveted my attention. It was a man with haggard face, and fettered arms, a prisoner under sentence of death. By his side was the jailor.

A painful tragedy had been recently enacted in our little town. The schoolmaster of a small hamlet in the county had beaten a child under his charge very severely — and for a very trifling error. The sufferer was a little girl, his own niece, and it was said that natural infirmity had prevented the child from clearly pronouncing certain words which her teacher required her to utter distinctly. To conquer what he considered the obstinacy of the child, this man continued to beat her so severely that she never recovered from the effects of the blows, and died some days after. The wretched man was arrested, tried for murder, condemned, and sentenced to the gallows. This was the first capital offence in Otsego County. It produced a very deep impression. The general character of the schoolmaster had been, until that evil hour, very good, in every way. He was deeply, and beyond all doubt unfeignedly, penitent for the crime into which he had been led, more, apparently, from false ideas of duty, than from natural severity of temper. He had been entirely unaware of the great physical injury he was doing the child. So great was his contrition, that public sympathy had been awakened in his behalf, and powerful petitions had been sent to the Governor of the State, in order to obtain a respite, if not a pardon. But the day named by the judge arrived without a return of the courier. The Governor was at his country-house, at least eighty miles beyond Albany. The petition had been kept to the last moment, for additional signatures, and the eighty miles to be travelled by the courier, after reaching Albany, had not been included in the calculation. No despatch was received, and there was every appearance that there would be no reprieve. The day arrived — throngs of people from Chenango, and Unadilla, and from the valley of the Mohawk, poured into the village, to witness the painful, and as yet unknown, spectacle of a public execution. In looking down, from an elevated position, upon the principal street of the village that day, it had seemed to me paved with human faces. The hour struck, the prisoner was taken from the jail, and, seated, as is usual, on his coffin, was carried to the place of execution, placed between two ministers of the gospel. His look of utter misery was beyond description. I have seen other offenders expiate for their crimes with life, but never have I beheld such agony, such a clinging to life, such mental horror at the nearness of death, as was betrayed by this miserable man. When he approached the gallows, he rose from his seat, and wringing his fettered hands, turned his back upon the fearful object, as if the view were too frightful for endurance. The ministers of the gospel succeeded at length in restoring him to a decent degree of composure. The last prayer was offered, and his own fervent "Amen!" was still sounding, hoarse, beseeching, and almost despairing, in the ears of the crowd, when the respite made its tardy appearance. A short reprieve was granted, and the prisoner was carried back to the miserable cell from which he had been drawn in the morning.

Such was the wretched man who had been brought from his dungeon that morning, to behold the grand phenomenon of the eclipse. During the twelve-month previous, he had seen the sun but once. The prisons of those days were literally dungeons, cut off from the light of day. That striking figure, the very picture of utter misery, his emotion, his wretchedness, I can never forget. I can see him now, standing at the window, pallid and emaciated by a year's confinement, stricken with grief, his cheeks furrowed with constant weeping, his whole frame attesting the deep and ravaging influences of conscious guilt and remorse. Here was a man drawn from the depths of human misery, to be immediately confronted with the grandest natural exhibition in which the Creator deigns to reveal his Omnipotence to our race. The wretched criminal, a murderer in fact, though not in intention, seemed to gaze upward at the awful spectacle, with an intentness and a distinctness of mental vision far beyond our own, and purchased by an agony scarcely less bitter than death. It seemed as if, for him, the curtain which veils the world beyond the grave, had been lifted. He stood immovable as a statue, with uplifted and manacled arms and clasped hands, the very image of impotent misery and wretchedness. Perhaps human invention could not have conceived of a more powerful moral accessory, to heighten the effect of the sublime movement of the heavenly bodies, than this spectacle of penitent human guilt afforded. It was an incident to stamp on the memory for life. It was a lesson not lost on me.

When I left the Court House, a sombre, yellowish, unnatural coloring was shed over the country. A great change had taken place. The trees on the distant heights had lost their verdure and their airy character; they were taking the outline of dark pictures graven upon an unfamiliar sky. The lake wore a lurid aspect, very unusual. All living creatures seemed thrown into a state of agitation. The birds were fluttering to and fro, in great excitement; they seemed to mistrust that this was not the gradual approach of evening, and were undecided in their movements. Even the dogs — honest creatures — became uneasy, and drew closer to their masters. The eager, joyous look of interest and curiosity, which earlier in the morning had appeared in almost every countenance, was now changed to an expression of wonder or anxiety or thoughtfulness, according to the individual character.

Every house now gave up its tenants. As the light failed more and more with every passing second, the children came flocking about their mothers in terror. The women themselves were looking about uneasily for their husbands. The American wife is more apt than any other to turn with affectionate confidence to the stronger arm for support. The men were very generally silent and grave. Many a laborer left his employment to be near his wife and children, as the dimness and darkness increased.

I once more took my position beside my father and my brothers, before the gates of our own grounds. The sun lay a little obliquely to the south and east, in the most favorable position possible for observation. I remember to have examined, in vain, the whole dusky canopy in search of a single cloud. It was one of those entirely unclouded days, less rare in America than in Europe. The steadily waning light, the gradual approach of darkness, became the more impressive as we observed this absolutely transparent state of the heavens. The birds, which a quarter of an hour earlier had been fluttering about in great agitation, seemed now convinced that night was at hand. Swallows were dimly seen dropping into the chimneys, the martins returned to their little boxes, the pigeons flew home to their dove- cots, and through the open door of a small barn we saw the fowls going to roost.

The usual flood of sunlight had now become so much weakened, that we could look upward long, and steadily, without the least pain. The sun appeared like a young moon of three or four days old, though of course with a larger and more brilliant crescent. Looking westward a moment, a spark appeared to glitter before my eye. For a second I believed it to be an optical illusion, but in another instant I saw it plainly to be a star. One after another they came into view, more rapidly than in the evening twilight, until perhaps fifty stars appeared to us, in a broad, dark zone of the heavens, crowning the pines on the western mountain. This wonderful vision of the stars, during the noontide hours of day, filled the spirit with singular sensations.

Suddenly one of my brothers shouted aloud, "The moon!" Quicker than thought, my eye turned eastward again, and there floated the moon, distinctly apparent, to a degree that was almost fearful. The spherical form, the character, the dignity, the substance of the planet, were clearly revealed as I have never beheld them before, or since. It looked grand, dark, majestic, and mighty, as it thus proved its power to rob us entirely of the sun's rays. We are all but larger children. In daily life we judge of objects by their outward aspect. We are accustomed to think of the sun, and also of the moon, as sources of light, as etherial, almost spiritual, in their essence. But the positive material nature of the moon was now revealed to our senses, with a force of conviction, a clearness of perception, that changed all our usual ideas in connection with the planet. This was no interposition of vapor, no deceptive play of shadow; but a vast mass of obvious matter had interposed between the sun above us and the earth on which we stood. The passage of two ships at sea, sailing on opposite courses, is scarcely more obvious than this movement of one world before another. Darkness like that of early night now fell upon the village.

My thoughts turned to the sea. A sailor at heart, already familiar with the face of the ocean, I seemed, in mental vision, to behold the grandeur of that vast pall of supernatural shadow falling suddenly upon the sea, during the brightest hour of the day. The play of light and shade upon the billows, always full of interest, must at that hour have been indeed sublime. And my fancy was busy with pictures of white-sailed schooners, and brigs, and ships, gliding like winged spirits over the darkened waves.

I was recalled by a familiar and insignificant incident, the dull tramp of hoofs on the village bridge. A few cows, believing that night had overtaken them, were coming homeward from the wild open pastures about the village. And no wonder the kindly creatures were deceived, the darkness was now much deeper than the twilight which usually turns their faces homeward; the dew was falling perceptibly, as much so as at any hour of the previous night, and the coolness was so great that the thermometer must have fallen many degrees from the great heat of the morning. The lake, the hills, and the buildings of the little town were swallowed up in the darkness. The absence of the usual lights in the dwellings rendered the obscurity still more impressive. All labor had ceased, and the hushed voices of the people only broke the absolute stillness by subdued whispering tones.

"Hist! The whippoorwill!" whispered a friend near me; and at the same moment, as we listened in profound silence, we distinctly heard from the eastern bank of the river the wild, plaintive note of that solitary bird of night, slowly repeated at intervals. The song of the summer birds, so full in June, had entirely ceased for the last half hour. A bat came flitting about our heads. Many stars were now visible, though not in sufficient number to lessen the darkness. At one point only in the far distant northern horizon, something of the brightness of dawn appeared to linger.

At twelve minutes past eleven, the moon stood revealed in its greatest distinctness — a vast black orb, so nearly obscuring the sun that the face of the great luminary was entirely and absolutely darkened, though a corona of rays of light appeared beyond. The gloom of night was upon us. A breathless intensity of interest was felt by all. There would appear to be something instinctive in the feeling with which man gazes at all phenomena in the heavens. The peaceful rainbow, the heavy clouds of a great storm, the vivid flash of electricity, the falling meteor, the beautiful lights of the aurora borealis, fickle as the play of fancy, — these never fail to fix the attention with something of a peculiar feeling, different in character from that with which we observe any spectacle on the earth. Connected with all grand movements in the skies there seems an instinctive sense of inquiry, of anxious expectation; akin to awe, which may possibly be traced to the echoes of grand Christian prophecies, whispering to our spirits, and endowing the physical sight with some mysterious mental prescience. In looking back to that impressive hour, such now seem to me the feelings of the youth making one of that family group, all apparently impressed with a sensation of the deepest awe — I speak with certainty — a clearer view than I had ever yet had of the majesty of the Almighty, accompanied with a humiliating, and, I trust, a profitable sense of my own utter insignificance.

That movement of the moon, that sublime voyage of the worlds, often recurs to my imagination, and even at this distant day, as distinctly, as majestically, and nearly as fearfully, as it was then beheld.

A group of silent, dusky forms stood near me; one emotion appeared to govern all. My father stood immovable, some fifteen feet from me, but I could not discern his features. Three minutes of darkness, all but absolute, elapsed. They appeared strangely lengthened by the intensity of feeling and the flood of overpowering thought which filled the mind.

Thus far the sensation created by this majestic spectacle had been one of humiliation and awe. It seemed as if the great Father of the Universe had visibly, and almost palpably, veiled his face in wrath. But, appalling as the withdrawal of light had been, most glorious, most sublime, was its restoration! The corona of light above the moon became suddenly brighter, the heavens beyond were illuminated, the stars retired, and light began to play along the ridges of the distant mountains. And then a flood of grateful, cheering, consoling brightness fell into the valley, with a sweetness and a power inconceivable to the mind, unless the eye has actually beheld it. I can liken this sudden, joyous return of light, after the eclipse, to nothing of the kind that is familiarly known. It was certainly nearest to the change produced by the swift passage of the shadow of a very dark cloud, but it was the effect of this instantaneous transition, multiplied more than a thousand fold. It seemed to speak directly to our spirits, with full assurance of protection, of gracious mercy, and of that

Divine love which has produced all the glorious combinations of matter for our enjoyment. It was not in the least like the gradual dawning of day, or the actual rising of the sun. There was no gradation in the change. It was sudden, amazing, like what the imagination would teach us to expect of the advent of a heavenly vision. I know that philosophically I am wrong; but, to me, it seemed that the rays might actually be seen flowing through the darkness in torrents, till they had again illuminated the forest, the mountains, the valley, and the lake with their glowing, genial touch.

There was another grand movement, as the crescent of the sun reappeared, and the moon was actually seen steering her course through the void. Venus was still shining brilliantly.

This second passage of the moon lasted but a moment, to the naked eye. As it ceased, my eye fell again on the scene around me. The street, now as distinctly seen as ever, was filled with the population of the village. Along the line of road stretching for a mile from the valley, against the side of the mountain, were twenty wagons bearing travellers, or teams from among the hills. All had stopped on their course, impelled, apparently, by unconscious reverence, as much as by curiosity, while every face was turned toward heaven, and every eye drank in the majesty of the sight. Women stood in the open street, near me, with streaming eyes and clasped hands, and sobs were audible in different directions. Even the educated and reflecting men at my side continued silent in thought. Several minutes passed, before the profound impressions of the spectacle allowed of speech. At such a moment the spirit of man bows in humility before his Maker.

The changes of the unwonted light, through whose gradations the full brilliancy of the day was restored, must have been very similar to those by which it had been lost, but they were little noted. I remember, however, marking the instant when I could first distinguish the blades of grass at my feet — and later again watching the shadows of the leaves on the gravel walk. The white lilies in my mother's flower-garden were observed by others among the first objects of the vegetation which could be distinguished from the windows of the house. Every living creature was soon rejoicing again in the blessed restoration of light after that frightful moment of a night at noon-day.

Men who witness any extraordinary spectacle together, are apt, in after-times, to find a pleasure in conversing on its impressions. But I do not remember to have ever heard a single being freely communicative on the subject of his individual feelings at the most solemn moment of the eclipse. It would seem as if sensations were aroused too closely connected with the constitution of the spirit to be irreverently and familiarly discussed. I shall only say that I have passed a varied and eventful life, that it has been my fortune to see earth, heavens, ocean, and man in most of their aspects; but never have I beheld any spectacle which so plainly manifested the majesty of the Creator, or so forcibly taught the lesson of humility to man as a total eclipse of the sun.

KURT VONNEGUT

Thanasphere
1950

At noon, Wednesday, July 26th, windowpanes in the small mountain town of Sevier County, Tennessee, were rattled by the shock and faint thunder of a distant explosion rolling down the northwest slopes of the Great Smokies. The explosion came from the general direction of the closely guarded Air Force experimental station in the forest ten miles northwest of Elkmont.

Said the Air Force Office of Public Information, "No comment."

That evening, amateur astronomers in Omaha, Nebraska, and Glenwood, Iowa, reported independently that a speck had crossed the face of the full moon at 9:57 p.m. There was a flurry of excitement on the news wires. Astronomers at the major North American observatories denied that they had seen it.

They lied.

In Boston, on the morning of Thursday, July 27th, an enterprising newsman sought out Dr. Bernard Groszinger, youthful rocket consultant for the Air Force. "Is it possible that what crossed the moon was a spaceship?" the newsman asked.

Dr. Groszinger laughed at the question. "My own opinion is that we're beginning another cycle of flying-saucer scares," he said. "This time everyone's seeing spaceships between us and the moon. You can tell your readers this, my friend: No rocket ship will leave the earth for at least another twenty years."

He lied.

He knew a great deal more than he was saying, but somewhat less than he himself thought. He did not believe in ghosts, for instance — and had yet to learn of the Thanasphere.

Dr. Groszinger rested his long legs on his cluttered desktop, and watched his secretary conduct the disappointed newsman through the locked door, past the armed guards. He lit a cigarette and tried to relax before going back into the stale air and tension of the radio room. IS YOUR SAFE LOCKED? asked a sign on the wall, tacked there by a diligent security officer. The sign annoyed him. Security officers, security regulations only served to slow his work, to make him think about things he had no time to think about.

The secret papers in the safe weren't secrets. They said what had been known for centuries: Given fundamental physics, it follows that a projectile fired into space in direction x, at y miles per hour, will travel in the arc z. Dr. Groszinger modified the equation: Given fundamental physics and one billion dollars.

Impending war had offered him the opportunity to try the experiment. The threat of war was an incident, the military men about him an irritating condition of work — *the experiment* was the heart of the matter.

There were no unknowns, he reflected, finding contentment in the dependability of the physical world. Young Dr. Groszinger smiled, thinking of Christopher Columbus and his crew, who hadn't known what lay ahead of them, who had been scared stiff by sea monsters that didn't exist. Maybe the average person of today felt the same way about space. The Age of Superstition still had a few years to run.

But the man in the spaceship two thousand miles from earth had no unknowns to fear. The sullen Major Allen Rice would have nothing surprising to report in his radio messages. He could only confirm what reason had already revealed about outer space.

The major American observatories, working closely with the project, reported that the ship was now moving around the earth in the predicted orbit at the predicted velocity. Soon, anytime now, the first message in history from outer space would be received in the radio room. The broadcast could be on an ultra-high-frequency band where no one had ever sent or received messages before.

The first message was overdue, but nothing had gone wrong — nothing *could* go wrong, Dr. Groszinger assured himself again. Machines, not men, were guiding the flight. The man was a mere observer, piloted to his lonely vantage point by infallible electronic brains, swifter than his own. He had controls in his ship, but only for gliding down through the atmosphere, when and if they brought him back from space. He was equipped to stay for several years.

Even the man was as much like a machine as possible, Dr. Groszinger thought with satisfaction. He was quick, strong, unemotional. Psychiatrists had picked Major Rice from a hundred volunteers, and predicted that he would function as perfectly as the rocket motors, the metal hull, and the electronic controls. His specifications: Husky, twenty-nine years of age, fifty-five missions over Europe during the Second World War without a sign of fatigue, a childless widower, melancholy and solitary, a career soldier, a demon for work.

The Major's mission? Simple: To report weather conditions over enemy territory, and to observe the accuracy of guided atomic missiles in the event of war.

Major Rice was fixed in the solar system, two thousand miles above the earth now — close by, really — the distance from New York to Salt Lake City, not far enough away to see much of the polar icecaps, even. With a telescope, Rice could pick out small towns and the wakes of ships without much trouble. It would be breathtaking to watch the enormous blue-and-green ball, to see night creeping around it, and clouds and storms growing and swirling over its face.

Dr. Groszinger tamped out his cigarette, absently lit another almost at once, and strode down the corridor to the small laboratory where the radio equipment had been set up.

Lieutenant General Franklin Dane, head of Project Cyclops, sat next to the radio operator, his uniform rumpled, his collar open. The General stared expectantly at the loudspeaker before him. The floor was littered with sandwich wrappings and cigarette butts. Coffee-filled paper cups stood before the General and the radio operator, and beside the canvas chair where Groszinger had spent the night waiting.

General Dane nodded to Groszinger and motioned with his hand for silence.

"Able Baker Fox, this is Dog Easy Charley. Able Baker Fox, this is Dog Easy Charley..." droned the radio operator wearily, using the code names. "Can you hear me, Able Baker Fox? Can you —"

The loudspeaker crackled, then, tuned to its peak volume, boomed: "This is Able Baker Fox. Come in, Dog Easy Charley. Over."

General Dane jumped to his feet and embraced Groszinger. They laughed idiotically and pounded each other on the back. The General snatched the microphone from the radio operator. "You made it. Able Baker Fox! Right on course! What's it like, boy? What's it feel like? Over." Groszinger, his arm draped around the General's shoulders, leaned forward eagerly, his ear a few inches from the speaker. The radio operator turned the volume down, so that they could hear something of the quality of Major Rice's voice.

The voice came through again, soft, hesitant. The tone disturbed Groszinger — he had wanted it to be crisp, sharp, efficient.

"This side of the earth's dark, very dark just now. And I feel like I'm falling — the way you said I would. Over."

"Is anything the matter?" asked the General anxiously. "You sound as though something —"

The Major cut in before he could finish: "There! Did you hear that?"

"Able Baker Fox, we can't hear anything," said the General, looking perplexed at Groszinger. "What is it — some kind of noise in your receiver? Over."

"A child," said the Major. "I hear a child crying. Don't you hear it? And now — listen! — now an old man is trying to comfort it." His voice seemed farther away, as though he were no longer speaking directly into his microphone.

"That's impossible, ridiculous!" said Groszinger. "Check your set, Able Baker Fox, check your set. Over."

"They're getting louder now. The voices are louder. I can't hear you very well above them. It's like standing in the middle of a crowd, with everybody trying to get my attention at once. It's like..." The message trailed off. They could hear a shushing sound in the speaker. The Major's transmitter was still on.

"Can you hear me, Able Baker Fox? Answer! Can you hear me?" called General Dane.

The shushing noise stopped. The General and Groszinger stared blankly at the speaker.

"Able Baker Fox, this is Dog Easy Charley," chanted the radio operator. "Able Baker Fox, this is Dog Easy Charley..."

Groszinger, his eyes shielded from the glaring ceiling light of the radio room by a newspaper, lay fully dressed on the cot that had been brought in for him. Every few minutes he ran his long, slender fingers through his tangled hair and swore. His machine had worked perfectly, *was* working perfectly. The one thing he had not designed, the damn man in it, had failed, had destroyed the whole experiment.

They had been trying for six hours to reestablish contact with the lunatic who peered down at earth from his tiny steel moon and heard voices.

"He's coming in again, sir," said the radio operator. "This is Dog Easy Charley. Come in, Able Baker Fox. Over."

"This is Able Baker Fox. Clear weather over Zones Seven, Eleven, Nineteen, and Twenty-three. Zones One, Two, Three, Four, Five, and Six overcast. Storm seems to be shaping up over Zones Eight and Nine, moving south by southwest at about eighteen miles an hour. Over."

"He's OK now," said the General, relieved.

Groszinger remained supine, his head still covered with the newspaper. "Ask him about the voices," he said.

"You don't hear the voices anymore, *do* you, Able Baker Fox?"

"What do you mean, I don't hear them? I can hear them better than I can hear you. Over."

"He's out of his head," said Groszinger, sitting up.

"I heard that," said Major Rice. "Maybe I am. It shouldn't be too hard to check. All you have to do is find out if an

241

Andrew Tobin died in Evansville, Indiana, on February 17, 1927. Over."

"I don't follow you, Able Baker Fox," said the General. "Who was Andrew Tobin? Over."

"He is one of the voices." There was an uncomfortable pause. Major Rice cleared his throat. "Claims his brother murdered him. Over."

The radio operator had risen slowly from his stool, his face chalk-white. Groszinger pushed him back down and took the microphone from the General's now limp hand.

"Either you've lost your mind, or this is the most sophomoric practical joke in history, Able Baker Fox," said Groszinger. "This is *Groszinger* you're talking to, and you're dumber than I think you are if you think you can kid me." He nodded. "Over."

"I can't hear you very well anymore, Dog Easy Charley. Sorry, but the voices are getting louder."

"Rice! Straighten out!" said Groszinger.

"There — I caught that: Mrs. Pamela Ritter wants her husband to marry again, for the sake of the children. He lives at —"

"Stop it!"

"He lives at 1577 Damon Place, in Scotia, New York. Over and out."

General Dane shook Groszinger's shoulder gently. "You've been asleep five hours," he said. "It's midnight." He handed him a cup of coffee. "We've got some more messages. Interested?"

242

Groszinger sipped the coffee. "Is he still raving?"

"He still hears the voices, if that's what you mean." The General dropped two unopened telegrams in Groszinger's lap. "Thought you might like to be the one to open these."

Groszinger laughed. "Went ahead and checked Scotia and Evansville, did you? God help this army, if all the generals are as superstitious as you, my friend."

"OK, OK, you're the scientist, you're the brain-box. That's why I want *you* to open the telegrams. I want you to tell me what in hell's going on."

Groszinger opened one of the telegrams.

HARVEY RITTER LISTED FOR 1577 DAMON PLACE, SCOTIA. GE ENGINEER. WIDOWER, TWO CHILDREN, DECEASED WIFE NAMED PAMELA. DO YOU NEED MORE INFORMATION? R.B. FAILEY, CHIEF, SCOTIA POLICE

He shrugged and handed the message to General Dane, then opened the other telegram:

RECORDS SHOW ANDREW TOBIN DIED IN HUNTING ACCIDENT FEBRUARY 17, 1927. BROTHER PAUL LEADING BUSINESSMAN. OWNS COAL BUSINESS STARTED BY ANDREW. CAN FURNISH FURTHER DETAILS IF NEEDED. F. B. JOHNSON, EVANSVILLE P.D.

"I'm not surprised," said Groszinger. "I expected something like this. I suppose you're firmly convinced now that our friend Major Rice has found outer space populated by ghosts?"

"Well, I'd say he's sure as hell found it populated by something," said the General.

Groszinger wadded the second telegram in his fist and threw it across the room, missing the wastebasket by a foot. He folded his hands and affected the patient, priestlike pose he used in lecturing freshman physics classes. "At first, my friend, we had two possible conclusions: Either Major Rice was insane, or he was pulling off a spectacular hoax." He twiddled his thumbs, waiting for the General to digest this intelligence. "Now that we know his spirit messages deal with real people, we've got to conclude that he has planned and is now carrying out some sort of hoax. He got his names and addresses before he took off. God knows what he hopes to accomplish by it. God knows what we can do to make him stop it. That's your problem I'd say."

The General's eyes narrowed. "So he's trying to jimmy the project, is he? We'll see, by God, we'll see." The radio operator was dozing. The General slapped him on the back. "On the ball, Sergeant, on the ball. Keep calling Rice till you get him, understand?"

The radio operator had to call only once.

"This is Able Baker Fox. Come in, Dog Easy Charley." Major Rice's voice was tired.

"This is Dog Easy Charley," said General Dane. "We've had enough of your voices, Able Baker Fox — do you understand? We don't want to hear any more about them. We're onto your little game. I don't know what your angle is, but I do know I'll bring you back down and slap you on a rock pile in Leavenworth so fast you'll leave your teeth up there. Do we understand each other?" The General bit the tip from a fresh cigar fiercely. "Over."

"Did you check those names and addresses? Over."

The general looked at Groszinger, who frowned and shook his head. "Sure we did. That doesn't prove anything. So you've got a list of names and addresses up there. So what does that prove? Over."

"You say those names checked? Over."

"I'm telling you to quit it, Rice. Right now. Forget the voices, do you hear? Give me a weather report. Over."

"Clear patches over Zones Eleven, Fifteen, and Sixteen. Looks like a solid overcast in One, Two, and Three. All clear in the rest. Over."

"That's more like it, Able Baker Fox," said the General. "We'll forget about the voices, eh? Over."

"There's an old woman calling out something in a German accent. Is Dr. Groszinger there? I think she's calling his name. She's asking him not to get too wound up in his work — not to —"

Groszinger leaned over the radio operator's shoulder and snapped off the switch on the receiver. "Of all the cheap, sickening stunts," he said.

"Let's hear what he has to say," said the General. "Thought you were a scientist."

Groszinger glared at him defiantly, snapped on the receiver, and stood back, his hands on his hips.

" — saying something in German," continued the voice of Major Rice. "Can't understand it. Maybe you can. I'll give it to you the way it sounds: '*Alles geben die Götter, die unendlichen, ihren Lieblingen, ganz. Alle —*'"

Groszinger turned down the volume. "'*Alle Freuden, die unendlichen, alle Schmerzen, die unendlichen, ganz,*'" he said faintly. "That's how it ends." He sat down on the cot. "It's my mother's favorite quotation — something from Goethe."

"I can threaten him again," said the General.

"What for?" Groszinger shrugged and smiled. "Outer space *is* full of voices." He laughed nervously. "*There's* something to pep up a physics textbook."

"An omen, sir — it's an omen," blurted the radio operator.

"What the hell do you mean, an omen?" said the General. "So outer space is filled with ghosts. That doesn't surprise me."

"Nothing would, then," said Groszinger.

"That's exactly right. I'd be a hell of a general if anything would. For all I know, the moon is made of green cheese. So what. All I want is a man out there to tell me that I'm hitting what I'm shooting at. I don't give a damn what's going on in outer space."

"Don't you see, sir?" said the radio operator. "Don't you see? It's an omen. When people find out about all the spirits out there they'll forget about war. They won't want to think about anything but the spirits."

"Relax, Sergeant," said the General. "Nobody's going to find out about them, understand?"

"You can't suppress a discovery like this," said Groszinger.

"You're nuts if you think I can't," said General Dane. "How're you going to tell anybody about this business without telling them we've got a rocket ship out there?"

"They've got a right to know," said the radio operator.

"If the world finds out we have that ship out there, that's the start of World War Three," said the General. "Now tell me you want that. The enemy won't have any choice but to try and blow the hell out of us before we can put Major Rice to any use. And there'd be nothing for us to do but try and blow the hell out of them first. Is that what you want?"

"No, sir," said the radio operator. "I guess not, sir."

"Well, we can experiment, anyway," said Groszinger. "We can find out as much as possible about what the spirits are like. We can send Rice into a wider orbit to find out how far out he can hear the voices, and whether —"

"Not on Air Force funds, you can't," said General Dane. "That isn't what Rice is out there for. We can't afford to piddle around. We need him right there."

"All right, all right," said Groszinger. "Then let's hear what he has to say."

"Tune him in, Sergeant," said the General.

"Yes, sir." The radio operator fiddled with the dials. "He doesn't seem to be transmitting now, sir." The shushing noise of a transmitter cut into the hum of the loudspeaker. "I guess he's coming in again. Able Baker Fox, this is Dog Easy Charley —"

"King Two X-ray William Love, this is William Five Zebra Zebra King in Dallas," said the loudspeaker. The voice had a soft drawl and was pitched higher than Major Rice's.

A bass voice answered: "This is King Two X-ray William Love in Albany. Come in W5ZZK, I hear you well. How do you hear me? Over."

"You're clear as a bell, K2XWL — twenty-five thousand megacycles on the button. I'm trying to cut down on my drift with a —"

The voice of Major Rice interrupted. "I can't hear you clearly, Dog Easy Charley. The voices are a steady roar now. I can catch bits of what they're saying. Grantland Whitman, the Hollywood actor, is yelling that his will was tampered with by his nephew Carl. He says —"

"Say again, K2XWL," said the drawling voice. "I must have misunderstood you. Over."

"I didn't say anything, W5ZZK. What was that about Grantland Whitman? Over."

"The crowd's quieting down," said Major Rice. "Now there's just one voice — a young woman, I think. It's so soft I can't make out what she's saying."

"What's going on, K2XWL? Can you hear me, K2XWL?"

"She's calling my name. Do you hear it? She's calling my name," said Major Rice.

"Jam the frequency, dammit!" cried the General. "Yell, whistle — do something!"

Early-morning traffic past the university came to a honking, bad-tempered stop, as Groszinger absently crossed the street against the light, on his way back to his office and the radio room. He looked up in surprise, mumbled an apology, and hurried to the curb. He had had a solitary breakfast in an all-night diner a block and a half from the laboratory building, and then he'd taken a long walk. He had hoped that getting away for a couple of hours would clear his head — but the feeling of confusion and helplessness was still with him. Did the world have a right to know, or didn't it?

There had been no more messages from Major Rice. At the General's orders, the frequency had been jammed. Now the unexpected eavesdroppers could hear nothing but a steady whine at 25,000 megacycles. General Dane had reported the dilemma to Washington shortly after midnight. Perhaps orders as to what to do with Major Rice had come through by now.

Groszinger paused in a patch of sunlight on the laboratory building's steps, and read again the front-page news story, which ran fancifully for a column, beneath the headline "Mystery Radio Message Reveals Possible Will Fraud." The story told of two radio amateurs, experimenting illegally on the supposedly unused ultra- high-frequency band, who had been amazed to hear a man chattering about voices and a will. The amateurs had broken the law, operating on an unassigned frequency, but they hadn't kept their mouths shut about their discovery. Now hams all over the world would be building sets so they could listen in, too.

"Morning, sir. Nice morning, isn't it?" said a guard coming off duty. He was a cheerful Irishman.

"Fine morning, all right," agreed Groszinger. "Clouding up a little in the west, maybe." He wondered what the guard would say if he told him what he knew. He would laugh, probably.

Groszinger's secretary was dusting off his desk when he walked in. "You could use some sleep, couldn't you?" she said. "Honestly, why you men don't take better care of yourselves I just don't know. If you had a wife, she'd make you —"

"Never felt better in my life," said Groszinger. "Any word from General Dane?"

"He was looking for you about ten minutes ago. He's back in the radio room now. He's been on the phone with Washington for half an hour."

She had only the vaguest notion of what the project was about. Again, Groszinger felt the urge to tell about Major Rice and the voices, to see what effect the news would have on someone else. Perhaps his secretary would react as he himself had reacted, with a shrug. Maybe that was the spirit of this era of the atom bomb, H-bomb, God-knows-what-next-bomb — to be amazed at nothing. Science had given humanity forces enough to destroy the earth, and politics had given humanity a fair assurance that the forces would be used. There could be no cause for awe to top *that* one. But proof of a spirit world might at least equal it. Maybe that was the shock the world needed, maybe word from the spirits could change the suicidal course of history.

General Dane looked up wearily as Groszinger walked into the radio room. "They're bringing him down," he said. "There's nothing else we can do. He's no damn good to us now." The loudspeaker, turned low, sang the monotonous hum of the jamming signal. The radio operator slept before the set, his head resting on his folded arms.

"Did you try to get through to him again?"

"Twice. He's clear off his head now. Tried to tell him to change his frequency, to code his messages, but he just went on jabbering like he couldn't hear me — talking about that woman's voice."

"Who's the woman? Did he say?"

The General looked at him oddly. "Says it's his wife, Margaret. Guess that's enough to throw anybody, wouldn't you say? Pretty bright, weren't we, sending up a guy with no family ties." He arose and stretched. "I'm going out for a minute. Just make sure you keep your hands off that set." He slammed the door behind him.

The radio operator stirred. "They're bringing him down," he said.

"I know," said Groszinger.

"That'll kill him, won't it?"

"He has controls for gliding her in, once he hits the atmosphere."

"If he wants to."

"That's right — if he wants to. They'll get him out of his orbit and back to the atmosphere under rocket power. After that, it'll be up to him to take over and make the landing."

They fell silent. The only sound in the room was the muted jamming signal in the loudspeaker.

"He don't want to live, you know that?" said the radio operator suddenly. "Would you want to?"

"Guess that's something you don't know until you come up against it," said Groszinger. He was trying to imagine the world of the future — a world in constant touch with the spirits, the living inseparable from the dead. It was bound to come. Other men, probing into space, were certain to find out. Would it make life heaven or hell? Every bum and genius, criminal and hero, average man and madman, now and forever part of humanity — advising, squabbling, conniving, placating...

The radio operator looked furtively toward the door. "Want to hear him again?"

Groszinger shook his head. "Everybody's listening to that frequency now. We'd all be in a nice mess if you stopped jamming." He didn't want to hear more. He was baffled, miserable. Would Death unmasked drive men to suicide, or bring new hope? he was asking himself. Would the living desert their leaders and turn to the dead for guidance? To Caesar... Charlemagne... Peter the Great... Napoleon... Bismarck... Lincoln... Roosevelt? To Jesus Christ? Were the dead wiser than —

Before Groszinger could stop him, the sergeant switched off the oscillator that was jamming the frequency.

Major Rice's voice came through instantly, high and giddy. "...thousands of them, thousands of them, all around me, standing on nothing, shimmering like northern lights — beautiful, curving off in space, all around the earth like a glowing fog. I can see them, do you hear? I can see them now. I can see Margaret. She's waving and smiling, misty, heavenly, beautiful. If only you could see it, if —"

The radio operator flicked on the jamming signal. There was a footfall in the hallway.

General Dane stalked into the radio room, studying his watch. "In five minutes they'll start him down," he said. he plunged his hands deep into his pockets and slouched dejectedly. "We failed this time. Next time, by God, we'll make it. The next man who goes up will know what he's up against — he'll be ready to take it."

He put his hand on Groszinger's shoulder. "The most important job you'll ever have to do, my friend, is to keep your mouth shut about those spirits out there, do you understand? We don't want the enemy to know we've had a ship out there, and we don't want them to know what they'll come across if they try it. The security of this country depends on that being our secret. Do I make myself clear?"

"Yes, sir," said Groszinger, grateful to have no choice but to be quiet. He didn't want to be the one to tell the world. He wished he had had nothing to do with sending Rice out into space. What discovery of the dead would do to humanity he didn't know, but the impact would be terrific. Now, like the rest, he would have to wait for the next wild twist of history.

The General looked at his watch again. "They're bringing him down," he said.

At 1:39 p.m., on Friday, July 28th, the British liner *Capricorn*, two hundred eighty miles out of New York City, bound for Liverpool, radioed that an unidentified object had crashed into the sea, sending up a towering geyser on the horizon to starboard of the ship. Several passengers were said to have seen something glinting as the thing fell from the sky. Upon reaching the scene of the crash, the *Capricorn* reported finding dead and stunned fish on the surface, and turbulent water, but no wreckage.

Newspapers suggested that the *Capricorn* had seen the crash of an experimental rocket fired out to sea in a test of range. The Secretary of Defense promptly denied that any such tests were being conducted over the Atlantic.

In Boston, Dr. Bernard Groszinger, young rocket consultant for the Air Force, told newsmen that what the *Capricorn* had observed might well have been a meteor.

"That seems quite likely," he said. "If it was a meteor, the fact that it reached the earth's surface should, I think, be one of the year's most important science news stories. Usually meteors burn to nothing before they're even through the stratosphere."

"Excuse me, sir," interrupted a reporter. "Is there anything out beyond the stratosphere — I mean, is there any name for it?"

"Well, actually the term 'stratosphere' is kind of arbitrary. It's the outer shell of the atmosphere. You can't say definitely where it stops. Beyond it is just, well — dead space."

"Dead space — that's the right name for it, eh?" said the reporter.

"If you want something fancier, maybe we could put it into Greek," said Groszinger playfully, "*Thanatos*, that's Greek for 'death,' I think. Maybe instead of 'dead space' you'd prefer 'Thanasphere.' Has a nice scientific ring to it, don't you think?"

The newsmen laughed politely.

"Dr. Groszinger, when's the first rocket ship going to make it into space?" asked another reporter.

"You people read too many comic books," said Groszinger. "Come back in twenty years, and maybe I'll have a story for you."

H.P. LOVECRAFT

Polaris
1918

Into the north window of my chamber glows the Pole Star with uncanny light. All through the long hellish hours of blackness it shines there. And in the autumn of the year, when the winds from the north curse and whine, and the red-leaved trees of the swamp mutter things to one another in the small hours of the morning under the horned waning moon, I sit by the casement and watch that star. Down from the heights reels the glittering Cassiopeia as the hours wear on, while Charles' Wain lumbers up from behind the vapour-soaked swamp trees that sway in the night-wind. Just before dawn Arcturus winks ruddily from above the cemetery on the low hillock, and Coma Berenices shimmers weirdly afar off in the mysterious east; but still the Pole Star leers down from the same place in the black vault, winking hideously like an insane watching eye which strives to convey some strange message, yet recalls nothing save that it once had a message to convey. Sometimes, when it is cloudy, I can sleep.

Well do I remember the night of the great Aurora, when over the swamp played the shocking coruscations of the daemon-light. After the beams came clouds, and then I slept.

And it was under a horned waning moon that I saw the city for the first time. Still and somnolent did it lie, on a strange plateau in a hollow betwixt strange peaks. Of ghastly marble were its walls and its towers, its columns, domes, and pavements. In the marble streets were marble pillars, the upper parts of which were carven into the images of grave bearded men. The air was warm and stirred not. And overhead, scarce ten degrees from the zenith, glowed that watching Pole Star. Long did I gaze on the city, but the day came not. When the red Aldebaran, which blinked low in the sky but never set, had crawled a quarter of the way around the horizon, I saw light and motion in the houses and the streets. Forms strangely robed, but at once noble and familiar, walked abroad, and under the horned waning moon men talked wisdom in a tongue which I understood, though it was unlike any language I had ever known. And when the red Aldebaran had crawled more than half way around the horizon, there were again darkness and silence.

When I awaked, I was not as I had been. Upon my memory was graven the vision of the city, and within my soul had arisen another and vaguer recollection, of whose nature I was not then certain. Thereafter, on the cloudy nights when I could sleep, I saw the city often; sometimes under that horned waning moon, and sometimes under the hot yellow rays of a sun which did not set, but which wheeled low around the horizon. And on the clear nights the Pole Star leered as never before.

Gradually I came to wonder what might be my place in that city on the strange plateau betwixt strange peaks. At first content to view the scene as an all-observant uncorporeal presence, I now desired to define my relation to it, and to speak my mind amongst the grave men who conversed each day in the public squares. I said to myself, "This is no dream, for by what means can I prove the greater reality of that other life in the house of stone and brick south of the sinister swamp and the cemetery on the low hillock, where the Pole Star peers into my north window each night?"

One night as I listened to the discourse in the large square containing many statues, I felt a change; and perceived that I had at last a bodily form. Nor was I a stranger in the streets of Olathoë, which lies on the plateau of Sarkis, betwixt the peaks Noton and Kadiphonek. It was my friend Alos who spoke, and his speech was one that pleased my soul, for it was the speech of a true man and patriot. That night had the news come of Daikos' fall, and of the advance of the Inutos; squat, hellish, yellow fiends who five years ago had appeared out of the unknown west to ravage the confines of our kingdom, and finally to besiege our towns. Having taken the fortified places at the foot of the mountains, their way now lay open to the plateau, unless every citizen could resist with the strength of ten men. For the squat creatures were mighty in the arts of war, and knew not the scruples of honour which held back our tall, grey-eyed men of Lomar from ruthless conquest.

Alos, my friend, was commander of all the forces on the plateau, and in him lay the last hope of our country. On this occasion he spoke of the perils to be faced, and exhorted the men of Olathoë, bravest of the Lomarians, to sustain the traditions of their ancestors, who when forced to move southward from Zobna before the advance of the great ice-sheet (even as our descendants must some day flee from the land of Lomar), valiantly and victoriously swept aside the hairy, long-armed, cannibal Gnophkehs that stood in their way. To me Alos denied a warrior's part, for I was feeble and given to strange faintings when subjected to stress and hardships. But my eyes were the keenest in the city, despite the long hours I gave each day to the study of the Pnakotic manuscripts and the wisdom of the Zobnarian Fathers; so my friend, desiring not to doom me to inaction, rewarded me with that duty which was second to nothing in importance. To the watch-tower of Thapnen he sent me, there to serve as the eyes of our army. Should the Inutos attempt to gain the citadel by the narrow pass behind the peak Noton, and thereby surprise the garrison, I was to give the signal of fire which would warn the waiting soldiers and save the town from immediate disaster.

Alone I mounted the tower, for every man of stout body was needed in the passes below. My brain was sore dazed with excitement and fatigue, for I had not slept in many days; yet was my purpose firm, for I loved my native land of Lomar, and the marble city of Olathoë that lies betwixt the peaks of Noton and Kadiphonek.

But as I stood in the tower's topmost chamber, I beheld the horned waning moon, red and sinister, quivering through the vapours that hovered over the distant valley of Banof. And through an opening in the roof glittered the pale Pole Star, fluttering as if alive, and leering like a fiend and tempter. Methought its spirit whispered evil counsel, soothing me to traitorous somnolence with a damnable rhythmical promise which it repeated over and over:

> *Slumber, watcher, till the spheres*
> *Six and twenty thousand years*
> *Have revolv'd, and I return*
> *To the spot where now I burn.*
> *Other stars anon shall rise*
> *To the axis of the skies;*
> *Stars that soothe and stars that bless*
> *With a sweet forgetfulness:*
> *Only when my round is o'er*
> *Shall the past disturb thy door.*

Vainly did I struggle with my drowsiness, seeking to connect these strange words with some lore of the skies which I had learnt from the Pnakotic manuscripts. My head, heavy and reeling, drooped to my breast, and when next I looked up it was in a dream; with the Pole Star grinning at me through a window from over the horrible swaying trees of a dream-swamp. And I am still dreaming.

In my shame and despair I sometimes scream frantically, begging the dream-creatures around me to waken me ere the Inutos steal up the pass behind the peak Noton and take the citadel by surprise; but these creatures are daemons, for they laugh at me and tell me I am not dreaming. They mock me whilst I sleep, and whilst the squat yellow foe may be creeping silently upon us. I have failed in my duty and betrayed the marble city of Olathoë; I have proven false to Alos, my friend and commander. But still these shadows of my dream deride me. They say there is no land of Lomar, save in my nocturnal imaginings; that in those realms where the Pole Star shines high and red Aldebaran crawls low around the horizon, there has been naught save ice and snow for thousands of years, and never a man save squat yellow creatures, blighted by the cold, whom they call "Esquimaux".

And as I writhe in my guilty agony, frantic to save the city whose peril every moment grows, and vainly striving to shake off this unnatural dream of a house of stone and brick south of a sinister swamp and a cemetery on a low hillock; the Pole Star, evil and monstrous, leers down from the black vault, winking hideously like an insane watching eye which strives to convey some strange message, yet recalls nothing save that it once had a message to convey.

PRIMO LEVI

Translated from the Italian by ANN GOLDSTEIN

A Tranquil Star

1978

Once upon a time, somewhere in the universe very far from here, lived a tranquil star, which moved tranquilly in the immensity of the sky, surrounded by a crowd of tranquil planets about which we have not a thing to report. This star was very big and very hot, and its weight was enormous: and here a reporter's difficulties begin. We have written "very far," "big," "hot," "enormous": Australia is very far, an elephant is big and a house is bigger, this morning I had a hot bath, Everest is enormous. It's clear that something in our lexicon isn't working.

If this story must be written, we must have the courage to eliminate all adjectives that tend to excite wonder: they would achieve the opposite effect, of impoverishing the narrative. For a discussion of stars our language is inadequate and seems laughable, as if someone were trying to plow with a feather. It's a language that was born with us, suitable for describing objects more or less as large and as long-lasting as we are; it has our dimensions, it's human. It doesn't go beyond what our senses tell us. Until two or three hundred years ago, small meant the scabies mite; there was nothing smaller, nor, as a result, was there an adjective to describe it.

The sea and the sky were big, in fact equally big; fire was hot. Not until the thirteenth century was the need felt to introduce into daily language a term suitable for counting "very" numerous objects, and, with little imagination, "million" was coined. A while later, with even less imagination, "billion" was coined, with no care being taken to give it a precise meaning, since the term today has different values in different countries.

Not even with superlatives does one get very far: how many times as high as a high tower is a very high tower? Nor can we hope for help from disguised superlatives, like "immense," "colossal," "extraordinary": to relate the things that we want to relate here, these adjectives are hopelessly unsuitable, because the star we started from was ten times as big as our sun, and the sun is "many" times as big and heavy as our Earth, whose size so overwhelms our own dimensions that we can represent it only with a violent effort of the imagination. There is, of course, the slim and elegant language of numbers, the alphabet of the powers of ten, but then this would not be a story in the sense in which it wants to be a story; that is, a fable that awakens echoes, and in which each of us can perceive distant reflections of himself and of the human race.

This tranquil star wasn't supposed to be so tranquil. Maybe it was too big: in the far-off original act in which everything was created, it had received an inheritance too demanding. Or maybe it contained in its heart an imbalance or an infection, as happens to some of us. It's customary among the stars to quietly burn the hydrogen they are made of, generously giving energy to the void, until they are reduced to a dignified thinness and end their career as modest white dwarfs. The star in question, however, when some billions of years had passed since its birth, and its companions began to rarefy, was not satisfied with its destiny and became restless — to such a point that its restlessness became visible even to those of us who are "very" distant and circumscribed by a "very" brief life.

Of this restlessness Arab and Chinese astronomers were aware. The Europeans no: the Europeans of that time, which was a time of struggle, were so convinced that the heaven of the stars was immutable, was in fact the paradigm and kingdom of immutability, that they considered it pointless and blasphemous to notice changes. There could be none — by definition there were none. But a diligent Arab observer, equipped only with good eyes, patience, humility, and the love of knowing the works of his God, had realized that this star, to which he was very attached, was not immutable. He had watched it for thirty years, and had noticed that the star oscillated between the fourth and the sixth of the six magnitudes that had been described many centuries earlier by a Greek, who was as diligent as he, and who, like him, thought that observing the stars was a route that would take one far. The Arab felt a little as if it were his star: he had wanted to place his mark on it, and in his notes he had called it Al-Ludra, which in his dialect means "the capricious one." Al-Ludra oscillated, but not regularly: not like a pendulum;

rather, like someone who is at a loss between two choices. It completed its cycle sometimes in one year, sometimes in two, sometimes in five, and it didn't always stop in its dimming at the sixth magnitude, which is the last visible to the naked eye: at times it disappeared completely. The patient Arab counted seven cycles before he died: his life had been long, but the life of a man is always pitifully brief compared with that of a star, even if the star behaves in such a way as to arouse suspicions about its eternity.

After the death of the Arab, Al-Ludra, although provided with a name, did not attract much interest, because the variable stars are so many, and also because, starting in 1750, it was reduced to a speck, barely visible with the best telescopes of the time. But in 1950 (and the message has only now reached us) the illness that must have been gnawing at it from within reached a crisis, and here, for the second time, our story, too, enters a crisis: now it is no longer the adjectives that fail but the facts themselves. We still don't know much about the convulsive death-resurrection of stars: we know that, fairly often, something flares up in the atomic mechanism of a star's nucleus and then the star explodes, on a scale not of millions or billions of years but of hours and minutes. We know that these events are among the most cataclysmic that the sky today holds; but we understand only — and approximately — the how, not the why. We'll be satisfied with the how.

An observer who, to his misfortune, found himself on October 19th of 1950, at ten o'clock our time, on one of the

270

silent planets of Al-Ludra would have seen, "before his very eyes," as they say, his gentle sun swell, not a little but "a lot," and would not have been present at the spectacle for long. Within a quarter of an hour he would have been forced to seek useless shelter against the intolerable heat — and this we can affirm independently of any hypothesis concerning the size and shape of this observer, provided that he was constructed, like us, of molecules and atoms — and in half an hour his testimony, and that of all his fellow-beings, would end. Therefore, to conclude this account we must base it on other testimony, that of our earthly instruments, for which the event, in its intrinsic horror, happened in a "very" diluted form and, besides being slowed down by the long journey through the realm of light that brought us the news. After an hour, the seas and ice (if there were any) of the no longer silent planet boiled up; after three, its rocks melted and its mountains crumbled into valleys in the form of lava. After ten hours, the entire planet was reduced to vapor, along with all the delicate and subtle works that the combined labor of chance and necessity, through innumerable trials and errors, had perhaps created there, and along with all the poets and wise men who had perhaps examined that sky, and had wondered what was the value of so many little lights, and had found no answer. That was the answer.

After one of our days, the surface of the star had reached the orbit of its most distant planets, invading their sky and, together with the remains of its tranquillity, spreading in all directions — a billowing wave of energy bearing the modulated news of the catastrophe.

Ramón Escojido was thirty-four and had two charming children. With his wife he had a complex and tense relationship: he was Peruvian and she was of Austrian origin, he solitary, modest, and lazy, she ambitious and eager for social life. But what social life can you dream of if you live in an observatory at an altitude of 2900 metres, an hour's flight from the nearest city and four kilometres from an Indian village, dusty in summer and icy in winter? Judith loved and hated her husband, on alternate days, sometimes even in the same instant. She hated his wisdom and his collection of shells; she loved the father of her children, and the man who was under the covers in the morning.

They reached a fragile accord on weekend outings. It was Friday evening, and they were getting ready with noisy delight for the next day's excursion. Judith and the children were busy with the provisions; Ramón went up to the observatory to prepare the photographic plate for the night. In the morning, he struggled to free himself from the children, who overwhelmed him with lighthearted questions: How far was the lake? Would it still be frozen? Had he remembered the rubber raft? He went into the darkroom to develop the plate, he dried it and placed it beside the plate that he had made seven days earlier. He examined both under the microscope: good, they were identical; he could leave in tranquillity. But then he had a scruple and looked more carefully, and realized that there was something new; not a big thing, a barely perceptible spot, but it wasn't there on the old plate. When these things happen, ninety-nine times out of a hundred it's a speck of dust (one can never be too clean while working) or a microscopic defect in the emulsion; but there is also the minuscule probability that it's a nova, and one has to make a report, subject to confirmation. Farewell, outing: he would have to retake the photograph on the following two nights. What would he tell Judith and the children?

PHILLIP K. DICK

Mr. Spaceship
1953

Kramer leaned back. "You can see the situation. How can we deal with a factor like this? The perfect variable."

"Perfect? Prediction should still be possible. A living thing still acts from necessity, the same as inanimate material. But the cause-effect chain is more subtle; there are more factors to be considered. The difference is quantitative, I think. The reaction of the living organism parallels natural causation, but with greater complexity."

Gross and Kramer looked up at the board plates, suspended on the wall, still dripping, the images hardening into place. Kramer traced a line with his pencil.

"See that? It's a pseudopodium. They're alive, and so far, a weapon we can't beat. No mechanical system can compete with that, simple or intricate. We'll have to scrap the Johnson Control and find something else."

"Meanwhile the war continues as it is. Stalemate. Checkmate. They can't get to us, and we can't get through their living minefield."

Kramer nodded. "It's a perfect defense, for them. But there still might be one answer."

"What's that?"

"Wait a minute." Kramer turned to his rocket expert, sitting with the charts and files. "The heavy cruiser that returned this week. It didn't actually touch, did it? It came close but there was no contact."

"Correct." The expert nodded. "The mine was twenty miles off. The cruiser was in space-drive, moving directly toward Proxima, line-straight, using the Johnson Control, of course. It had deflected a quarter of an hour earlier for reasons unknown. Later it resumed its course. That was when they got it."

"It shifted," Kramer said. "But not enough. The mine was coming along after it, trailing it. It's the same old story, but I wonder about the contact."

"Here's our theory," the expert said. "We keep looking for contact, a trigger in the pseudopodium. But more likely we're witnessing a psychological phenomena, a decision without any physical correlative. We're watching for something that isn't there. The mine decides to blow up. It sees our ship, approaches, and then decides."

"Thanks." Kramer turned to Gross. "Well, that confirms what I'm saying. How can a ship guided by automatic relays escape a mine that decides to explode? The whole theory of mine penetration is that you must avoid tripping the trigger. But here the trigger is a state of mind in a complicated, developed life-form."

"The belt is fifty thousand miles deep," Gross added. "It solves another problem for them, repair and maintenance.

The damn things reproduce, fill up the spaces by spawning into them. I wonder what they feed on?"

"Probably the remains of our first-line. The big cruisers must be a delicacy. It's a game of wits, between a living creature and a ship piloted by automatic relays. The ship always loses." Kramer opened a folder. "I'll tell you what I suggest."

"Go on," Gross said. "I've already heard ten solutions today. What's yours?"

"Mine is very simple. These creatures are superior to any mechanical system, but only because they're alive. Almost any other life-form could compete with them, any higher life-form. If the yuks can put out living mines to protect their planets, we ought to be able to harness some of our own life-forms in a similar way. Let's make use of the same weapon ourselves."

"Which life-form do you propose to use?"

"I think the human brain is the most agile of known living forms. Do you know of any better?"

"But no human being can withstand outspace travel. A human pilot would be dead of heart failure long before the ship got anywhere near Proxima."

"But we don't need the whole body," Kramer said. "We need only the brain."

"What?"

"The problem is to find a person of high intelligence who would contribute, in the same manner that eyes and arms are volunteered."

"But a brain...."

"Technically, it could be done. Brains have been transferred several times, when body destruction made it necessary. Of course, to a spaceship, to a heavy outspace cruiser, instead of an artificial body, that's new."

The room was silent.

"It's quite an idea," Gross said slowly. His heavy square face twisted. "But even supposing it might work, the big question is *whose* brain?"

It was all very confusing, the reasons for the war, the nature of the enemy. The Yucconae had been contacted on one of the outlying planets of Proxima Centauri. At the approach of the Terran ship, a host of dark slim pencils had lifted abruptly and shot off into the distance. The first real encounter came between three of the yuk pencils and a single exploration ship from Terra. No Terrans survived. After that it was all out war, with no holds barred.

Both sides feverishly constructed defense rings around their systems. Of the two, the Yucconae belt was the better. The ring around Proxima was a living ring, superior to anything Terra could throw against it. The standard equipment by which Terran ships were guided in outspace, the Johnson Control, was not adequate. Something more was needed. Automatic relays were not good enough.

— Not good at all, Kramer thought to himself, as he stood looking down the hillside at the work going on below him. A warm wind blew along the hill, rustling the weeds and grass. At the bottom, in the valley, the mechanics had almost finished; the last elements of the reflex system had been removed from the ship and crated up.

All that was needed now was the new core, the new central key that would take the place of the mechanical system. A human brain, the brain of an intelligent, wary human being. But would the human being part with it? That was the problem.

Kramer turned. Two people were approaching him along the road, a man and a woman. The man was Gross, expressionless, heavy-set, walking with dignity. The woman was — He stared in surprise and growing annoyance. It was Dolores, his wife. Since they'd separated he had seen little of her....

"Kramer," Gross said. "Look who I ran into. Come back down with us. We're going into town."

"Hello, Phil," Dolores said. "Well, aren't you glad to see me?"

He nodded. "How have you been? You're looking fine." She was still pretty and slender in her uniform, the blue-grey of Internal Security, Gross' organization.

"Thanks." She smiled. "You seem to be doing all right, too. Commander Gross tells me that you're responsible for this project, Operation Head, as they call it. Whose head have you decided on?"

"That's the problem." Kramer lit a cigarette. "This ship is to be equipped with a human brain instead of the Johnson system. We've constructed special draining baths for the brain, electronic relays to catch the impulses and magnify them, a continual feeding duct that supplies the living cells with everything they need. But —"

"But we still haven't got the brain itself," Gross finished. They began to walk back toward the car. "If we can get that we'll be ready for the tests."

"Will the brain remain alive?" Dolores asked. "Is it actually going to live as part of the ship?"

"It will be alive, but not conscious. Very little life is actually conscious. Animals, trees, insects are quick in their responses, but they aren't conscious. In this process of ours the individual personality, the ego, will cease. We only need the response ability, nothing more."

Dolores shuddered. "How terrible!"

"In time of war everything must be tried," Kramer said absently. "If one life sacrificed will end the war it's worth it. This ship might get through. A couple more like it and there wouldn't be any more war."

They got into the car. As they drove down the road, Gross said, "Have you thought of anyone yet?"

Kramer shook his head. "That's out of my line."

"What do you mean?"

"I'm an engineer. It's not in my department."

"But all this was your idea."

"My work ends there."

Gross was staring at him oddly. Kramer shifted uneasily.

"Then who is supposed to do it?" Gross said. "I can have my organization prepare examinations of various kinds, to determine fitness, that kind of thing —"

"Listen, Phil," Dolores said suddenly.

"What?"

She turned toward him. "I have an idea. Do you remember that professor we had in college. Michael Thomas?"

Kramer nodded.

"I wonder if he's still alive." Dolores frowned. "If he is he must be awfully old."

"Why, Dolores?" Gross asked.

"Perhaps an old person who didn't have much time left, but whose mind was still clear and sharp —"

"Professor Thomas." Kramer rubbed his jaw. "He certainly was a wise old duck. But could he still be alive? He must have been seventy, then."

"We could find that out," Gross said. "I could make a routine check."

"What do you think?" Dolores said. "If any human mind could outwit those creatures —"

"I don't like the idea," Kramer said. In his mind an image had appeared, the image of an old man sitting behind a desk, his bright gentle eyes moving about the classroom. The old man leaning forward, a thin hand raised —

"Keep him out of this," Kramer said.

"What's wrong?" Gross looked at him curiously.

"It's because I suggested it," Dolores said.

"No." Kramer shook his head. "It's not that. I didn't expect anything like this, somebody I knew, a man I studied under. I remember him very clearly. He was a very distinct personality."

"Good," Gross said.

"He sounds fine."

"We can't do it. We're asking his death!"

"This is war," Gross said, "and war doesn't wait on the needs of the individual. You said that yourself. Surely he'll volunteer; we can keep it on that basis."

"He may already be dead," Dolores murmured.

"We'll find that out," Gross said speeding up the car. They drove the rest of the way in silence.

For a long time the two of them stood studying the small wood house, overgrown with ivy, set back on the lot behind an enormous oak. The little town was silent and sleepy; once in awhile a car moved slowly along the distant highway, but that was all.

"This is the place," Gross said to Kramer. He folded his arms. "Quite a quaint little house."

Kramer said nothing. The two Security Agents behind them were expressionless.

Gross started toward the gate. "Let's go. According to the check he's still alive, but very sick. His mind is agile, however. That seems to be certain. It's said he doesn't leave the house. A woman takes care of his needs. He's very frail."

They went down the stone walk and up onto the porch. Gross rang the bell. They waited. After a time they heard slow footsteps. The door opened. An elderly woman in a shapeless wrapper studied them impassively.

"Security," Gross said, showing his card. "We wish to see Professor Thomas."

"Why?"

"Government business." He glanced at Kramer.

Kramer stepped forward. "I was a pupil of the Professor's," he said. "I'm sure he won't mind seeing us."

The woman hesitated uncertainly. Gross stepped into the doorway. "All right, mother. This is war time. We can't stand out here."

The two Security agents followed him, and Kramer came reluctantly behind, closing the door. Gross stalked down the hall until he came to an open door. He stopped, looking in. Kramer could see the white corner of a bed, a wooden post and the edge of a dresser.

He joined Gross.

In the dark room a withered old man lay, propped up on endless pillows. At first it seemed as if he were asleep; there was no motion or sign of life. But after a time Kramer saw with a faint shock that the old man was watching them intently, his eyes fixed on them, unmoving, unwinking.

"Professor Thomas?" Gross said. "I'm Commander Gross of Security. This man with me is perhaps known to you —"

The faded eyes fixed on Kramer.

"I know him. Philip Kramer.... You've grown heavier, boy." The voice was feeble, the rustle of dry ashes. "Is it true you're married now?"

"Yes. I married Dolores French. You remember her." Kramer came toward the bed. "But we're separated. It didn't work out very well. Our careers —"

"What we came here about, Professor," Gross began, but Kramer cut him off with an impatient wave.

"Let me talk. Can't you and your men get out of here long enough to let me talk to him?"

Gross swallowed. "All right, Kramer." He nodded to the two men. The three of them left the room, going out into the hall and closing the door after them.

The old man in the bed watched Kramer silently. "I don't think much of him," he said at last. "I've seen his type before. What's he want?"

"Nothing. He just came along. Can I sit down?" Kramer found a stiff upright chair beside the bed. "If I'm bothering you —"

"No. I'm glad to see you again, Philip. After so long. I'm sorry your marriage didn't work out."

"How have you been?"

"I've been very ill. I'm afraid that my moment on the world's stage has almost ended." The ancient eyes studied the younger man reflectively. "You look as if you have been doing well. Like everyone else I thought highly of. You've gone to the top in this society."

Kramer smiled. Then he became serious. "Professor, there's a project we're working on that I want to talk to you about. It's the first ray of hope we've had in this whole war. If it works, we may be able to crack the yuk defenses, get some ships into their system. If we can do that the war might be brought to an end."

"Go on. Tell me about it, if you wish."

"It's a long shot, this project. It may not work at all, but we have to give it a try."

"It's obvious that you came here because of it," Professor Thomas murmured. "I'm becoming curious. Go on."

After Kramer finished the old man lay back in the bed without speaking. At last he sighed.

"I understand. A human mind, taken out of a human body." He sat up a little, looking at Kramer. "I suppose you're thinking of me."

Kramer said nothing.

"Before I make my decision I want to see the papers on this, the theory and outline of construction. I'm not sure I like it. — For reasons of my own, I mean. But I want to look at the material. If you'll do that —"

"Certainly." Kramer stood up and went to the door. Gross and the two Security Agents were standing outside, waiting tensely. "Gross, come inside."

They filed into the room.

"Give the Professor the papers," Kramer said. "He wants to study them before deciding."

Gross brought the file out of his coat pocket, a manila envelope. He handed it to the old man on the bed. "Here it is, Professor. You're welcome to examine it. Will you give us your answer as soon as possible? We're very anxious to begin, of course."

"I'll give you my answer when I've decided." He took the envelope with a thin, trembling hand. "My decision depends on what I find out from these papers. If I don't like what I find, then I will not become involved with this work in any shape or form." He opened the envelope with shaking hands. "I'm looking for one thing."

"What is it?" Gross said.

"That's my affair. Leave me a number by which I can reach you when I've decided."

Silently, Gross put his card down on the dresser. As they went out Professor Thomas was already reading the first of the papers, the outline of the theory.

Kramer sat across from Dale Winter, his second in line. "What then?" Winter said.

"He's going to contact us." Kramer scratched with a drawing pen on some paper. "I don't know what to think."

"What do you mean?" Winter's good-natured face was puzzled.

"Look." Kramer stood up, pacing back and forth, his hands in his uniform pockets. "He was my teacher in college. I respected him as a man, as well as a teacher. He was more than a voice, a talking book. He was a person, a calm, kindly person I could look up to. I always wanted to be like him, someday. Now look at me."

"So?"

"Look at what I'm asking. I'm asking for his life, as if he were some kind of laboratory animal kept around in a cage, not a man, a teacher at all."

"Do you think he'll do it?"

"I don't know." Kramer went to the window. He stood looking out. "In a way, I hope not."

"But if he doesn't — "

"Then we'll have to find somebody else. I know. There would be somebody else. Why did Dolores have to — "

The vidphone rang. Kramer pressed the button.

"This is Gross." The heavy features formed. "The old man called me. Professor Thomas."

"What did he say?" He knew; he could tell already, by the sound of Gross' voice.

"He said he'd do it. I was a little surprised myself, but apparently he means it. We've already made arrangements for his admission to the hospital. His lawyer is drawing up the statement of liability."

Kramer only half heard. He nodded wearily. "All right. I'm glad. I suppose we can go ahead, then."

"You don't sound very glad."

"I wonder why he decided to go ahead with it."

"He was very certain about it." Gross sounded pleased. "He called me quite early. I was still in bed. You know, this calls for a celebration."

"Sure," Kramer said. "It sure does."

Toward the middle of August the project neared completion. They stood outside in the hot autumn heat, looking up at the sleek metal sides of the ship. Gross thumped the metal with his hand. "Well, it won't be long. We can begin the test any time."

"Tell us more about this," an officer in gold braid said. "It's such an unusual concept."

"Is there really a human brain inside the ship?" a dignitary asked, a small man in a rumpled suit. "And the brain is actually alive?"

"Gentlemen, this ship is guided by a living brain instead of the usual Johnson relay-control system. But the brain is not conscious. It will function by reflex only. The practical difference between it and the Johnson system is this: a human brain is far more intricate than any man-made structure, and its ability to adapt itself to a situation, to respond to danger, is far beyond anything that could be artificially built."

Gross paused, cocking his ear. The turbines of the ship were beginning to rumble, shaking the ground under them with a deep vibration. Kramer was standing a short distance away from the others, his arms folded, watching silently. At the sound of the turbines he walked quickly around the ship to the other side. A few workmen were clearing away the last of the waste, the scraps of wiring and scaffolding. They glanced up at him and went on hurriedly with their work. Kramer mounted the ramp and entered the control cabin of the ship. Winter was sitting at the controls with a Pilot from Space-transport.

"How's it look?" Kramer asked.

"All right." Winter got up. "He tells me that it would be best to take off manually. The robot controls —" Winter hesitated. "I mean, the built-in controls, can take over later on in space."

"That's right," the Pilot said. "It's customary with the Johnson system, and so in this case we should —"

"Can you tell anything yet?" Kramer asked.

"No," the Pilot said slowly. "I don't think so. I've been going over everything. It seems to be in good order. There's only one thing I wanted to ask you about." He put his hand on the control board. "There are some changes here I don't understand."

"Changes?"

"Alterations from the original design. I wonder what the purpose is."

Kramer took a set of the plans from his coat. "Let me look." He turned the pages over. The Pilot watched carefully over his shoulder.

"The changes aren't indicated on your copy," the Pilot said. "I wonder —" He stopped. Commander Gross had entered the control cabin.

"Gross, who authorized alterations?" Kramer said. "Some of the wiring has been changed."

"Why, your old friend." Gross signaled to the field tower through the window.

"My old friend?"

"The Professor. He took quite an active interest." Gross turned to the Pilot. "Let's get going. We have to take this out past gravity for the test they tell me. Well, perhaps it's for the best. Are you ready?"

"Sure." The Pilot sat down and moved some of the controls around. "Anytime."

"Go ahead, then," Gross said.

"The Professor —" Kramer began, but at that moment there was a tremendous roar and the ship leaped under him. He grasped one of the wall holds and hung on as best he could. The cabin was filling with a steady throbbing, the raging of the jet turbines underneath them.

The ship leaped. Kramer closed his eyes and held his breath. They were moving out into space, gaining speed each moment.

"Well, what do you think?" Winter said nervously. "Is it time yet?"

"A little longer," Kramer said. He was sitting on the floor of the cabin, down by the control wiring. He had removed the metal covering-plate, exposing the complicated maze of relay wiring. He was studying it, comparing it to the wiring diagrams.

"What's the matter?" Gross said.

"These changes. I can't figure out what they're for. The only pattern I can make out is that for some reason —"

"Let me look," the Pilot said. He squatted down beside Kramer. "You were saying?"

"See this lead here? Originally it was switch controlled. It closed and opened automatically, according to temperature change. Now it's wired so that the central control system operates it. The same with the others. A lot of this was still mechanical, worked by pressure, temperature, stress. Now it's under the central master."

"The brain?" Gross said. "You mean it's been altered so that the brain manipulates it?"

Kramer nodded. "Maybe Professor Thomas felt that no mechanical relays could be trusted. Maybe he thought that things would be happening too fast. But some of these could close in a split second. The brake rockets could go on as quickly as —"

"Hey," Winter said from the control seat. "We're getting near the moon stations. What'll I do?"

They looked out the port. The corroded surface of the moon gleamed up at them, a corrupt and sickening sight. They were moving swiftly toward it.

"I'll take it," the Pilot said. He eased Winter out of the way and strapped himself in place. The ship began to move away from the moon as he manipulated the controls. Down below them they could see the observation stations dotting the surface, and the tiny squares that were the openings of the underground factories and hangars. A red blinker winked up at them and the Pilot's fingers moved on the board in answer.

"We're past the moon," the Pilot said, after a time. The moon had fallen behind them; the ship was heading into outer space. "Well, we can go ahead with it."

Kramer did not answer.

"Mr. Kramer, we can go ahead any time."

Kramer started. "Sorry. I was thinking. All right, thanks." He frowned, deep in thought.

"What is it?" Gross asked.

"The wiring changes. Did you understand the reason for them when you gave the okay to the workmen?"

Gross flushed. "You know I know nothing about technical material. I'm in Security."

"Then you should have consulted me."

"What does it matter?" Gross grinned wryly. "We're going to have to start putting our faith in the old man sooner or later."

The Pilot stepped back from the board. His face was pale and set. "Well, it's done," he said. "That's it."

"What's done?" Kramer said.

"We're on automatic. The brain. I turned the board over to it — to him, I mean. The Old Man." The Pilot lit a cigarette and puffed nervously. "Let's keep our fingers crossed."

The ship was coasting evenly, in the hands of its invisible pilot. Far down inside the ship, carefully armoured and protected, a soft human brain lay in a tank of liquid, a thousand minute electric charges playing over its surface. As the charges rose they were picked up and amplified, fed into relay systems, advanced, carried on through the entire ship —

Gross wiped his forehead nervously. "So he is running it, now. I hope he knows what he's doing."

Kramer nodded enigmatically. "I think he does."

"What do you mean?"

"Nothing." Kramer walked to the port. "I see we're still moving in a straight line." He picked up the microphone. "We can instruct the brain orally, through this." He blew against the microphone experimentally.

"Go on," Winter said.

"Bring the ship around half-right," Kramer said. "Decrease speed."

They waited. Time passed. Gross looked at Kramer. "No change. Nothing."

"Wait."

Slowly, the ship was beginning to turn. The turbines missed, reducing their steady beat. The ship was taking up its new course, adjusting itself. Nearby some space debris rushed past, incinerating in the blasts of the turbine jets.

"So far so good," Gross said.

They began to breathe more easily. The invisible pilot had taken control smoothly, calmly. The ship was in good hands. Kramer spoke a few more words into the microphone, and they swung again. Now they were moving back the way they had come, toward the moon.

"Let's see what he does when we enter the moon's pull," Kramer said. "He was a good mathematician, the old man. He could handle any kind of problem."

The ship veered, turning away from the moon. The great eaten-away globe fell behind them.

Gross breathed a sigh of relief. "That's that."

"One more thing." Kramer picked up the microphone. "Return to the moon and land the ship at the first space field," he said into it.

"Good Lord," Winter murmured. "Why are you —"

"Be quiet." Kramer stood, listening. The turbines gasped and roared as the ship swung full around, gaining speed.

They were moving back, back toward the moon again. The ship dipped down, heading toward the great globe below.

"We're going a little fast," the Pilot said. "I don't see how he can put down at this velocity."

The port filled up, as the globe swelled rapidly. The Pilot hurried toward the board, reaching for the controls. All at once the ship jerked. The nose lifted and the ship shot out into space, away from the moon, turning at an oblique angle. The men were thrown to the floor by the sudden change in course. They got to their feet again, speechless, staring at each other.

The Pilot gazed down at the board. "It wasn't me! I didn't touch a thing. I didn't even get to it."

The ship was gaining speed each moment. Kramer hesitated. "Maybe you better switch it back to manual."

The Pilot closed the switch. He took hold of the steering controls and moved them experimentally. "Nothing." He turned around. "Nothing. It doesn't respond."

No one spoke.

"You can see what has happened," Kramer said calmly. "The old man won't let go of it, now that he has it. I was afraid of this when I saw the wiring changes. Everything in this ship is centrally controlled, even the cooling system, the hatches, the garbage release. We're helpless."

"Nonsense." Gross strode to the board. He took hold of the wheel and turned it. The ship continued on its course, moving away from the moon, leaving it behind.

"Release!" Kramer said into the microphone. "Let go of the controls! We'll take it back. Release."

"No good," the Pilot said. "Nothing." He spun the useless wheel. "It's dead, completely dead."

"And we're still heading out," Winter said, grinning foolishly. "We'll be going through the first-line defense belt in a few minutes. If they don't shoot us down —"

"We better radio back." The Pilot clicked the radio to send. "I'll contact the main bases, one of the observation stations."

"Better get the defense belt, at the speed we're going. We'll be into it in a minute."

"And after that," Kramer said, "we'll be in outer space. He's moving us toward outspace velocity. Is this ship equipped with baths?"

"Baths?" Gross said.

"The sleep tanks. For space-drive. We may need them if we go much faster."

"But good God, where are we going?" Gross said. "Where — where's he taking us?"

The Pilot obtained contact. "This is Dwight, on ship," he said. "We're entering the defense zone at high velocity. Don't fire on us."

"Turn back," the impersonal voice came through the speaker. "You're not allowed in the defense zone."

"We can't. We've lost control."

"Lost control?"

"This is an experimental ship."

Gross took the radio. "This is Commander Gross, Security. We're being carried into outer space. There's nothing we can do. Is there any way that we can be removed from this ship?"

A hesitation. "We have some fast pursuit ships that could pick you up if you wanted to jump. The chances are good they'd find you. Do you have space flares?"

"We do," the Pilot said. "Let's try it."

"Abandon ship?" Kramer said. "If we leave now we'll never see it again."

"What else can we do? We're gaining speed all the time. Do you propose that we stay here?"

"No." Kramer shook his head. "Damn it, there ought to be a better solution."

"Could you contact him?" Winter asked. "The Old Man? Try to reason with him?"

"It's worth a chance," Gross said. "Try it."

"All right." Kramer took the microphone. He paused a moment. "Listen! Can you hear me? This is Phil Kramer. Can you hear me, Professor. Can you hear me? I want you to release the controls."

There was silence.

"This is Kramer, Professor. Can you hear me? Do you remember who I am? Do you understand who this is?"

Above the control panel the wall speaker made a sound, a sputtering static. They looked up.

"Can you hear me, Professor. This is Philip Kramer. I want you to give the ship back to us. If you can hear me, release the controls! Let go, Professor. Let go!"

Static. A rushing sound, like the wind. They gazed at each other. There was silence for a moment.

"It's a waste of time," Gross said.

"No—listen!"

The sputter came again. Then, mixed with the sputter, almost lost in it, a voice came, toneless, without inflection, a mechanical, lifeless voice from the metal speaker in the wall, above their heads.

"... Is it you, Philip? I can't make you out. Darkness.... Who's there? With you...."

"It's me, Kramer." His fingers tightened against the microphone handle. "You must release the controls, Professor. We have to get back to Terra. You must."

Silence. Then the faint, faltering voice came again, a little stronger than before. "Kramer. Everything so strange. I was right, though. Consciousness result of thinking. Necessary result. Cognito ergo sum. Retain conceptual ability. Can you hear me?"

"Yes, Professor —"

"I altered the wiring. Control. I was fairly certain.... I wonder if I can do it. Try...."

Suddenly the air-conditioning snapped into operation. It snapped abruptly off again. Down the corridor a door slammed. Something thudded. The men stood listening. Sounds came from all sides of them, switches shutting, opening. The lights blinked off; they were in darkness. The lights came back on, and at the same time the heating coils dimmed and faded.

"Good God!" Winter said.

Water poured down on them, the emergency fire-fighting system. There was a screaming rush of air. One of the escape hatches had slid back, and the air was roaring frantically out into space.

The hatch banged closed. The ship subsided into silence. The heating coils glowed into life. As suddenly as it had begun the weird exhibition ceased.

"I can do — everything," the dry, toneless voice came from the wall speaker. "It is all controlled. Kramer, I wish to talk to you. I've been — been thinking. I haven't seen you in many years. A lot to discuss. You've changed, boy. We have much to discuss. Your wife—"

The Pilot grabbed Kramer's arm. "There's a ship standing off our bow. Look."

They ran to the port. A slender pale craft was moving along with them, keeping pace with them. It was signal-blinking.

"A Terran pursuit ship," the Pilot said. "Let's jump. They'll pick us up. Suits —"

He ran to a supply cupboard and turned the handle. The door opened and he pulled the suits out onto the floor.

"Hurry," Gross said. A panic seized them. They dressed frantically, pulling the heavy garments over them. Winter staggered to the escape hatch and stood by it, waiting for the others. They joined him, one by one.

"Let's go!" Gross said. "Open the hatch."

Winter tugged at the hatch. "Help me."

They grabbed hold, tugging together. Nothing happened. The hatch refused to budge.

"Get a crowbar," the Pilot said.

"Hasn't anyone got a blaster?" Gross looked frantically around. "Damn it, blast it open!"

"Pull," Kramer grated. "Pull together."

"Are you at the hatch?" the toneless voice came, drifting and eddying through the corridors of the ship. They looked up, staring around them. "I sense something nearby, outside. A ship? You are leaving, all of you? Kramer, you are leaving, too? Very unfortunate. I had hoped we could talk. Perhaps at some other time you might be induced to remain."

"Open the hatch!" Kramer said, staring up at the impersonal walls of the ship. "For God's sake, open it!"

There was silence, an endless pause. Then, very slowly, the hatch slid back. The air screamed out, rushing past them into space.

One by one they leaped, one after the other, propelled away by the repulsive material of the suits. A few minutes later they were being hauled aboard the pursuit ship. As the last one of them was lifted through the port, their own ship pointed itself suddenly upward and shot off at tremendous speed. It disappeared.

Kramer removed his helmet, gasping. Two sailors held onto him and began to wrap him in blankets. Gross sipped a mug of coffee, shivering.

"It's gone," Kramer murmured.

"I'll have an alarm sent out," Gross said.

"What's happened to your ship?" a sailor asked curiously. "It sure took off in a hurry. Who's on it?"

"We'll have to have it destroyed," Gross went on, his face grim. "It's got to be destroyed. There's no telling what it — what he has in mind." Gross sat down weakly on a metal bench. "What a close call for us. We were so damn trusting."

"What could he be planning," Kramer said, half to himself. "It doesn't make sense. I don't get it."

As the ship sped back toward the moon base they sat around the table in the dining room, sipping hot coffee and thinking, not saying very much.

"Look here," Gross said at last. "What kind of man was Professor Thomas? What do you remember about him?"

Kramer put his coffee mug down. "It was ten years ago. I don't remember much. It's vague."

He let his mind run back over the years. He and Dolores had been at Hunt College together, in physics and the life sciences. The College was small and set back away from the momentum of modern life. He had gone there because it was his home town, and his father had gone there before him.

Professor Thomas had been at the College a long time, as long as anyone could remember. He was a strange old man, keeping to himself most of the time. There were many things that he disapproved of, but he seldom said what they were.

"Do you recall anything that might help us?" Gross asked. "Anything that would give us a clue as to what he might have in mind?"

Kramer nodded slowly. "I remember one thing...."

One day he and the Professor had been sitting together in the school chapel, talking leisurely.

"Well, you'll be out of school, soon," the Professor had said. "What are you going to do?"

"Do? Work at one of the Government Research Projects, I suppose."

"And eventually? What's your ultimate goal?"

Kramer had smiled. "The question is unscientific. It presupposes such things as ultimate ends."

"Suppose instead along these lines, then: What if there were no war and no Government Research Projects? What would you do, then?"

"I don't know. But how can I imagine a hypothetical situation like that? There's been war as long as I can remember. We're geared for war. I don't know what I'd do. I suppose I'd adjust, get used to it."

The Professor had stared at him. "Oh, you do think you'd get accustomed to it, eh? Well, I'm glad of that. And you think you could find something to do?"

Gross listened intently. "What do you infer from this, Kramer?"

"Not much. Except that he was against war."

"We're all against war," Gross pointed out.

"True. But he was withdrawn, set apart. He lived very simply, cooking his own meals. His wife died many years ago. He was born in Europe, in Italy. He changed his name when he came to the United States. He used to read Dante and Milton. He even had a Bible."

"Very anachronistic, don't you think?"

"Yes, he lived quite a lot in the past. He found an old phonograph and records, and he listened to the old music. You saw his house, how old-fashioned it was."

"Did he have a file?" Winter asked Gross.

"With Security? No, none at all. As far as we could tell he never engaged in political work, never joined anything or even seemed to have strong political convictions."

"No," Kramer agreed. "About all he ever did was walk through the hills. He liked nature."

"Nature can be of great use to a scientist," Gross said. "There wouldn't be any science without it."

"Kramer, what do you think his plan is, taking control of the ship and disappearing?" Winter said.

"Maybe the transfer made him insane," the Pilot said. "Maybe there's no plan, nothing rational at all."

"But he had the ship rewired, and he had made sure that he would retain consciousness and memory before he even agreed to the operation. He must have had something planned from the start. But what?"

"Perhaps he just wanted to stay alive longer," Kramer said. "He was old and about to die. Or—"

"Or what?"

"Nothing." Kramer stood up. "I think as soon as we get to the moon base I'll make a vidcall to earth. I want to talk to somebody about this."

"Who's that?" Gross asked.

"Dolores. Maybe she remembers something."

"That's a good idea," Gross said.

"Where are you calling from?" Dolores asked, when he succeeded in reaching her.

"From the moon base."

"All kinds of rumors are running around. Why didn't the ship come back? What happened?"

"I'm afraid he ran off with it."

"He?"

"The Old Man. Professor Thomas." Kramer explained what had happened. Dolores listened intently. "How strange. And you think he planned it all in advance, from the start?"

"I'm certain. He asked for the plans of construction and the theoretical diagrams at once."

"But why? What for?"

"I don't know. Look, Dolores. What do you remember about him? Is there anything that might give a clue to all this?"

"Like what?"

"I don't know. That's the trouble."

On the vidscreen Dolores knitted her brow. "I remember he raised chickens in his back yard, and once he had a goat." She smiled. "Do you remember the day the goat got loose and wandered down the main street of town? Nobody could figure out where it came from."

"Anything else?"

"No." He watched her struggling, trying to remember. "He wanted to have a farm, sometime, I know."

"All right. Thanks." Kramer touched the switch. "When I get back to Terra maybe I'll stop and see you."

"Let me know how it works out."

He cut the line and the picture dimmed and faded. He walked slowly back to where Gross and some officers of the Military were sitting at a chart table, talking.

"Any luck?" Gross said, looking up.

"No. All she remembers is that he kept a goat."

"Come over and look at this detail chart." Gross motioned him around to his side. "Watch!"

Kramer saw the record tabs moving furiously, the little white dots racing back and forth.

"What's happening?" he asked.

"A squadron outside the defense zone has finally managed to contact the ship. They're maneuvering now, for position. Watch."

The white counters were forming a barrel formation around a black dot that was moving steadily across the board, away from the central position. As they watched, the white dots constricted around it.

"They're ready to open fire," a technician at the board said. "Commander, what shall we tell them to do?"

Gross hesitated. "I hate to be the one who makes the decision. When it comes right down to it —"

"It's not just a ship," Kramer said. "It's a man, a living person. A human being is up there, moving through space. I wish we knew what —"

"But the order has to be given. We can't take any chances. Suppose he went over to them, to the yuks."

Kramer's jaw dropped. "My God, he wouldn't do that."

"Are you sure? Do you know what he'll do?"

"He wouldn't do that."

Gross turned to the technician. "Tell them to go ahead."

"I'm sorry, sir, but now the ship has gotten away. Look down at the board."

Gross stared down, Kramer over his shoulder. The black dot had slipped through the white dots and had moved off at an abrupt angle. The white dots were broken up, dispersing in confusion.

"He's an unusual strategist," one of the officers said. He traced the line. "It's an ancient maneuver, an old Prussian device, but it worked."

The white dots were turning back. "Too many yuk ships out that far," Gross said. "Well, that's what you get when you don't act quickly." He looked up coldly at Kramer. "We should have done it when we had him. Look at him go!" He jabbed a finger at the rapidly moving black dot. The dot came to the edge of the board and stopped. It had reached the limit of the chartered area. "See?"

— Now what? Kramer thought, watching. So the Old Man had escaped the cruisers and gotten away. He was alert, all right; there was nothing wrong with his mind. Or with his ability to control his new body.

Body —The ship was a new body for him. He had traded in the old dying body, withered and frail, for this hulking frame of metal and plastic, turbines and rocket jets. He was strong, now. Strong and big. The new body was more powerful than a thousand human bodies. But how long would it last him? The average life of a cruiser was only ten years. With careful handling he might get twenty out of it, before some essential part failed and there was no way to replace it.

And then, what then? What would he do, when something failed and there was no one to fix it for him? That would be the end. Someplace, far out in the cold darkness of space, the ship would slow down, silent and lifeless, to exhaust its last heat into the eternal timelessness of outer space. Or perhaps it would crash on some barren asteroid, burst into a million fragments.

It was only a question of time.

"Your wife didn't remember anything?" Gross said.

"I told you. Only that he kept a goat, once."

"A hell of a lot of help that is."

Kramer shrugged. "It's not my fault."

"I wonder if we'll ever see him again." Gross stared down at the indicator dot, still hanging at the edge of the board. "I wonder if he'll ever move back this way."

"I wonder, too," Kramer said.

That night Kramer lay in bed, tossing from side to side, unable to sleep. The moon gravity, even artificially increased, was unfamiliar to him and it made him uncomfortable. A thousand thoughts wandered loose in his head as he lay, fully awake.

What did it all mean? What was the Professor's plan? Maybe they would never know. Maybe the ship was gone for good; the Old Man had left forever, shooting into outer space.

They might never find out why he had done it, what purpose — if any — had been in his mind.

Kramer sat up in bed. He turned on the light and lit a cigarette. His quarters were small, a metal-lined bunk room, part of the moon station base. The Old Man had wanted to talk to him. He had wanted to discuss things, hold a conversation, but in the hysteria and confusion all they had been able to think of was getting away. The ship was rushing off with them, carrying them into outer space. Kramer set his jaw. Could they be blamed for jumping? They had no idea where they were being taken, or why. They were helpless, caught in their own ship, and the pursuit ship standing by waiting to pick them up was their only chance. Another half hour and it would have been too late.

But what had the Old Man wanted to say? What had he intended to tell him, in those first confusing moments when the ship around them had come alive, each metal strut and wire suddenly animate, the body of a living creature, a vast metal organism?

It was weird, unnerving. He could not forget it, even now. He looked around the small room uneasily. What did it signify, the coming to life of metal and plastic? All at once they had found themselves inside a living creature, in its stomach, like Jonah inside the whale.

It had been alive, and it had talked to them, talked calmly and rationally, as it rushed them off, faster and faster into outer space. The wall speaker and circuit had become the vocal cords and mouth, the wiring the spinal cord and nerves, the hatches and relays and circuit breakers the muscles.

They had been helpless, completely helpless. The ship had, in a brief second, stolen their power away from them and left them defenseless, practically at its mercy. It was not right; it made him uneasy. All his life he had controlled machines, bent nature and the forces of nature to man and man's needs. The human race had slowly evolved until it was in a position to operate things, run them as it saw fit. Now all at once it had been plunged back down the ladder again, prostrate before a Power against which they were children.

Kramer got out of bed. He put on his bathrobe and began to search for a cigarette. While he was searching, the vidphone rang.

He snapped the vidphone on.

"Yes?"

The face of the immediate monitor appeared. "A call from Terra, Mr. Kramer. An emergency call."

"Emergency call? For me? Put it through." Kramer came awake, brushing his hair back out of his eyes. Alarm plucked at him.

From the speaker a strange voice came. "Philip Kramer? Is this Kramer?"

"Yes. Go on."

"This is General Hospital, New York City, Terra. Mr. Kramer, your wife is here. She has been critically injured in an accident. Your name was given to us to call. Is it possible for you to —"

"How badly?" Kramer gripped the vidphone stand. "Is it serious?"

"Yes, it's serious, Mr. Kramer. Are you able to come here? The quicker you can come the better."

"Yes." Kramer nodded. "I'll come. Thanks."

The screen died as the connection was broken. Kramer waited a moment. Then he tapped the button. The screen relit again. "Yes, sir," the monitor said.

"Can I get a ship to Terra at once? It's an emergency. My wife —"

"There's no ship leaving the moon for eight hours. You'll have to wait until the next period."

"Isn't there anything I can do?"

"We can broadcast a general request to all ships passing through this area. Sometimes cruisers pass by here returning to Terra for repairs."

"Will you broadcast that for me? I'll come down to the field."

"Yes sir. But there may be no ship in the area for awhile. It's a gamble." The screen died.

Kramer dressed quickly. He put on his coat and hurried to the lift. A moment later he was running across the general receiving lobby, past the rows of vacant desks and conference tables. At the door the sentries stepped aside and he went outside, onto the great concrete steps.

The face of the moon was in shadow. Below him the field stretched out in total darkness, a black void, endless, without form. He made his way carefully down the steps and along the ramp along the side of the field, to the control tower. A faint row of red lights showed him the way.

Two soldiers challenged him at the foot of the tower, standing in the shadows, their guns ready.

"Kramer?"

"Yes."

A light was flashed in his face.

"Your call has been sent out already."

"Any luck?" Kramer asked.

"There's a cruiser nearby that has made contact with us. It has an injured jet and is moving slowly back toward Terra, away from the line."

"Good." Kramer nodded, a flood of relief rushing through him. He lit a cigarette and gave one to each of the soldiers. The soldiers lit up.

"Sir," one of them asked, "is it true about the experimental ship?"

"What do you mean?"

"It came to life and ran off?"

"No, not exactly," Kramer said. "It had a new type of control system instead of the Johnson units. It wasn't properly tested."

"But sir, one of the cruisers that was there got up close to it, and a buddy of mine says this ship acted funny. He never saw anything like it. It was like when he was fishing once on Terra, in Washington State, fishing for bass. The fish were smart, going this way and that —"

"Here's your cruiser," the other soldier said. "Look!"

An enormous vague shape was setting slowly down onto the field. They could make nothing out but its row of tiny green blinkers. Kramer stared at the shape.

"Better hurry, sir," the soldiers said. "They don't stick around here very long."

"Thanks." Kramer loped across the field, toward the black shape that rose up above him, extended across the width of the field. The ramp was down from the side of the cruiser and he caught hold of it. The ramp rose, and a moment later Kramer was inside the hold of the ship. The hatch slid shut behind him.

As he made his way up the stairs to the main deck the turbines roared up from the moon, out into space.

Kramer opened the door to the main deck. He stopped suddenly, staring around him in surprise. There was nobody in sight. The ship was deserted.

"Good God," he said. Realization swept over him, numbing him. He sat down on a bench, his head swimming. "Good God."

The ship roared out into space leaving the moon and Terra farther behind each moment.

And there was nothing he could do.

"So it was you who put the call through," he said at last. "It was you who called me on the vidphone, not any hospital on Terra. It was all part of the plan." He looked up and around him. "And Dolores is really —"

"Your wife is fine," the wall speaker above him said tonelessly. "It was a fraud. I am sorry to trick you that way,

Philip, but it was all I could think of. Another day and you would have been back on Terra. I don't want to remain in this area any longer than necessary. They have been so certain of finding me out in deep space that I have been able to stay here without too much danger. But even the purloined letter was found eventually."

Kramer smoked his cigarette nervously. "What are you going to do? Where are we going?"

"First, I want to talk to you. I have many things to discuss. I was very disappointed when you left me, along with the others. I had hoped that you would remain." The dry voice chuckled. "Remember how we used to talk in the old days, you and I? That was a long time ago."

The ship was gaining speed. It plunged through space at tremendous speed, rushing through the last of the defense zone and out beyond. A rush of nausea made Kramer bend over for a moment.

When he straightened up the voice from the wall went on, "I'm sorry to step it up so quickly, but we are still in danger. Another few moments and we'll be free."

"How about yuk ships? Aren't they out here?"

"I've already slipped away from several of them. They're quite curious about me."

"Curious?"

"They sense that I'm different, more like their own organic mines. They don't like it. I believe they will begin to withdraw from this area, soon. Apparently they don't want to get involved with me. They're an odd race, Philip. I would have liked to study them closely, try to learn something about them. I'm of the opinion that they use no inert material. All their equipment and instruments are alive, in some form or other. They don't construct or build at all. The idea of making is foreign to them. They utilize existing forms. Even their ships —"

"Where are we going?" Kramer said. "I want to know where you are taking me."

"Frankly, I'm not certain."

"You're not certain?"

"I haven't worked some details out. There are a few vague spots in my program, still. But I think that in a short while I'll have them ironed out."

"What is your program?" Kramer said.

"It's really very simple. But don't you want to come into the control room and sit? The seats are much more comfortable than that metal bench."

Kramer went into the control room and sat down at the control board. Looking at the useless apparatus made him feel strange.

"What's the matter?" the speaker above the board rasped.

Kramer gestured helplessly. "I'm — powerless. I can't do anything. And I don't like it. Do you blame me?"

"No. No, I don't blame you. But you'll get your control back, soon. Don't worry. This is only a temporary expedient, taking you off this way. It was something I didn't contemplate. I forgot that orders would be given out to shoot me on sight."

"It was Gross' idea."

"I don't doubt that. My conception, my plan, came to me as soon as you began to describe your project, that day at my house. I saw at once that you were wrong; you people have no understanding of the mind at all. I realized that the transfer of a human brain from an organic body to a complex artificial space ship would not involve the loss of the intellectualization faculty of the mind. When a man thinks, he is.

"When I realized that, I saw the possibility of an age-old dream becoming real. I was quite elderly when I first met you, Philip. Even then my life-span had come pretty much to its end. I could look ahead to nothing but death, and with it the extinction of all my ideas. I had made no mark on the world, none at all. My students, one by one, passed from me into the world, to take up jobs in the great Research Project, the search for better and bigger weapons of war.

"The world has been fighting for a long time, first with itself, then with the Martians, then with these beings from Proxima Centauri, whom we know nothing about. The human society has evolved war as a cultural institution, like the science of astronomy, or mathematics. War is a part of our lives, a career, a respected vocation. Bright, alert young men and women move into it, putting their shoulders to the wheel as they did in the time of Nebuchadnezzar. It has always been so.

"But is it innate in mankind? I don't think so. No social custom is innate. There were many human groups that did not go to war; the Eskimos never grasped the idea at all, and the American Indians never took to it well.

"But these dissenters were wiped out, and a cultural pattern was established that became the standard for the whole planet. Now it has become ingrained in us.

"But if someplace along the line some other way of settling problems had arisen and taken hold, something different than the massing of men and material to —"

"What's your plan?" Kramer said. "I know the theory. It was part of one of your lectures."

"Yes, buried in a lecture on plant selection, as I recall. When you came to me with this proposition I realized that perhaps my conception could be brought to life, after all. If my theory were right that war is only a habit, not an instinct, a society built up apart from Terra with a minimum of cultural roots might develop differently. If it failed to absorb our outlook, if it could start out on another foot, it might not arrive at the same point to which we have come: a dead end, with nothing but greater and greater wars in sight, until nothing is left but ruin and destruction everywhere.

"Of course, there would have to be a Watcher to guide the experiment, at first. A crisis would undoubtedly come very quickly, probably in the second generation. Cain would arise almost at once.

"You see, Kramer, I estimate that if I remain at rest most of the time, on some small planet or moon, I may be able to keep functioning for almost a hundred years. That would be time enough, sufficient to see the direction of the new colony. After that—Well, after that it would be up to the colony itself.

"Which is just as well, of course. Man must take control eventually, on his own. One hundred years, and after that they will have control of their own destiny. Perhaps I am wrong, perhaps war is more than a habit. Perhaps it is a law of the universe, that things can only survive as groups by group violence.

"But I'm going ahead and taking the chance that it is only a habit, that I'm right, that war is something we're so accustomed to that we don't realize it is a very unnatural thing. Now as to the place! I'm still a little vague about that. We must find the place, still.

"That's what we're doing now. You and I are going to inspect a few systems off the beaten path, planets where the trading prospects are low enough to keep Terran ships away. I know of one planet that might be a good place. It was reported by the Fairchild Expedition in their original manual. We may look into that, for a start."

The ship was silent.

Kramer sat for a time, staring down at the metal floor under him. The floor throbbed dully with the motion of the turbines. At last he looked up.

"You might be right. Maybe our outlook is only a habit." Kramer got to his feet. "But I wonder if something has occurred to you?"

"What is that?"

"If it's such a deeply ingrained habit, going back thousands of years, how are you going to get your colonists to make the break, leave Terra and Terran customs? How about this generation, the first ones, the people who found the colony? I think you're right that the next generation would be free of all this, if there were an —" He grinned. " — An Old Man Above to teach them something else instead."

Kramer looked up at the wall speaker. "How are you going to get the people to leave Terra and come with you, if by your own theory, this generation can't be saved, it all has to start with the next?"

The wall speaker was silent. Then it made a sound, the faint dry chuckle.

"I'm surprised at you, Philip. Settlers can be found. We won't need many, just a few." The speaker chuckled again. "I'll acquaint you with my solution."

At the far end of the corridor a door slid open. There was sound, a hesitant sound. Kramer turned.

"Dolores!"

Dolores Kramer stood uncertainly, looking into the control room. She blinked in amazement. "Phil! What are you doing here? What's going on?"

They stared at each other.

"What's happening?" Dolores said. "I received a vidcall that you had been hurt in a lunar explosion —"

The wall speaker rasped into life. "You see, Philip, that problem is already solved. We don't really need so many people; even a single couple might do."

Kramer nodded slowly. "I see," he murmured thickly. "Just one couple. One man and woman."

"They might make it all right, if there were someone to watch and see that things went as they should. There will be quite a few things I can help you with, Philip. Quite a few. We'll get along very well, I think."

Kramer grinned wryly. "You could even help us name the animals," he said. "I understand that's the first step."

"I'll be glad to," the toneless, impersonal voice said. "As I recall, my part will be to bring them to you, one by one. Then you can do the actual naming."

"I don't understand," Dolores faltered. "What does he mean, Phil? Naming animals. What kind of animals? Where are we going?"

Kramer walked slowly over to the port and stood staring silently out, his arms folded. Beyond the ship a myriad fragments of light gleamed, countless coals glowing in the dark void. Stars, suns, systems. Endless, without number. A universe of worlds. An infinity of planets, waiting for them, gleaming and winking from the darkness.

He turned back, away from the port. "Where are we going?" He smiled at his wife, standing nervous and frightened, her large eyes full of alarm. "I don't know where we are going," he said. "But somehow that doesn't seem too important right now.... I'm beginning to see the Professor's point, it's the result that counts."

And for the first time in many months he put his arm around Dolores. At first she stiffened, the fright and nervousness still in her eyes. But then suddenly she relaxed against him and there were tears wetting her cheeks.

"Phil ... do you really think we can start over again — you and I?"

He kissed her tenderly, then passionately.

And the spaceship shot swiftly through the endless, trackless eternity of the void....

RAY BRADBURY

The End of the Beginning
1959

He stopped the lawn mower in the middle of the yard, because he felt that the sun at just that moment had gone down and the stars come out. The fresh-cut grass that had showered his face and body died softly away. Yes, the stars were there, faint at first, but brightening in the clear desert sky. He heard the porch screen door tap shut and felt his wife watching him as he watched the night.

"Almost time," she said.

He nodded; he did not have to check his watch. In the passing moments he felt very old, then very young, very cold, then very warm, now this, now that. Suddenly he was miles away. He was his own son talking steadily, moving briskly to cover his pounding heart and the resurgent panics as he felt himself slip into fresh uniform, check food supplies, oxygen flasks, pressure helmet, space-suiting, and turn as every man on Earth tonight turned, to gaze at the swiftly filling sky.

Then, quickly, he was back, once more the father of the son, hands gripped to the lawn-mower handle. His wife called, "Come sit on the porch."

"I've got to keep busy!"

She came down the steps and across the lawn. "Don't worry about Robert; he'll be all right."

"But it's all so new," he heard himself say. "It's never been done before. Think of it—a manned rocket going up tonight to build the first space station. Good Lord, it can't be done, it doesn't exist, there's no rocket, no proving ground, no take-off time, no technicians. For that matter, I don't even have a son named Bob. The whole thing's too much for me!"

"Then what are you doing out here, staring?"

He shook his head. "Well, late this morning, walking to the office, I heard someone laugh out loud. It shocked me, so I froze in the middle of the street. It was me, laughing! Why? Because finally I really knew what Bob was going to do tonight; at last I *believed* it. 'Holy' is a word I never use, but that's how I felt stranded in all that traffic. Then, middle of the afternoon, I caught myself humming. You know the song. 'A wheel in a wheel. Way in the middle of the air.' I laughed again. The space station, of course, I thought. The big wheel with hollow spokes where Bob'll live six or eight months, then get along to the Moon. Walking home, I remembered more of the song. 'Little wheel run by faith, big wheel run by the grace of God.' I wanted to jump, yell, and flame-out myself!"

His wife touched his arm. "If we stay out here, let's at least be comfortable."

They placed two wicker rockers in the center of the lawn and sat quietly as the stars dissolved out of darkness in pale crushings of rock salt strewn from horizon to horizon.

"Why," said his wife, at last, "it's like waiting for the fireworks at Sisley Field every year."

"Bigger crowd tonight..."

"I keep thinking — a billion people watching the sky right now, their mouths all open at the same time."

They waited, feeling the earth move under their chairs.

"What time is it now?"

"Eleven minutes to eight."

"You're always right; there must be a clock in your head."

"I can't be wrong, tonight. I'll be able to tell you one second before they blast off. Look! The ten-minute warning!"

On the western sky they saw four crimson flares open out, float shimmering down the wind above the desert, then sink silently to the extinguishing earth.

In the new darkness the husband and wife did not rock in their chairs.

After a while he said, "Eight minutes." A pause. "Seven minutes." What seemed a much longer pause. "Six..."

His wife, her head back, studied the stars immediately above her and murmured, "Why?" She closed her eyes. "Why the rockets, why tonight? Why all this? I'd like to know."

He examined her face, pale in the vast powdering light of the Milky Way. He felt the stirring of an answer, but let his wife continue.

"I mean it's not that old thing again, is it, when people asked why men climbed Mt. Everest and they said, 'Because it's there'? I never understood. That was no answer to me."

Five minutes, he thought. Time ticking... his wristwatch... a wheel in a wheel... little wheel run by... big wheel run by... way in the middle of... four minutes!... The men snug in the rocket by now, the hive, the control board flickering with light...

"All I know is it's really the end of the beginning. The Stone Age, Bronze Age, Iron Age; from now on we'll lump all those together under one big name for when we walked on Earth and heard the birds at morning and cried with envy. Maybe we'll call it the Earth Age, or maybe the Age of Gravity. Millions of years we fought gravity. When we were amoebas and fish we struggled to get out of the sea without gravity crushing us. Once safe on the shore we fought to stand upright without gravity breaking our new invention, the spine, tried to walk without stumbling, run without falling. A billion years Gravity kept us home, mocked us with wind and clouds, cabbage moths and locusts. That's what's so God-awful big about tonight...it's the end of old man Gravity and the age we'll remember him by, for once and all. I don't know where they'll divide the ages, at the Persians, who dreamt of flying carpets, or the Chinese, who all unknowing celebrated birthdays and New Years with strung ladyfingers and high skyrockets, or some minute, some incredible second in the next hour. But we're in at the end of a billion years trying, the end of something long and to us humans, anyway, honorable."

Three minutes... two minutes fifty-nine seconds... two minutes fifty-eight seconds...

"But," said his wife, "I still don't know why."

Two minutes, he thought. *Ready? Ready? Ready?* The far radio voice calling. *Ready! Ready! Ready!* The quick, faint replies from the humming rocket. *Check! Check! Check!*

Tonight, he thought, even if we fail with this first, we'll send a second and a third ship and move on out to all the planets and later, all the stars. We'll just keep going until the big words like 'immortal' and 'forever' take on meaning. Big words, yes, that's what we want. Continuity. Since our tongues first moved in our mouths we've asked, What does it all mean? No other question made sense, with death breathing down our necks. But just let us settle in on ten thousand worlds spinning around ten thousand alien suns and the question will fade away. Man will be endless and infinite, even as space is endless and infinite. Man will go on, as space goes on, forever. Individuals will die as always, but our history will reach as far as we'll ever need to see into the future, and with the knowledge of our survival for all time to come, we'll know security and thus the answer we've always searched for. Gifted with life, the least we can do is preserve and pass on the gift to infinity. That's a goal worth shooting for.

The wicker chairs whispered ever so softly on the grass.

One minute.

"One minute," he said aloud.

"Oh!" His wife moved suddenly to seize his hands.

"I hope that Bob..."

"He'll be all right!"

"Oh, God, take care..."

Thirty seconds.

"Watch now."

Fifteen, ten, five...

"Watch!"

Four, three, two, one.

"There! There! Oh, there, there!"

They both cried out. They both stood. The chairs toppled back, fell flat on the lawn. The man and his wife swayed, their hands struggled to find each other, grip, hold. They saw the brightening color in the sky and, ten seconds later, the great uprising comet burn the air, put out the stars, and rush away in fire flight to become another star in the returning profusion of the Milky Way. The man and wife held each other as if they had stumbled on the rim of an incredible cliff that faced an abyss so deep and dark there seemed no end to it. Staring up, they heard themselves sobbing and crying. Only after a long time were they able to speak.

"It got away, it did, *didn't* it?"

"Yes..."

"It's all right, isn't it?"

"Yes... yes..."

"It didn't fall back...?"

"No, no it's all right, Bob's all right, it's all right."

They stood away from each other at last.

He touched his face with his hand and looked at his wet fingers. "I'll be damned," he said. "I'll be damned."

They waited another five and then ten minutes until the darkness in their heads, the retina, ached with a million specks of fiery salt. Then they had to close their eyes.

"Well," she said, "now let's go in."

He could not move. Only his hand reached a long way out by itself to find the lawn-mower handle. He saw what his hand had done and said, "There's just a little more to do..."

"But you can't see."

"Well enough," he said. "I must finish this. Then we'll sit on the porch awhile before we turn in."

He helped her put the chairs on the porch and sat her down and then walked back out to put his hands on the guide bar of the lawn mower. The lawn mower. A wheel in a wheel. A simple machine which you held in your hands, which you sent on ahead with a rush and a clatter while you walked behind with your quiet philosophy. Racket, followed by warm silence. Whirling wheel, then soft footfall of thought.

I'm a billion years old, he told himself; I'm one minute old. I'm one inch, no ten thousand *miles*, tall. I look down and can't see my feet they're so far off and gone away below.

He moved the lawn mower. The grass showering up fell softly around him, he relished and savored it and felt that he was all mankind bathing at last in the fresh waters of the fountain of youth.

Thus bathed, he remembered the song again about the wheels and the faith and the grace of God being way up there in the middle of the sky where that single star, among a million motionless stars, dared to move and keep on moving.

Then he finished cutting the grass.

LEO TOLSTOY

Translated from the Russian by LOUISE and AYLMAR MAUDE

The Coffee-House of Surat

(After Bernardin de Saint-Pierre)

1893

In the town of Surat, in India, was a coffee-house where many travelers and foreigners from all parts of the world met and conversed.

One day a learned Persian theologian visited this coffee-house. He was a man who had spent his life studying the nature of the Deity, and reading and writing books upon the subject. He had thought, read, and written so much about God, that eventually he lost his wits, became quite confused, and ceased even to believe in the existence of a God. The Shah, hearing of this, had banished him from Persia.

After having argued all his life about the First Cause, this unfortunate theologian had ended by quite perplexing himself, and instead of understanding that he had lost his own reason, he began to think that there was no higher Reason controlling the universe.

This man had an African slave who followed him everywhere. When the theologian entered the coffee-house, the slave remained outside, near the door, sitting on a stone in the glare of the sun, and driving away the flies that buzzed around him. The Persian having settled down on a divan in the coffee-house, ordered himself a cup of opium. When he had drunk it and the opium had begun to quicken the workings of his brain, he addressed his slave through the open door:

"Tell me, wretched slave," said he, "do you think there is a God, or not?"

"Of course there is," said the slave, and immediately drew from under his girdle a small idol of wood.

"There," said he, "that is the God who has guarded me from the day of my birth. Every one in our country worships the fetish tree, from the wood of which this God was made."

This conversation between the theologian and his slave was listened to with surprise by the other guests in the coffee-house. They were astonished at the master's question, and yet more so at the slave's reply.

One of them, a Brahmin, on hearing the words spoken by the slave, turned to him and said:

"Miserable fool! Is it possible you believe that God can be carried under a man's girdle? There is one God — Brahma, and he is greater than the whole world, for he created it. Brahma is the One, the mighty God, and in His honour are built the temples on the Ganges' banks, where his true priests, the Brahmins, worship him. They know the true God, and none but they. A thousand score of years have passed, and yet through revolution after revolution these priests have held their sway, because Brahma, the one true God, has protected them."

So spoke the Brahmin, thinking to convince every one; but a Jewish broker who was present replied to him, and said:

"No! the temple of the true God is not in India. Neither does God protect the Brahmin caste. The true God is not the God of the Brahmins, but of Abraham, Isaac, and Jacob. None does He protect but His chosen people, the Israelites. From the commencement of the world, our nation has been beloved of Him, and ours alone. If we are now scattered over the whole earth, it is but to try us; for God has promised that He will one day gather His people together in Jerusalem. Then, with the Temple of Jerusalem — the wonder of the ancient world — restored to its splendor, shall Israel be established a ruler over all nations."

So spoke the Jew, and burst into tears. He wished to say more, but an Italian missionary who was there interrupted him.

"What you are saying is untrue," said he to the Jew. "You attribute injustice to God. He cannot love your nation above the rest. Nay rather, even if it be true that of old He favored the Israelites, it is now nineteen hundred years since they angered Him, and caused Him to destroy their nation and scatter them over the earth, so that their faith makes no converts and has died out except here and there. God shows preference to no nation, but calls all who wish to be saved to the bosom of the Catholic Church of Rome, the one outside whose borders no salvation can be found."

So spoke the Italian. But a Protestant minister, who happened to be present, growing pale, turned to the Catholic missionary and exclaimed:

"How can you say that salvation belongs to your religion? Those only will be saved, who serve God according to the Gospel, in spirit and in truth, as bidden by the word of Christ."

Then a Turk, an office-holder in the custom-house at Surat, who was sitting in the coffee-house smoking a pipe, turned with an air of superiority to both the Christians.

"Your belief in your Roman religion is vain," said he. "It was superseded twelve hundred years ago by the true faith: that of Mohammed! You cannot but observe how the true Mohammed faith continues to spread both in Europe and Asia, and even in the enlightened country of China. You say yourselves that God has rejected the Jews; and, as a proof, you quote the fact that the Jews are humiliated and their faith does not spread. Confess then the truth of Mohammedanism, for it is triumphant and spreads far and wide. None will be saved but the followers of Mohammed, God's latest prophet; and of them, only the followers of Omar, and not of Ali, for the latter are false to the faith."

To this the Persian theologian, who was of the sect of Ali, wished to reply; but by this time a great dispute had arisen among all the strangers of different faiths and creeds present. There were Abyssinian Christians, Llamas from Thibet, Ismailians and Fireworshippers. They all argued about the nature of God, and how He should be worshipped. Each of them asserted that in his country alone was the true God known and rightly worshipped.

Every one argued and shouted, except a Chinaman, a student of Confucius, who sat quietly in one corner of the coffee-house, not joining in the dispute. He sat there drinking tea and listening to what the others said, but did not speak himself.

The Turk noticed him sitting there, and appealed to him, saying:

"You can confirm what I say, my good Chinaman. You hold your peace, but if you spoke I know you would uphold my opinion. Traders from your country, who come to me for assistance, tell me that though many religions have been introduced into China, you Chinese consider Mohammedanism the best of all, and adopt it willingly. Confirm, then, my words, and tell us your opinion of the true God and of His prophet."

"Yes, yes," said the rest, turning to the Chinaman, "let us hear what you think on the subject."

The Chinaman, the student of Confucius, closed his eyes, and thought a while. Then he opened them again, and drawing his hands out of the wide sleeves of his garment, and folding them on his breast, he spoke as follows, in a calm and quiet voice.

Sirs, it seems to me that it is chiefly pride that prevents men agreeing with one another on matters of faith. If you care to listen to me, I will tell you a story which will explain this by an example.

I came here from China on an English steamer which had been round the world. We stopped for fresh water, and landed on the east coast of the island of Sumatra. It was midday, and some of us, having landed, sat in the shade of some cocoanut palms by the seashore, not far from a native village. We were a party of men of different nationalities.

As we sat there, a blind man approached us. We learned afterwards that he had gone blind from gazing too long and too persistently at the sun, trying to find out what it is, in order to seize its light.

He strove a long time to accomplish this, constantly looking at the sun; but the only result was that his eyes were injured by its brightness, and he became blind.

Then he said to himself:

"The light of the sun is not a liquid; for if it were a liquid it would be possible to pour it from one vessel into another, and it would be moved, like water, by the wind. Neither is it fire; for if it were fire, water would extinguish it. Neither is light a spirit, for it is seen by the eye; nor is it matter, for it cannot be moved. Therefore, as the light of the sun is neither liquid, nor fire, nor spirit, nor matter, it is--nothing!"

So he argued, and, as a result of always looking at the sun and always thinking about it, he lost both his sight and his reason. And when he went quite blind, he became fully convinced that the sun did not exist.

With this blind man came a slave, who after placing his master in the shade of a cocoanut tree, picked up a cocoanut from the ground, and began making it into a night-light. He twisted a wick from the fibre of the cocoanut: squeezed oil from the nut in the shell, and soaked the wick in it.

As the slave sat doing this, the blind man sighed and said to him:

"Well, slave, was I not right when I told you there is no sun? Do you not see how dark it is? Yet people say there is a sun.... . But if so, what is it?"

"I do not know what the sun is," said the slave. "That is no business of mine. But I know what light is. Here I have made a night-light, by the help of which I can serve you and find anything I want in the hut."

And the slave picked up the cocoanut shell, saying: "This is my sun."

A lame man with crutches, who was sitting near by, heard these words, and laughed:

"You have evidently been blind all your life," said he to the blind man, "not to know what the sun is. I will tell you what it is. The sun is a ball of fire, which rises every morning out of the sea and goes down again among the mountains of our island each evening. We have all seen this, and if you had had your eyesight you too would have seen it."

A fisherman, who had been listening to the conversation said:

"It is plain enough that you have never been beyond your own island. If you were not lame, and if you had been out as I have in a fishing-boat, you would know that the sun does not set among the mountains of our island, but as it rises from the ocean every morning so it sets again in the sea every night.

What I am telling you is true, for I see it every day with my own eyes."

Then an Indian who was of our party, interrupted him by saying:

"I am astonished that a reasonable man should talk such nonsense. How can a ball of fire possibly descend into the water and not be extinguished? The sun is not a ball of fire at all, it is the Deity named Deva, who rides for ever in a chariot round the golden mountain, Meru. Sometimes the evil serpents Ragu and Ketu attack Deva and swallow him: and then the earth is dark. But our priests pray that the Deity may be released, and then he is set free. Only such ignorant men as you, who have never been beyond their own island, can imagine that the sun shines for their country alone."

Then the master of an Egyptian vessel, who was present, spoke in his turn.

"No," said he, "you also are wrong. The sun is not a Deity, and does not move only round India and its golden mountain. I have sailed much on the Black Sea, and along the coasts of Arabia, and have been to Madagascar and to the Philippines. The sun lights the whole earth, and not India alone. It does not circle round one mountain, but rises far in the East, beyond the Isles of Japan, and sets far, far away in the West, beyond the islands of England. That is why the Japanese call their country 'Nippon,' that is, 'the birth of the sun.' I know this well, for I have myself seen much, and heard more from my grandfather, who sailed to the very ends of the sea."

He would have gone on, but an English sailor from our ship interrupted him.

"There is no country," he said "where people know so much about the sun's movements as in England. The sun, as every one in England knows, rises nowhere and sets nowhere. It is always moving round the earth. We can be sure of this for we have just been round the world ourselves, and nowhere knocked up against the sun. Wherever we went, the sun showed itself in the morning and hid itself at night, just as it does here."

And the Englishman took a stick and, drawing circles on the sand, tried to explain how the sun moves in the heavens and goes round the world. But he was unable to explain it clearly, and pointing to the ship's pilot said:

"This man knows more about it than I do. He can explain it properly."

The pilot, who was an intelligent man, had listened in silence to the talk till he was asked to speak. Now every one turned to him, and he said:

"You are all misleading one another, and are yourselves deceived. The sun does not go round the earth, but the earth goes round the sun, revolving as it goes, and turning towards the sun in the course of each twenty-four hours, not only Japan, and the Philippines, and Sumatra where we now are, but Africa, and Europe, and America, and many lands besides. The sun does not shine for some one mountain, or for some one island, or for some one sea, nor even for one earth alone, but for other planets as well as our earth. If you would only look up at the heavens, instead of at the ground beneath your own feet, you might all understand this, and would then no longer suppose that the sun shines for you, or for your country alone."

Thus spoke the wise pilot, who had voyaged much about the world, and had gazed much upon the heavens above.

"So on matters of faith," continued the Chinaman, the student of Confucius, "it is pride that causes error and discord among men. As with the sun, so it is with God. Each man wants to have a special God of his own, or at least a special God for his native land. Each nation wishes to confine in its own temples Him, whom the world cannot contain.

"Can any temple compare with that which God Himself has built to unite all men in one faith and one religion?

"All human temples are built on the model of this temple, which is God's own world. Every temple has its fonts, its vaulted roof, its lamps, its pictures or sculptures, its inscriptions, its books of the law, its offerings, its altars and its priests. But in what temple is there such a font as the ocean; such a vault as that of the heavens; such lamps as the sun, moon, and stars; or any figures to be compared with living, loving, mutually-helpful men? Where are there any records of God's goodness so easy to understand as the blessings which God has strewn abroad for man's happiness? Where is there any book of the law so clear to each man as that written in his heart? What sacrifices equal the self-denials which loving men and women make for one another? And what altar can be compared with the heart of a good man, on which God Himself accepts the sacrifice?

"The higher a man's conception of God, the better will he know Him. And the better he knows God, the nearer will he draw to Him, imitating His goodness, His mercy, and His love of man.

"Therefore, let him who sees the sun's whole light filling the world, refrain from blaming or despising the superstitious man, who in his own idol sees one ray of that same light. Let him not despise even the unbeliever who is blind and cannot see the sun at all."

So spoke the Chinaman, the student of Confucius; and all who were present in the coffee-house were silent, and disputed no more as to whose faith was the best.

SLOOH

Since 2003, Slooh has promoted communal exploration of the universe through its global network of telescopes. Our automated observatories develop celestial images in real-time for broadcast to the internet, enabling anyone to explore the cosmos. Our live shows illuminate spectacular celestial events such as eclipses, comets, transits, solar activity, and potentially hazardous asteroids, and feature narration and explanation by astronomy experts.

We are dedicated to creating goodwill among humankind by celebrating our common existence under a shared sky. We believe in a multitude of perspectives about the universe, including those fueled by spirituality and imagination. We are as much about the reflection of light in a telescope as the reflection on a person's face when they are looking through it. We believe in the authenticity of a *live* experience, over simulations and animations, in order to capture the ephemeral ebb and flow of nature. We are inspired by our universe, and want to make this inspiration a key driver of society, connecting it to all human endeavors including literature.

Slooh is space for everyone.

www.slooh.com

ACKNOWLEDGEMENTS

Hans Christian Anderson: "The Comet" appears in English in AUNT JUDY'S CHRISTMAS VOLUME, 6-7 for Young People. Edited by Mrs. Alfred Gatty. London: Bell and Daldy, York Street, Covent Garden (1871).

Margaret Atwood: "Homelanding" from GOOD BONES AND SIMPLE MURDERS, by Margaret Atwood, copyright ©1983, 1992, 1994, by O.W. Todd Ltd. Used by permission of Nan A. Talese, and imprint of the Knopf Doubleday Publishing Company, a division of Penguin Random House LLC. All rights reserved.

J.G. Ballard: "The Message from Mars". Copyright © 1992 by J.G. Ballard, from THE COMPLETE STORIES OF J.G. BALLARD, by J.G. Ballard. Used by permission of W.W. Norton & Company, Inc.

Stephen Baxter: "Last Contact" copyright © Stephan Baxter 2007. Published by permission of Stephen Baxter c/o Selectric Artists LLC.

Ray Bradbury: "Kaleidescope" and "The End of the Beginning" are reprinted by permission of Don Congdon Associates, Inc. KALEIDESCOPE © 1949 By *Standard Magazines*, renewed 1976 by Ray Bradbury. THE END OF THE BEGINNING © 1956, renewed 1984 by Ray Bradbury.

Don DeLillo: "Human Moments in World War III" is reprinted with the permission of Scribner, a division of Simon & Schuster, Inc., from THE ANGEL ESMERALDA: NINE STORIES, by Don DeLillo. "Human Moments in World War III" originally appeared in *Esquire*, July 1983. Copyright © 1983, 2011 by Don DeLillo. All rights reserved.

Phillip K. Dick: "Mr. Spaceship" was first published in the January 1953 edition of *Imagination*, a fantasy and science fiction magazine.

James Fennimore Cooper: "The Eclipse" was first published posthumously in the September 1869 issue of *Putnam's Monthly Magazine*. (It was written between 1833 and 1838).

Selma Lagerlof: "The Eclipse" was first published in the December 1922 *American-Scandinavian* Review in a translation by Velma Swanston Howard.

Stanislaw Lem: "The Seventh Voyage" from THE STAR DIARIES by Stanislaw Lem, translated from Polish by Michael Kandel. English translation copyright © 1976 by Continuum Publishing Corporation. Reprinted by permission of Houghton Mifflin Harcourt Publishing Company. All rights reserved.

Primo Levi: "A Tranquil Star". Copyright © 2007 by W.W. Norton & Company. English translations copyright © 2007 by Ann Goldstein and Alessandra Bastagli, from COMPLETE WORKS OF PRIMO LEVI, by Primo Levi. Used by permission of Liveright Publishing Corporation.

C. S. Lewis: "Forms of Things Unknown" from OF OTHER WORLDS by C.S. Lewis. Copyright © 1966, renewed 1994 by C.S. Lewis Pte Ltd. Reprinted by permission of Houghton Mifflin Harcourt Publishing Company. All rights reserved.

H.P. Lovecraft: "Polaris" was written in 1918 and first published in the December 1920 issue of *The Philosopher*, an amateur journal.

Reginald McKnight: "Uncle Moustapha's Eclipse" from MOUSTAPHA'S ECLIPSE, by Reginald McKnight, © 1988. Reprinted by permission of the University of Pittsburgh Press.

Stephen Millhauser: "The Invasion From Outer Space," copyright © 2009 by Steven Millhauser, from WE OTHERS; NEW AND COLLECTED STORIES, by Steven Millhauser. Used by permission of Alfred A. Knopf, an imprint of Knopf Doubleday Publishing Group, a division of Penguin Random House LLC. All rights reserved.

Leo Tolstoy: "The Coffee-House of Surat" was written in 1887 and first published in Russian in the literary magazine *Severny Vestnik* in 1893. It was translated by Louise and Aylmar Maude as part of Twenty-Three Tales, Henry Frowde, Oxford University Press (1906).

John Updike: "Conjunction" from THE AFTERLIFE AND OTHER STORIES by John Updike, copyright © 1994 by John Updike. Used by permission of Alfred A. Knopf, an imprint of the Knopf Doubleday Publishing Group, a division of Penguin Random House LLC. All rights reserved.

Kurt Vonnegut: "Thanasphere" is from BAGOMBO SNUFF BOX: UNCOLLECTED SHORT FICTION by Kurt Vonnegut, copyright © 1999 by Kurt Vonnegut. Used by permission of G.P. Putnam's Sons, an imprint of Penguin Publishing Group, a division of Penguin Random House LLC.

H.G. Wells: "The Star" was first published in the December 1897 edition of *The Graphic*, a British weekly illustrated newspaper.